He knelt slowly and laid Shelby down on the sun-warmed ground, then rose back to his full height. "Great. Now I'm talking to myself." Propping his hands on his hips, the dark brim of his hat pulled low on his forehead, Cody stared down at her and wished for the hundredth time that she had never come to the Double K.

At least he hadn't fallen in love with her yet. He liked her well enough, and his body ached for her, but that was all. It wasn't love. And if he could convince her to leave, as he knew she would eventually, anyway, the feelings wouldn't have time to turn into love. Angry with himself, he let his gaze fall on the horizon. He felt like a man trying to straddle a picket fence that had cactus on one side and angry bulls on the other.

Cody kicked a heel at the dirt. "Ah, hell. Who am I trying to kid, anyhow?" Shelby Hill had already stolen his heart, and he knew damn well he'd probably never get it back.

CHERYL BIGGS

Denim And Lace

ZEBRA BOOKS
KENSINGTON PUBLISHING CORP.

ZEBRA BOOKS

are published by

Kensington Publishing Corp.
475 Park Avenue South
New York, NY 10016

First printing: November, 1992

Printed in the United States of America

This book is dedicated solely to my dad, who gave me a love of cowboys, horses, and everything to do with the Old West. Thanks, Dad.

Chapter One

Shelby turned the sleek red sports car onto the gravel drive and pulled to a stop. Her gaze moved from the pristine white gates, which stood open, to the brick pillars that supported them, then over the endless green plains that stretched as far as she could see. She could hardly believe she was really here, and that all this was now hers.

She looked up at the wooden arch overhead, where Double K Ranch was spelled out in barn-red letters. Tears filled her eyes and a sob she was unable to hold back caught in her throat. It was still hard to accept that Katie was really gone. Shelby remembered the morning two months earlier when the police had come to her door to tell her. She'd been convinced they'd made a mistake, that they were at the wrong house, that there must be some other Shelby Hill whose sister had just been killed in an automobile accident. But there'd been no mistake. Her beautiful sister, Katie, her laughing lighthearted brother-in-law, Ken, and their eight-year-old twins, Josh and Joey, were dead.

The next day had held yet another shock: a telephone call from her sister's attorney informing her that she was the sole heir to Katie and Ken's estate. As their only living relative, she shouldn't have been surprised, but she was. Before she'd had time even to accept the fact of the accident, she had become the owner of the Montana ranch they'd worked so hard for. Together Katie and Ken had turned the Double K into the best dude ranch in the country.

Along with the ranch they left Shelby all their assets. There were stocks and bonds, plus enough money for her to live comfortably *and* keep the place running for quite a long time.

Shelby's first thought had been to sell the ranch. After all, Katie had been the one who was crazy about horses and country life. Shelby had always preferred the city, with its creature comforts and luxuries. Besides, she already had a full-time job as executive sales coordinator with one of San Francisco's best public relations firms. Of course, that was only a fancy title for a glorified gofer, but it was the first job she'd had in a long time that she liked. She couldn't possibly keep the ranch.

But then the letter had come, forwarded by the attorney. Her little sister had written it a year earlier, to accompany the will.

Shelby had placed it on her bureau, not wanting to open it. Somehow, it seemed that the longer she put off opening that letter, the longer she could deny Katie's death. But the letter was impossible to ignore. Its presence nagged at her, beckoning, looming up so that eventually, whenever she entered her bedroom, that small white envelope was the only thing she saw.

Finally she'd been unable to avoid it any longer. She opened the letter with trembling hands, her heart pounding so furiously she thought it might explode. . . .

Shelby reached a hand into the pocket of her safari jacket and her fingers closed around the now-crumpled, worn envelope. She didn't need to look at the letter within to know what it said; she had every line, every word, memorized. The last line rang in her ears: *Keep the ranch going, Shelby. Please, take my dream and make it your own.*

Shelby sighed and leaned forward to rest her head against the steering wheel. She wasn't sure she could do what her sister had asked, but she'd try.

Suddenly a car horn blasted behind her, startling Shelby and jerking her from her thoughts. She looked in the rear-view mirror, but all she could see was a brilliantly shiny silver grill.

The horn sounded again, an obvious expression of its owner's impatience.

"All right already!" Shelby muttered. Her melancholy was instantly replaced by irritation at the occupants of the "monster" behind her. Some people thought they owned the world. She grabbed the stick shift and rammed the car into gear. With a loud grinding noise, the sports car bucked forward and the engine died. Shelby felt a flush of heat spread across her cheeks. She'd forgotten to use the clutch.

The driver behind her leaned on the horn again . . . for several long seconds.

Shelby twisted around in her seat. She stared at the long white limousine, its occupants safely hidden behind darkly tinted glass, and had the insane urge to stick out her tongue. Instead she turned back to grip the steering wheel, and mumbled a curse. She carefully pushed in the clutch pedal, restarted the car, and slowly steered it to the side of the dirt drive.

The limousine instantly pulled around her and zoomed past, spraying dust and gravel in its wake.

"Oh, well, thank you!" Shelby sputtered at the disappearing car. She waved at the cloud of dirt settling upon her and her shiny new car. "I knew I should have left the top up. I knew it." The fact of the matter was, the previous day she'd managed to jam the canvas roof into its open position and was now unable to get it back up, but that completely slipped her mind. "Why in heaven's name I even bought a convertible is beyond me. All it does is leave you a target for wind, dirt, and suicidal bugs!"

She pulled back onto the entry and drove slowly down the road, enjoying the lush scenery. There wasn't a skyscraper or a freeway in sight. Thirty minutes and a lot of winding road later, the Double K ranch house and its surrounding outbuildings finally came into view. She'd forgotten how pretty the ranch was. All the buildings were made from rough-hewn logs, with roofs of green tile, so the structures blended with the enveloping land-scape of rolling plains, forests, and mountains. Behind and to one side of the two-story ranch house, there was a swimming pool that Shelby hadn't seen before, its waters glistening silver beneath the hot summer sun. Two more guest cottages had been added as well, since the last time she'd visited.

That had been a couple of years ago, and she'd stayed only a few days. Country life, she'd told Katie at least twenty times during that visit and a thousand times afterward, was just not her cup of tea.

"So what am I doing here now?" she muttered as the car slowly rolled toward the house. But she knew why she was here: she had resolved to keep Katie's dream alive.

Shelby pulled the car up before the wide entry steps of the ranch house. "All right, Katie," she whispered, gazing at the big house, "I'm going to try. I promise. I'm really going to try."

Brushing away the tears that filled her eyes at the thought of her sister, Shelby opened the car door, swung her legs out, and made to rise.

"Can I help you, ma'am?"

She looked up to see a weathered old face smiling down at her from beneath a straw cowboy hat that had obviously seen better days. Its owner held out a gnarled hand, and after a second's hesitation, Shelby placed her hand in his.

"Thank you." She rose to discover that even wearing flats, she was a good two inches taller than the old cowboy. "I'm Shelby Hill."

"I know. We met when you were here before. Been a long time. I'm Jake." He smiled. "Assistant to the foreman," he added. He shut the car door behind her as she stepped away.

"Jake . . . oh, yes, of course. Jake," Shelby mumbled, trying to remember him. She brushed a hand across her skirt and moved to the trunk to retrieve her luggage, but paused as another wrangler stepped up beside her.

"Billy will take your luggage into the house, Miss Shelby," Jake said.

She handed Billy the keys and began to look around again, trying to familiarize herself with the setting, with each building. Several wranglers in a nearby corral had stopped whatever it was they were doing and were staring at her with obvious curiosity.

Shelby smiled and started to turn back toward the ranch house, but a tall cowboy leaning casually against a hitching post at the opposite end of the house caught her eye. He, too, was watching her, but not with curiosity. His gaze was more assessing, as if he were sizing her up. He had one long, lean leg crossed over the other, and the well-worn, faded jeans he had on hugged his form. His pale blue, linen shirt was stretched taut across wide shoulders. His face was shadowed by a wide-brimmed, black Stetson, pulled low, but not low enough to obscure his rugged features. With a seemingly careless gesture, he unfolded his arms, reached up, and pushed the hat back off his forehead.

Every cowboy hero in every cowboy movie

Shelby had endured while she and Katie were kids flashed before her as their eyes met and locked. For one endless moment she was mesmerized, unable to look away, and wondered if she'd ever seen eyes such a dark, dazzling blue, or hair such a rich, lustrous gold.

Not until the cowboy pushed himself away from the hitching rack and walked toward her, his gait slow and insolent, was Shelby able to pull her gaze from his. She lowered her eyes and ordered herself to remain calm, while all she really wanted to do was turn and run.

He paused before her, and she took a step back, putting some distance between them.

With a swift movement he swept the hat from his head and held out his other hand toward her. "I'm Cody Farlowe, Miss Hill. Foreman of the Double K."

For the next five days Shelby threw herself into learning everything she could about the ranch, though she did her best to avoid Cody Farlowe.

The first morning after her arrival, she went over the books, pulling back into mind what she'd learned in her few accounting classes in college. After a few hours of trying to decipher thousands of numbers, she knew she'd have to pore over the figures a second time just to understand them . . . forget about auditing them. Hiring a bookkeeper was most likely the logical answer, she'd decided.

The second morning she rose at the crack of dawn and trudged down to the kitchen, intending to help Marie, the cook, with breakfast. She figured she needed to learn all aspects of running the place, even though cooking had never been one of her strong points. She pushed open the kitchen door, while trying to stifle a yawn, and stared in disbelief at the mountain of food piled on the counter. "What's all that for?"

"Breakfast," Marie answered simply. A wide smile curved her generously full lips. A long black braid that hung down the middle-aged woman's back swung like a pendulum as she turned from the refrigerator and moved back to the counter.

"Marie, there's enough food here for an army!"

The woman's dark eyes danced with laughter. "Ah, but between the guests and the ranch hands, Miss Shelby, we *do* have an army to feed. Still want to help?"

"I've got to learn," she answered, trying to sound cheerier than she felt. For some reason she'd envisioned several assistants running around the kitchen, not just *one* cook. She picked up a knife and began to cut away the fat on the steaks, promptly slicing a good bit of skin off one of her fingers. "Ouch! Damn!" She shoved her finger under the tap, twisted the faucet hastily, and hissed beneath her breath as cold water splashed down onto the small wound.

Marie chuckled. "Here, you beat the eggs and scramble them on the grill. I'll cook the steaks."

The two women worked side by side for more than an hour and by the time the ranch hands had filed through the back door to sit at the kitchen table, breakfast was ready. Mountains of steaks,

14

scrambled eggs, fried potatoes, toast, and two huge bowls of fresh fruit sat in the center of the table.

Shelby placed a pot of coffee before Jake just as Cody, the last to enter the room, sat down at the head of the table. She glanced at him, and immediately wished she hadn't. A slightly wicked grin curved his lips and a gleam that could only be described as devilish sparkled in his eyes as he caught her gaze.

Twenty minutes later, when the ranch hands filed back out the door, not a scrap of food was left on the table . . . and Shelby's nerves were completely shot. The entire time the wranglers had been in the kitchen, she'd tried to keep busy and ignore the burning sensation of Cody's gaze on her back. She'd been busy enough, but she'd been aware of Cody's presence every moment. Each time she'd snuck a glance at him he'd caught her. She hadn't blushed so much since she was twelve and Rodney Wagstaff had shown the mushy valentine card she'd sent him to all the boys in school.

The process of serving breakfast was repeated an hour later for the guests, who gathered in the huge main dining room. And it was no sooner over than Marie started to pull out food for lunch.

By the end of her second day at the Double K, Shelby was astounded that Marie did all the cooking at the ranch. The preparation of breakfast alone had been exhausting, and Marie did three meals a day. Which was actually six, because the guests and ranch hands ate separately.

Three days later, Shelby was starting to feel

more comfortable at the ranch, except when Cody was around. At those times, it seemed, she turned into a klutz, dropping plates, tripping over small rocks or twigs, and once even running smack into a closed door.

Chapter Two

Shelby stared at the Western saddle straddling the stall railing and knew she was in trouble. But, then, she'd been in trouble since the moment the attorney had informed her she'd inherited her sister's world-famous Montana dude ranch. If she'd been smart she would have sold the place immediately, which had been her first instinct, and set herself up in a luxury condo in San Francisco. After all, what did she know about catering to wealthy jet-setters and Hollywood types who wanted a taste of the Old West? For that matter, what did she know of the Old West?

But of course she couldn't do that. She couldn't let her sister's dream die.

"You managing okay there, boss lady?" Cody asked.

His lazy drawl was edged with humor, Shelby noted. He'd obviously found her efforts to acquaint herself with country life since arriving at the Double K amusing. She gripped the saddle, pulled it from the railing, and nearly toppled backward. The blasted thing weighed a ton, and with all the straps and buckles and doodads that hung from it, she found it difficult to carry the saddle and walk at the same time without tripping.

She glanced across the barn at Cody. "What do they do, stuff these things with lead?"

He chuckled and shook his head as he tightened the cinch around the belly of his horse. "You sure you want to go on this roundup? It's going to be a lot of time in the saddle for someone who's never done much riding."

"Who says I haven't done much riding? I'll have you know I'm a very good rider." She bit down on her bottom lip and hoped her fib wasn't too obvious. But, then, it wasn't really a fib, just an exaggeration. She hadn't been on a horse in more than ten years, not since she'd stop taking lessons with Katie. Of course, Katie had been learning to ride Western. Shelby, who had taken the lessons only at her mother's insistence, had stubbornly demanded to ride English-style . . . quite different, she knew, from Western, and in her mind classier.

Cody shrugged. "You're the boss." He glanced across the barn and saw her struggling to get the saddle onto her horse's back. "Leave it on the rail. I'll saddle Lady for you when I'm done here."

Shelby was tempted to take him up on his offer. She seemed to recall that she'd been able to carry an English saddle with one hand. This thing was as heavy as a truck! How was she ever going to get it up onto the horse? She was about to accept Cody's offer of help, when she stopped herself. She'd

18

never make a go of it on the Double K by letting Cody and the ranch hands do everything for her.

"Thanks, I'll manage," she finally said with some bravado. A stray lock of auburn hair dangled from her forehead and tickled her nose. She blew a stream of air upward in an effort to rid herself of it, but the rebellious curl fell back instantly onto the tip of her nose. Trying to ignore the annoying tendril, Shelby sidled into the stall, moving slowly and cautiously down the narrow space between the chestnut horse, which looked monstrous, and the stall rail. With a lot of huffing and puffing, she managed to wrestle the saddle onto the horse's back.

"You forgot the blanket," Cody said.

"What?" Shelby stared at him in confusion. "Who needs a blanket the way the heat is around here? It's boiling."

He patted his horse on the rump and walked toward Shelby. "The blanket goes under the saddle. Put that thing on Lady without one and you'll rub her back raw."

"Oh." Lord, what else had she forgotten about riding in the past ten years? She stepped aside as Cody effortlessly lifted the saddle from the mare and sat it on the stall rail. From the same rail he grabbed a colorful Indian-print blanket and threw it over Lady's back, then began deftly to saddle her.

Shelby felt her cheeks warm. If Cody Farlowe didn't know before that she hadn't been around horses much recently, if at all, she was certain he knew it now.

She tried to look away, and found her eyes stubbornly refuse to cooperate. Giving up the struggle, she let her gaze wander over Cody's tall body. A plaid chambray shirt covered his broad shoulders, the sleeves rolled to reveal well-tanned and muscular arms. His long legs were encased in a pair of snug-fitting jeans that were so well used the knees and back pockets had turned white. His boots had pointed toes and wedged heels, and were work-worn to the point that discerning their original color was impossible.

He straightened and turned toward her, leaning one bent arm against the top of the saddle. With his other hand, he reached up and pushed the black Stetson from his forehead, using the tip of his thumb. "There you go. Now, climb up onto Lady and I'll adjust your stirrups."

Shelby stuck her left foot in the leather stirrup, grabbed the horn of the saddle, and, after three bouncing tries, finally made it up onto Lady's back. The mare did a nervous little side step, and shook her head, sending her long mane spraying through the air, almost into Shelby's face. At a few soothing words from Cody, the horse settled down, and Shelby glanced around from her perch. She looked toward the ground and instantly wished she hadn't. The hard-packed dirt floor appeared miles away.

Cody led Lady to the center of the barn and then paused, turning to look at Shelby. "Stand up in the stirrups, then sit down and take your feet out of them so I can adjust them to where you'll need them."

"I need them on the ground," she mumbled.

Cody chuckled softly, but made no other response. When she was settled back in the saddle, he began to adjust the footings. Shelby watched him, and for the umpteenth time since her arrival felt a simmering warmth of attraction for the handsome foreman of the Double K. And for the umpteenth time she tried to deny it. He hadn't spoken to her twice since she'd arrived, except to tell her what she was doing wrong or to laugh at her mistakes, which, unfortunately, were many. It appeared that the only thing she and Cody had in common, besides their desire to see the Double K continue to operate, was the fact that both their first names ended with a *y*. Nevertheless she found him to be one of the sexiest men she'd ever met, and in her travels she'd met many.

Everything about him radiated strength and virility, a sensual power that was almost overpowering. His face was a contrast of square cuts, smooth planes, and sweeping hollows, all combining to form a rugged perfection. Long hours under the sun had turned his skin a burnished bronze, which accentuated the brilliant blue of his eyes and the golden waves of hair that curled raggedly over the top of his ears and shirt collar.

"Okay, boss lady, that's it. Time to hit the trail," Cody said.

Shelby groaned silently, something she was starting to do with extreme regularity. This is what she'd been dreading since the moment she had heard about the trail drive.

Planning "authentic Western cuisine" for twenty

people and overseeing its preparation was one thing. Making sure all the cabins were cleaned, the guest activities were running smoothly, the guides and workers were on the ball, and the Olympic-size pool and two hot tubs were always spick-and-span was another. Helping out in the Double K's general store, which carried designer-name Western outfits at outrageous prices, was yet another. But riding a horse in the wilderness for four days and trying to herd cows from pasture A to pasture B was something entirely different, and she wasn't sure she was ready for it.

She wasn't looking forward to it, but the guests expected her to host the roundup. Actually, they expected Katie Hill-Randall, whose smiling face graced the front of the Double K's colorful brochures. But Katie wasn't here anymore . . . Shelby was. Tears stung her eyes as thoughts of Katie filled her mind, and she blinked rapidly to force them away. Now wasn't the time to break down.

The roundup was a special attraction at the ranch, and one of the main reasons many of the wealthy, jet-setting guests chose the Double K over other dude ranches in the area. They wanted to get a taste of the Old West. If she was going to keep Katie's dream alive and make a life for herself here, she had to go on this roundup. She had to be strong.

She almost laughed out loud at that last thought. Strength had never been one of her dominant characteristics. She'd lost more than her share of jobs because of her inability to make a decision, act on it, then stand behind it. Even some of her relationships had failed because she'd rarely felt able to voice her opinion or demand a choice. It had always been easier just to walk away.

The first rays of the morning sun crept through the tall, open doors of the barn, spreading their warmth as they penetrated the shadows. "This isn't even a decent hour to be awake, let alone perched on the back of a horse," Shelby grumbled.

Cody whistled and his horse, a huge bay with black mane and tail, sauntered from the stall out into the center of the barn. "Okay, Soldier, time to hit the road."

Shelby watched Cody swing easily up and onto his saddle, and cringed. He mounted a horse with fluid grace, while she looked as if she were struggling to climb the Rocky Mountains. Cody touched his heels to the side of his mount and the animal moved toward the open door of the barn. Lady immediately followed, with no encouragement from Shelby.

Jake had just finished saddling the last of the corral horses and was shouting at two wranglers to help the guests mount. The area hummed with confusion and excitement as twenty-two people, ranging in age from ten to sixty, struggled to climb onto their horses. Obviously, most had never ridden before coming to the Double K.

Well, at least I'm in good company, Shelby thought just as Lance Murdock, Hollywood superstar, sidled his mount up beside hers. He had apologized profusely for his limo practically running her over at the gate the day of her arrival, and had been flirting outrageously ever since.

23

"Hi, beautiful. How about being my trail partner?" He flashed her the real-life version of his seductively wicked screen smile and winked one amber-laced brown eye.

Shelby smiled back. He'd probably already made the same proposal to at least half the other women on the drive, but she was flattered all the same. It wasn't every day a movie star propositioned her. And such a handsome one, she mused, admiring his Greek-god looks. A dark brown Stetson, almost the same shade as his hair, sat at a jaunty angle and cast his wide forehead, high cheekbones, and aristocratic nose in shadow, while the smiling mouth and strong jaw remained in sunlight. He wore a white linen shirt with brown cord trim and onyx snap buttons, the collar left open just enough to allow several curly dark strands of hair below the hollow of his throat to peek out. His color-coordinated brown jeans hadn't even lost their crease yet, and his eelskin cowboy boots, with their steel-tipped toes and high-wedged heels, shone brilliantly.

He looked great, but more ready for a parade than a trail drive, Shelby thought, glancing at the well-worn jeans and plain work shirts most of the wranglers wore.

"Sorry, Murdock. Miss Hill rides with me," Cody said.

Shelby spun around, surprised at the rather curt tone Cody had used toward a guest, but was then equally surprised to see him smiling.

"Well, perhaps we can get together later, Shelby." Lance's gaze made a caressing, very suggestive sweep from Shelby's eyes to her breasts and back again. "A warm, crackling campfire, a full summer moon overhead, and the serenading lullaby of crickets and hoot owls. Sound good?"

"We'll see," Shelby answered softly, painfully conscious of Cody behind her.

Jake led two of the mounted guests to where Shelby and Cody waited. She was forced to turn her head away, hiding a smile that threatened to erupt into a laugh. Eva Montalvo, a New York socialite who, Shelby guessed, was fifty if she was a day, was dressed in a sunflower yellow jumpsuit with leather fringe hanging the length of her sleeves, down the outseam of her pants, and across the sloping front of her bustline. A stiff white cowboy hat sat nestled amid her bouncing blond curls, and her feet were encased in stylish white cowboy boots with very high heels.

Shelby stared at the fancy boots and silently hoped the woman had shown some common sense and packed a more sensible pair of shoes in her saddlebags.

"Oh, this is going to be such fun!" Eva said, flashing Cody a huge smile and batting long mascara-coated lashes.

Shelby looked back just in time to catch Eva's flirtatious gesture toward the Double K's foreman, and saw him return the smile. She looked away again, suddenly wondering if she should have worn something a little fancier than her plain jeans and Western-style shirt with its floral print trim. She'd discovered the shirt in the general store boutique while supposedly there to go over the inventory, and had fallen in love with it. She thought of the closetful of designer clothes she'd bought just before leaving San Francisco. The shopping trip had been an impulse, spurred on by a yearning to dull the intense grief and loneliness the news of the accident had brought on. Despite the new wardrobe, this morning she'd nearly panicked when she realized she had no riding boots. She'd burrowed into Katie's closet in a frenzy and finally found hers — luckily she and Katie had worn the same size. Shelby hadn't gotten around to cleaning out Katie's closet yet; truth be told, she'd deliberately avoided the task.

Eva Montalvo's musical laugh drew her attention and pulled her from the threat of sad thoughts.

"Oh, Randolph, loosen up. You'll enjoy it, I promise," Eva said, speaking to the heavyset balding man on the mount beside hers.

"I just hope you realize what you've gotten us into this time," he grumbled.

Eva laughed. "Tut-tut, Randolph. Remember, you're my friend, not my husband."

Shelby saw the man's brow furrow deeply. Obviously this was one pampered guest who was not enthused about being a "cowboy." Or maybe his displeasure had to do with the fact he was Eva's friend and not her husband, as Eva had so blithely reminded him.

Within minutes the ranch hands had led the rest of the guests from the corral and all were gathered in a wide semicircle before Shelby and Cody. Excited chatter filled the air.

Cody stood up in his stirrups. "All right, people, listen up." He waited a minute while everyone quieted. "We're going to do a lot of work on this ride, and I hope have a little fun. There are about two hundred cows out there that have to be moved from the east valley to the west ridge. It'll take us most of the day to get to the valley they're at now. We'll stop for lunch, a rest about halfway, and make camp for the night in the hills that overlook the valley. First thing in the morning we'll start moving the herd westward. Tomorrow and the day after, we ride all day, pushing them to the ridge. We finish up the move the day after that. We should be back at the ranch house by dinnertime Sunday. That is, if none of you gets lost."

A wicked little smile curved his lips at his last comment, and nervous chuckles came from the guests.

Shelby noticed several of the ranch hands mount their horses, which had been tied to a rack beside the corral, and move up behind the guests. She turned to Cody. "Tom will have the truck wherever it is we're going to stop for lunch, won't he?"

Cody grinned and turned his horse around. "Stop worrying, boss lady. He'll probably have the picnic blankets laid out and the food cooked and served when we ride up."

Lady turned automatically to follow Cody and Soldier.

Shelby clutched the saddle horn so hard her knuckles turned white. "Cody?" Owing to the combination of the eight or nine inches he had on her own five-foot-five and Soldier's three or four

27

inches over Lady, Shelby was forced to look up in order to meet Cody's eyes.

"Yeah?"

"Do you think you could stop calling me 'boss lady'?"

"Sure, *Ms Hill.*"

She heard the tinkle of amusement in his tone again and felt like punching his arm. The man was maddening. For the past six days, ever since he'd greeted her in front of the ranch house, he'd kept her in alternating states of laughter, piqued indignation, or red-hot fury. Casual, relaxed conversation was something she carried on with everyone else at the ranch—workers and guests alike—but not with Cody Farlowe.

"Really, Cody. I'd rather you call me 'Shelby.' "

"Okay, if you'll call me 'Mr. Farlowe.' "

She stared at him in openmouthed surprise.

Cody burst out laughing, a deep mellifluous sound that sent a tingle of warmth from Shelby's boot-enclosed toes, through her body, to the top of her auburn-tressed head. Then she began to laugh, her softer pitch blending with his in the quiet morning air.

For more than an hour they rode side by side in silence, the others trailing behind them, a cacophony of chatter, grumbles, and laughter floating in the air. The ranch hands mingled with the guests, making sure all were okay and having a good time, and that no one wandered away from the group.

The open fields of tall golden grass gave way to sloping hills and shallow valleys; pine trees dotted the landscape, along with redwoods and scrub oaks. Squirrels perched in high branches scolded the group passing below, and a hawk flew overhead, shrieking its irritation at their invasion of his hunting grounds.

Shelby was mesmerized by the raw beauty of the land, the clear blue sky, and the fresh air. She'd been in cities so long she had forgotten fresh air even existed. No smog, no exhaust fumes, no heavy layer of dirty gray on the horizon. The sky was crystal clear, the air clean and pure. She breathed deeply and sighed. Her nephews must have loved growing up here. The thought brought a pang of grief and Shelby pushed it aside, knowing that if she didn't, tears would quickly follow.

"Anyone ever tell you that your eyes are the same color as the trees?" Cody said.

His comment surprised her and she turned to look at him, but he was staring straight ahead, a slight frown pulling at his brow.

"I'm going to ride ahead a bit, boss—uh, Shelby. We had a landslide a couple of months ago on the trail that curves around the next hill. It was cleared out, but I want to make sure no other trees have fallen, or are about to." With that Cody touched his heels to Soldier's side and the horse broke into a lope.

Shelby held tight to the reins in an effort to prevent Lady from following. The horse shook her head and pranced in a little dance that told Shelby in no uncertain terms that she was not happy with being left behind by Soldier. "Whoa, horse, whoa," Shelby said, praying the animal wouldn't decide to ignore her and bolt into a gallop. She

could see the headline now: NEW OWNER OF DOU-
BLE K DUDE RANCH DISAPPEARS IN MONTANA
WILDERNESS ON RUNAWAY HORSE.

Chapter Three

Shelby shifted position in the saddle, trying to find a spot on her rear end that wasn't sore. Her tailbone felt as if someone had used it for a battering ram, and she didn't know if she'd ever be able to sit down again. In the four hours since they'd left the ranch house, the saddle seemed to have transformed itself from a curved piece of leather into hard, flat rock. And in her ever-increasing pain, the beauty of the landscape had long since lost its attraction.

Too bad she hadn't arranged for the Double K's resident masseuse to accompany them on the trail drive, she thought. At least then she might have had a *slight* chance of being able to walk again once she got off of this horse.

It was nearing noon before Cody returned to the group. He'd been gone for well over an hour and Shelby, in spite of herself, had been unable to think of anything or anyone else during his absence.

"How's the slide area?" she asked as he pulled up to ride beside her.

"Huh? Oh, it's all right. Nothing to worry

about." He wasn't about to admit that he'd checked the area only the day before, and that the real reason he'd ridden off was that he'd found himself starting to wonder what it would be like to lean over and brush his lips across hers.

A short while later the group crested a small hill, and Cody raised a hand to indicate they all stop. He turned in his saddle to look back at the gathering of weary riders. "Okay, folks, we're almost there. Today's halfway point. The chuck truck's parked at the bottom of this hill, the blankets are laid out, and the food's on."

A soft hum of mumbles, moans, and grumbles filtered back in response from the saddle-sore guests. Most of the laughter had ceased more than an hour earlier. Cody grinned and urged Soldier back into motion.

Lance rode up beside Shelby. "I promised to lunch with a couple of the other guests, but I'm counting the hours till sundown and our date, beautiful. Only seven. Then we can get off these beasts and get to know each other a little better."

He winked conspiratorially, a gesture that, Shelby knew, would have sent any number of Lance Murdock's female fans into near hysteria.

"I'm looking forward to it," she fibbed graciously, and smiled. Whatever was the matter with her? she wondered. Normally she would have been one of those swooning females, ready to walk on hot coals for the chance to get near someone like Lance Murdock, and here she was, flattered by his compliments and attention but otherwise totally unmoved. Had she suddenly gone frigid or something?

She glanced across the herd to where Cody was riding with one of the female guests . . . a very pretty female guest. Shelby felt a spark of jealousy. No, she definitely hadn't turned frigid.

She looked back at Lance. "I'd best see what I can do to help us make camp." She nudged her heels against Lady's ribs. "See you tonight, Lance." The mare broke into a sudden trot, obviously anxious to catch up with Soldier. Shelby was thrown backward. Her feet flew upward, taking the stirrups with them, and in an effort to right herself, she pulled on the reins. Lady shook her head in revolt at the bit jerking against her mouth, and Shelby was forced to grab hold of the saddle horn to keep from falling off.

Within minutes the group was beside Tom's chuck truck and dismounting. The ranch hands took the guests horses and tied them to a hitching rack that had been built some time ago between two tall pine trees. The aroma of barbecued hamburgers and baked beans filled the air, and Shelby thought she'd never smelled anything so good in her entire life. She saw that next to the portable barbecue grill Tom had set up beneath a copse of pines was a picnic table piled high with condiments, beflowered paper plates, a huge bowl of potato salad, green salad, and a bucket filled with ice, canned drinks, and sparkling waters.

"Need any help, Shelby?" Cody asked as she brought Lady up beside the battered red pickup truck that served as a modern-day chuck wagon.

"Thanks, I'm sure I can get down on my own." She gripped the saddle horn and swung her right leg

33

over the mare's rump. When she had both feet on the ground, she groaned loudly as she felt her legs begin to collapse beneath her weight. No, not in front of Cody! her mind screamed.

Cody swooped to catch her in his arms, and her flailing hand knocked the brim of his hat and sent it flying to the ground. "That's not exactly the way we get off a horse around here, Shelby."

His smile, and the twinkling humor she saw in his eyes, softened the stinging reference to her ungainly dismount. With a toss of her head she removed the long strands of hair that blocked her vision and set her knocked-askew hat back on her head. His face was only inches from her own.

Her gaze locked with his, forest green melding with mountain-lake blue. Suddenly Shelby was painfully conscious of her breasts crushed against the hard breadth of Cody's chest, his arms, like bands of hot steel, wrapped around her, holding her to him. She felt the beating of his heart, a rapid pounding that matched her own thump for thump, smelled the spicy fragrance of his cologne blended with the scent of horseflesh and leather, and saw his smile vanish as he looked down at her.

The arm beneath her legs disappeared and her feet swung down to touch the ground, but his other arm still remained firmly in place around her back, holding her tightly against him.

"Are you all right now? Can you stand?"

Both his tone and his attitude seemed to have suddenly turned sullen, Shelby thought. "Yes, I'm fine." She pushed herself from his embrace, and instantly felt an agonizingly long moment of panic.

Her legs, which seemed irreversibly bowed, were shaking like a dry leaf in a winter storm.

Cody had turned away to tie her horse to a nearby bush.

Shelby's aching legs trembled and then seemed to melt beneath her weight. She lost the struggle to remain upright and collapsed to the ground, her saddle-sore derriere hitting the weed-covered earth with a solid *whumpf.*

The sound caught Cody's attention and he jerked around in her direction. "What the hel—?"

Shelby glared at him. "Don't you dare laugh, Cody Farlowe, or so help me I'll fire you," she threatened with a lot more aplomb than she felt. Her face was warm and she knew she'd just turned as red as a ripe tomato. She determinedly fought back the tears stinging her eyes.

Without even a trace of a grin, Cody scooped her up in his arms and carried her to one of the picnic blankets Tom had laid out beside a nearby creek. He deposited her on the plaid square with less than a gentle hand. "Stay here," he ordered brusquely, then straightened and walked back toward the truck.

Shelby watched his retreating back, while trying to ignore the throbbing ache of her limbs. The man had more moods than a kaleidoscope had colors, she thought, and he changed them just as quickly. Which was driving her nuts.

Something moved behind her, effectively blocking the sun and throwing a shadow across both her and the blanket. She turned. "Oh, hi, Lance."

He bent down beside her, pushing the brim of his hat from his forehead. A lock of dark hair fell forward, giving his already strikingly handsome face a rakish appeal. "Great ride, wasn't it? Of course, so is a zip in my Ferrari."

Shelby smiled, a bit surprised that Lance wasn't limping around like some of the other guests or complaining. "Have you done this before? Ride, I mean?"

"Yeah. I have a ranch up in Malibu with a full stable."

"So why'd you come to the Double K?"

Lance smiled. "My agent thought I needed a change of scenery and pace. A little relaxation. She knows I love horses, so she made me the reservation here."

"Well, I'm glad she did," Shelby answered truthfully. Lance was a nice man. He didn't make her blood boil or her heart sing, which was a little disappointing, but his attentions certainly didn't do her wavering ego any damage. Quite the contrary.

"You ever ride on a beach in the moonlight, Shelby?"

She laughed. "No, I can't say that I have, though it sounds wonderfully romantic."

"It is. Maybe you could come down to my place sometime. I know you'd —"

"Laaance, I'm hungry."

A tall redhead moved up to stand beside him, a pout pulling at her full lower lip. Shelby recognized her as one of the single women in a group that had arrived at the ranch two days earlier.

Lance winked at Shelby and stood. "See you this evening, beautiful," he said softly, his voice too low for the redhead to hear. "Duty calls."

"Lance, I . . ." But before she could finish the sentence, he was gone.

"Hollywood seems pretty taken with you."

Shelby jumped and turned around. Cody stared down at her, a food-laden plate in each hand.

"Oh, poo. Lance Murdock could have any woman on the face of the earth. Or any other planet in the universe, for that matter. He's just being nice to me because I own the Double K, that's all."

"Yeah, right." Though his words were of agreement, his drippingly sarcastic tone said otherwise.

Cody sat down cross-legged beside Shelby on the blanket and handed her one of the plates. It held a huge hamburger plus all the trimmings, a sea of steaming baked beans, a mountain of potato salad, some kind of fruit salad, and a few carrot and celery sticks. Shelby stared at the food in disbelief. She'd worked up an appetite, but this was ridiculous.

From his shirt pockets Cody pulled two cans of Canadian beer. He handed her one, snapped the tab of his own, and took a long swallow.

Shelby looked at the can in her hand and wrinkled her nose. Beer was not one of her favorite drinks, even if it was imported, but it was cold and wet — two things that, at the moment, made it appealing. It would do in this heat, she decided. She pulled the tab and hurriedly took a sip as foam began to bubble up through the small hole. She shuddered involuntarily at the sharp taste.

"I guess you would have preferred one of those bottles of fancy water," Cody said when Shelby sat her can of beer on the ground.

"Uh, no. This is okay."

He stared at her, an unrelenting stare that made her nervous and caused her to fidget.

"Thank you for catching me," she said finally, hating herself for having had to be rescued in the first place.

"Shelby, I've been thinking. Maybe you'd better ride back to the ranch house in the truck with Tom. Help Marie with the cooking and cleaning and stuff till we get back. There're more guests arriving every day."

Her muffled protest was lost in the mound of hamburger and bun she had just bitten down on. She chewed furiously, getting unreasonably angrier with each passing second, and finally swallowed. "I'm not going back to the ranch house."

Cody sighed. "Shelby, there's no reason to torture yourself out here. The boys and I can handle the drive and the guests."

With each word he spoke her indignation grew, and with it, her stubbornness. "Now, you listen here, Cody Farlowe. Ever since I came to the Double K you've tried to persuade me to leave. Not in so many words, mind you, but I've heard the hints and insinuations. And let me tell you, they're not going to work. My sister left me this place, and I'm here to stay, whether you like it or not!" Shelby tried to brave Cody's irate stare, found she couldn't after a few agonizing long seconds, and lowered her eyes.

"You don't belong here."

Her head shot up at the harsh words. "Katie thought otherwise, and . . . and so do I." A cloud of doubt hovered at the back of her mind and she pushed it away. This was the first place in years she could actually call home. Since her parents had died and she'd finished college, she'd been unable to find a job or a place that held her interest for more than a few months. Oh, she'd done all right in the advertising field, but it had never excited her the way she'd thought it would. Now she had Katie's dream to hang on to, and no one, not even Cody Farlowe, was going to make her give it up.

"I doubt Katie would have expected you to go on this roundup, Shelby." His tone softened. "Be reasonable. You don't know how to ride, and by the time we make camp tonight you probably won't remember how to walk."

"I'll be fine."

An angry glint clouded the clear blue eyes and a frown nettled his forehead, pulling the golden brows together. "Yeah, right. *Fine*. Look at you — you're already a mess. Another few hours in the saddle and you'll be screaming that you're crippled for life. Admit it, Shelby. You're not up to this and you know it. You're a city girl."

He said the last sentence as if the words disgusted him, and Shelby did not miss the tone. "Katie trusted me," she shot back.

"Go home, Shelby. Sell the Double K to someone who knows what they're doing. To someone who can run it."

Shelby felt her anger growing, and at the same time her self-confidence wavered. Was he right? Was she just fooling herself by believing she could run the Double K? She stiffened and forced her apprehension away. Katie had wanted her here; otherwise she and Ken would have found some distant relative of his to name in their will, or left the ranch to charity, or stipulated it be sold and the money given to Shelby. She felt a new surge of resolve. Just who in the hell did Cody Farlowe think he was, anyway? Maybe she was just a city girl, and maybe Cody, or someone else, could take care of and run the Double K better than she could, but she'd never let her little sister down in the past and she wasn't about to start now. Even if Katie wasn't here to realize it.

Shelby slammed the hamburger down on the paper plate and glowered at Cody. "I have no intention of going back to California, Cody. Not now or ever. Katie worked hard to make the Double K the best and classiest dude ranch in the country, and I intend to keep it just that, with or without your help."

Cody took another long swallow of his beer, wadded up the napkin that had been wrapped around his hamburger, and grinned at her.

The boyish smile, so innocent and beguiling, was almost Shelby's undoing. Her anger disappeared like so much smoke on the wind, and she found herself suddenly wondering what it would be like to feel his lips on hers.

"Well, darlin', we'll see. For now, if you really insist on sticking it out here, then I've got a couple of suggestions for you. First, you'd best find something soft to put between you and the saddle this afternoon 'cause it's going to be a long ride. And second, I'd get off that pretty rear of yours and start moving around. Otherwise, in another few minutes your legs are going to be so stiff you won't be able to move." That said, Cody got up. He began to walk away, paused, and looked back over his shoulder. "You might get a couple of aspirin from Tom, unless the guests have already gobbled them all up. He usually hands them out with their lunch. First-day aches, you know."

Shelby wanted to throw her hamburger at him; instead, she took a healthy bite out of it and ground the meat viciously between her teeth. This time she wouldn't quit. This time she'd see the situation through, no matter what. If for no other reason than to show Cody Farlowe he was wrong about her, she'd stick it out on this trail drive, and she'd make it without any help from him.

A few minutes later, Shelby clenched her teeth at the pain that coursed through her legs when she shifted her weight, and struggled to her feet. Damn. If she felt like this after only four hours in the saddle, what was she going to be like by the time they made camp for the night?

She stumbled toward the creek: at its edge, she glanced over her shoulder. Most of the guests were either still eating or lying flat on their backs on the picnic blankets. Obviously they weren't in any better shape than she was. She moved behind a cluster of large rocks at the creek's edge and sat down, out of sight. Within seconds she had her boots and socks off, and had peeled out of her Levi's. Daring, she knew, but at the moment it seemed like a good idea. She stood in a crouched position, and another glance over the rocks told her no one had seen her escape. She was still safe.

She waded into the stream. Its mountain iciness jolted her, but oh, Lord it felt good. She sat down

41

and let the cold water wash over her aching legs and backside, numbing them. She closed her eyes and turned her face skyward, allowing the sun to caress her from the hips up and the slowly moving water from the hips down.

"Hey, guess what Miss Hill's doing!"

Shelby jumped and looked around. A small boy of about ten was standing on one of the rocks, gazing down at her.

With no time to escape, she watched, aghast, as the edge of the creek quickly crowded with guests from the Double K. The moment they saw their hostess sitting in the water, the idea seemed to become unanimously accepted. Boots and socks went flying through the air. The kids ripped off their jeans and practically threw themselves into the water, while most of the adults, being a little more modest, rolled up their pant legs and waded in. A few even sat down in the creek fully clothed.

Shelby, though a good twenty feet from everyone else, felt trapped. Not wanting to stand up with nothing on below her waist but her tiger-striped bikini panties, she inched her way back toward the rocks, and stretched out a hand in search of her Levi's.

"Looking for these, boss lady?"

Chapter Four

Cody sat on the highest of a cluster of large rocks, one arm draped across his bent knee, Shelby's rolled jeans dangling from the fingers of one hand. A wicked grin curved his lips.

Her heart jumped into her throat. "Gi-give me those," she ordered, and instinctively crossed her legs. "And stop gawking at me. Haven't you ever seen a woman before?"

Cody laughed, and the warm sound wrapped around her like a blanket of soft velvet.

"Sure, I've seen my share. I just don't think I've ever encountered one who could start near riots out in the middle of nowhere without saying a word."

Shelby threw a quick glance at the rollicking guests, then looked back at Cody. A wave of guilt swept over her. She'd probably thrown the rest of the day's schedule off. "I guess this will make us late meeting Tom with tonight's chuck truck."

"Some. A few steaks might be well done instead of rare, and somebody's going to have to explain to the old grump why we're late, but other than that—" he shrugged "—we'll manage okay."

"It's my fault. I'll explain to him what happened."

Cody reached behind him and grabbed a rolled-up towel he'd carried to the rocks when he'd figured out what was going on. "Come on out and dry yourself off, then help me try to talk the guests back into their saddles, if that's possible."

"Turn around."

"What?" He arched his brows in disbelief.

"You heard me." She stretched her arm toward him, pointed a finger down, and moved it in a circle, as if instructing a child. "Turn around."

With a soft chuckle Cody tossed her the towel, rose to his feet, and turned his back to her. Damned if she wasn't driving him crazy, and had been since the moment she'd driven up to the ranch house in that snazzy little red sports car of hers. He'd taken one look at Shelby Hill as her lithe form emerged from the low-slung car, the light of the afternoon turning her hair to glistening strands of fire, and it had been all over. He'd started having visions of that exquisite body wrapped securely within his embrace, the smooth, sun-kissed skin shed of its clothing and open to his touch, and her full, sensuous lips returning his passion.

He felt a surge of desire coil within the lower region of his body and purposely countered the heated thoughts with memory of the love lesson he'd learned not so long ago. He'd been down that road once with someone very much like Shelby

Hill, and it had proven too rocky and treacherous for his tastes. He wasn't about to travel it again. Not for anybody.

Shelby stood up and walked from the creek, using the towel to quickly dry her legs. "I'm sorry about the guests, Cody. I didn't mean for anything like this to happen. I honestly didn't think anyone would see me back here."

Without thinking he turned around, and nearly dropped his jaw. His gaze raked Shelby from head to foot and back again, the long length of her legs drawing his eyes like a bear to honey. They went on forever, exquisite golden calves that turned to exquisite golden thighs that gave way to—

He pulled himself up short. She was off-limits. He had to remember that, keep telling himself that. She was a city girl, and always had been. And he knew as surely as he knew his own name, that's exactly what she'd stay. Sooner or later, she'd hightail it back to the bright lights. Hadn't Katie told him numerous stories about how different she and her sister had always been? While Katie had cherished pony rides, old Western movies, and picnics in the country, Shelby had taken to roller skates, bicycles, and superhero cartoons.

Cody's hands were clenched into fists. City women and country men don't mix. He'd found that out the hard way. But damn, she sure was easy on the eyes—all subtle curves and seductive planes, and hair the rich color of the bark on an ancient redwood. Her lips seemed always arched in a smile beneath a nose that he could only describe as turned-up sassy. And her eyes . . . He'd found himself nearly mesmerized by her eyes, which were the deep green of a pine forest, shot through with tiny slivers of gold.

She was the kind of woman a man could lose himself to before he even knew what had happened.

Shelby looked up and saw Cody's gaze on her. Her cheeks warmed, and her pulse raced. She knew she was turning every shade of red imaginable, and tried desperately to ignore her embarrassment, telling herself that the bikini she used to swim in at the apartment pool didn't cover much more than the panties she had on now. But for some reason standing in front of Cody Farlowe with nothing on below her hips but a tiny strip of fancy nylon cloth just seemed so . . . so . . . intimate. She grabbed her pants from his outstretched hand and hastily struggled into them, then sat down to pull on her socks and boots.

When she stood, finally ready to meet his gaze, he was gone.

After climbing several steep mountain ridges and putting several miles between himself and the group from the Double K, Cody gave Soldier his head, letting the horse set the pace and trail. The dark gelding's strong legs stretched outward, muscles flexing, the lope an effortless run that both horse and rider enjoyed. The breeze, caused by their speed, whipped at Soldier's black mane and tail, sending the silken tendrils flying. The warm air brushed against Cody's face and pushed at the brim of his hat.

He'd had to get away from Shelby, needed some time to bring his wayward, spiraling emotions under control. If he'd stayed on that rock, staring down at her, it would only have been a matter of seconds before the taut leash he held on his simmering passion broke. How a woman could get under his skin in such a short time he didn't know, but that's exactly what she'd done. And what was worse, he knew she wasn't even aware of it.

His gaze roamed the passing landscape, and he tried to forget about Shelby Hill. He loved the open countryside of Montana, the ruggedness of the raw land and majestic mountains, and he'd missed it. Damn, but he'd missed it. How had he ever thought he could live in the city? It had been an insane idea. But, then, love—or what he'd thought was love—had prompted him to do some crazy, unbelievable things, things that ordinarily he would never even have considered.

He remembered the crowded streets of New York, people hurrying along the concrete, pushing past one another in their rush to get to wherever they were going. And all of them staring straight ahead, afraid to acknowledge one another or just plain not caring to.

Cody had felt lost in New York. He'd yearned for open space and clean air, for endless pastures and snowcapped mountains. Instead he'd been surrounded by car-locked streets, an overhead blanket of smog, and sky-spiraling buildings of steel and glass. Every time he'd seen a policeman on horseback he'd become horribly homesick, and a walk in Central Park had always left him sullen and depressed.

Even worse than the city had been watching his relationship with Lisa crumble. He'd been unable to fit in to her life, to find a job that paid him half what she made as a high-powered model. The fact that he couldn't accept her making most of the money had been reason for many a night's argument, until she'd finally told him it was over, that he should pack up and go back where he belonged.

Shelby Hill was the same type of woman as Lisa: beautiful, city bred, and far more financially secure than he could ever hope to be.

Soldier jumped a small gully and the movement pulled Cody from his thoughts. He drew up on the reins and the gelding stopped. Cody stood in the stirrups and surveyed his surroundings, lost in the splendor of the land he called home. He knew he would never leave again.

A living collage of brilliant colors, contrasting textures, and virgin freshness spread out before him for miles. Years passed, and the rest of the country changed, grew, and modernized, until nature was almost totally squeezed out, a forgotten luxury of man's past, but not here, not in this place. The wildcat still roamed Montana's mountains, as did the grizzly, the coyote, and the mountain goat. Even the buffalo were still here, in fewer numbers than a hundred years earlier, but once again they were thriving and coming back into their own.

God's country, Cody thought. An old cliché,

but a true one.

If only Shelby could feel about the land as he did, but that was too much to expect, or even hope for. Why was he always attracted to the wrong women?

A shadow passed over Cody and he looked up, shielding his eyes from the sun with one hand. A hawk soared high overhead, its dark wings spread wide, its body held taut and straight as it glided across the clear blue stretch of sky. Then, most likely spotting its prey, the bird swooped low and disappeared within a thick grove of pine trees.

Cody pulled Soldier's reins slightly to the right and the horse turned east; then, at a nudge of his rider's heels, Soldier broke into a lope back in the direction of the group from the Double K.

After covering more than a half-dozen miles, Cody began to worry. Where the hell was everybody? The Double K party should have been in sight by now, well on the down-slope side of the ridge, but they weren't. There was no sign of anyone, let alone a group of pampered jet-setters who wanted to be weekend cowboys. He spurred the dark gelding to a faster pace. Something was wrong. He could feel it. Damn it all to hell, he should never have left them.

Lance jerked on the leather thong that held his rope to the saddle; at the same time he slid from his horse's back. He hit the ground and was already forming a lasso as he ran toward the edge of the road, pushing some of the Double K wranglers out of his way.

"Hang on, beautiful, I'm coming," he called, sliding to a stop where the road ended. Nothing more than open air stretched ahead. He looked over the side, nodded, and positioned himself only inches from where the earth dropped off in a sheer cliff to a canyon far below. Raising his arm high, he began to move his rope through the air until it was circling over his head.

Jake tried to approach him, and was nearly hit by the spinning lasso. "Damn it, man, get away from there. Whadya think you're doing with that fool thing? This ain't no trick movie stunt."

"Stay out of my way, old man," Lance ordered.

Everyone stared, the wranglers in disbelief at what he was attempting, the guests in awe, having seen him in many a Western part and assuming he knew exactly what he was doing.

Lance's arm suddenly arched back, then forward, and the lasso lifted up and flew through the air before him. With the forward movement, he lost his balance.

In the flash of less than a second, Lance Murdock went from graceful and efficient cowboy, to city slicker on the verge of getting himself killed.

His arms flapped at the air like featherless wings. His body arched and twisted in a series of contortions as he tried to regain his balance and keep from plunging over the cliff. His screams cut through the silence of the countryside and spurred the Double K crew to action. A dead guest was bad for business. Especially a dead Western-movie-star guest.

Two wranglers darted forth and grabbed at his arms, another secured a handful of Lance's expensive shirt in his fist, and Jake dove for the star's legs, wrapping his arms around his thighs and pulling him back to safety.

They all landed in the dirt in a tangled heap, sputtering a colorful variety of curses, entwined legs and arms flailing, hats flying, and dust rising up around them in billowy clouds.

Jake was the first to disentangle himself from the group. "Dag nab it!" He rose to his feet, slapping at the dust that clung to his pants and glaring down at Lance. "Didn't I tell you not to do that?"

He didn't wait for an answer. Instead he whirled on his heel and strode toward the other ranch hands, who had retrieved their own ropes and were dropping them over the side of the cliff.

Soldier charged around a curve in the wide path, dirt and pebbles flying through the air behind him as his hooves pounded the ground. Cody jerked up on the reins, his heart practically lodging in his throat at the sight that met his eyes. "Whoa, boy, hold on there," he ordered. Soldier's front legs stiffened and his hooves dug into the ground. Cody's right leg swung over the saddle and he jumped to the ground even before they'd come to a complete stop. He ran past the huddled gathering of tourists, past Lance Murdock, who was busy brushing himself off, and toward the group of cowhands standing at the edge of the road. He knew the road dropped off into a deep canyon.

"What the hell happened?" He shouldered his

way past several of the men.

Jake Tosby grabbed Cody's shoulder and pulled him back. "Don't get too near the edge, Cody. It shakes the rocks loose on her."

Cody looked back at Jake. "On who?" He knew the answer even before he'd asked the question. He felt a sinking feeling in the pit of his stomach. "Oh, no. Not Shelby."

Jake nodded.

"Son of a—" Cody caught himself. "Is she all right? Is she hurt?"

"She's okay, Cody, just scared, and probably a little bruised and scratched up. Thankfully she didn't fall all the way. Wouldn't have been much we coulda done for her if she had. She landed on a little ledge that juts out about thirty feet down."

Cody inched carefully toward the edge of the road and peered into the canyon. It was almost a straight drop to the narrow valley three hundred feet below, and the face of the wall was nearly a sheer drop. "Oh, Lord." Cody slammed one gloved fist into the palm of his other hand. He leaned forward in an effort to see her. "Shelby, can you hear me?"

Silence hung heavy on the hot afternoon air.

"Shelby?" Cody called again, a hint of urgency in his voice now.

Still nothing.

"Shelby, answer me, damn it. Are you all right?"

"Cody?" A mingling of relief and fear ringed her voice. "Cody, get me out of here, or I swear I'll fire you." Her words were blustery and brave, but her voice was as tremulous as a newborn kitten's meow.

He chuckled and turned back to Jake, relief sweeping over him like a tidal wave. "She's okay. Can the boys pull her up?"

The older man shook his head. "She won't reach for the ropes . . . too afraid to move. Murdock there—" Jake jabbed a thumb toward Lance, who was standing nearby "—tried to throw down a lasso and we almost lost him, too. Slipped and fell half over the edge. If Jamie hadn't caught his arm we'd have two people down there. One most likely at the bottom."

Cody threw Lance a dismissive glance and then turned back to Jake.

"Someone's gonna have to go down and get her," Jake said, looking pointedly at Cody.

"Ah, hell. How'd I know you were going to say that?" Cody handed his Stetson to one of the other men. "All right, give me a rope."

One of the wranglers handed him the requested rope and Cody proceeded to loop one end around his waist. "Damn it, Shelby," he mumbled, "you couldn't have done something easy like just fall on your rump. Oh, no. You have to go and topple over a damn cliff. And I have to play Sir Galahad." He jerked on the knot and, satisfied that it was solid, walked over to Soldier, looped the other end over the saddle horn, and tied it off. "Okay, boy, you stand here nice and quiet like." He turned back to Jake. "When I yell, have Soldier back up . . . slow."

He tugged on his gloves, pulling the leather snug, and began to back himself over the edge of the cliff releasing a few inches of rope as he went. "Shelby, I'm coming down. Just don't move."

"Don't worry, I won't," she called back.

He inched his way steadily down the face of the wall, the soles of his boots dislodging dirt and pieces of rock with each step.

"Ouch!" Shelby cringed at the shower of rock and dirt. "What are you doing?"

He jumped onto the ledge. The impact of his weight on the narrow cliff sent up a cloud of dust and caused the jut of earthen rock to shake.

"Be careful!" She pressed herself against the rock wall at her back. "I haven't been waiting here for rescue just so you can come down and send us plummeting to our deaths."

"Grateful little thing, aren't you?" he taunted. "Maybe I should go back up and let you find your own way to the top."

"You wouldn't."

Cody tightened his hold on the rope and moved to brace a foot against the cliff.

"Cody."

He lowered his foot and looked back at her. "Yeah?"

Shelby made to stand up, glanced down, and thought better of it. "Just get us out of here. Please?"

"Okay, since you asked so nice. But first, take off your belt."

Shelby's eyes widened. "This isn't the time or place for that, Cody Farlowe, even if I was inclined. Which I'm not."

"At the moment, neither am I. Now, take off

your belt or I'm going back up this rope alone."

Shelby hurriedly unbuckled her belt and pulled it from the loops of her jeans. "Okay, now what?"

"Now, stand up."

She rose slowly to her feet, staring down into the canyon and hugging the wall the entire time.

"Stop looking down. You're only scaring yourself."

"I can't help it." Knowing he was right, she managed to draw her gaze away from the floor of the canyon far below and looked up, straight into Cody's blue eyes. Shelby felt a tingle of desire and was amazed that she could experience such a thing while standing on the precipice of certain death.

All business and no nonsense, Cody fastened the buckle of her belt to one end of his, then looped the whole thing under her arms. Moving carefully, he turned his back to her and brought the belt around his waist. Shelby was pulled away from the wall and up against Cody, her breasts crushed to his back, the plane of her stomach pressed to the tight contour of his behind.

"Wrap your arms around me and hold on. We're going up."

"Like this?"

"You got any better ideas?"

Shelby wrapped her arms around his chest.

"And don't move your legs. Trip me and we'll both be at the bottom of this canyon, with Soldier on top of us." He leaned back and looked up at the top of the ledge. "Okay, Jake, we're ready. Back Soldier up. Slow."

The belt began to tighten beneath Shelby's arms, and she felt her feet start to lift away from the ground. "Wait!" she screamed.

"Jake, stop!" Cody looked over his shoulder at her. "What's wrong?"

"I'm going to be hanging out in the air."

Cody took a deep breath and forced himself to count to ten. "It's the only way, Shelby. Now, are you ready?"

She wasn't, but she nodded, anyway.

Cody turned back to look up toward the ledge. "Okay, Jake, let's do it."

The rope grew taut in Cody's hands and the belt tightened again. He began to climb the wall, bracing his feet against it and moving slow. Shelby clung to his back, her legs dangling in midair. She pressed her face against Cody's spine and kept her eyes scrunched tightly closed. Every nerve in her body was quivering, her muscles were rigid with fear, and she was so anxious she could hardly breathe.

"Are we there yet?" she asked weakly.

"A little farther, darlin'."

She shifted her hold on Cody and the belt beneath her arms suddenly slipped. Her body slid down his . . . only an inch, but enough to fire sheer panic through her veins. Her eyes shot open and she grappled to find a grip on the front of Cody's shirt. "Ohhh! Cody, help! We're falling!" She kicked the air in an effort to run up his back.

"Stop moving!" Cody yelled. The muscles in his arms ached with the strain of clinging to the rope and resisting the pull of Shelby on his back.

Shelby's legs grappled with his as she tried to wrap them around him, while her fingers clung to the front of his shirt. Several of its buttons tore away in her frantic struggle to grasp the material, and one of her fingernails left a long scratch down the front of his chest, a ragged red line that wove its way across bronzed skin and through a mat of short golden curls.

Her flailing hand struck Cody's left elbow and it buckled. His hold on the rope loosened and they slid several inches down the canyon wall before he was able to regain his grip and stop them.

Shelby screamed. Cody reached behind him with one hand to grab her and Jake, afraid he was losing them both, hurriedly pushed Soldier backward.

Chapter Five

Shelby and Cody shot several feet up the face of the cliff, bouncing against its hard, rough surface on their swift ascent.

"Jake, stop!" Cody shouted. "Don't pull—" The rest of his sentence was abruptly cut off when his shoulder slammed against the rock wall. He heard Shelby's gasp of pain as she, too, came into contact with the hard surface, but her tight grip on him didn't loosen this time.

The spiraling upward pull suddenly stopped, and they hung motionless in midair, halfway between the jutting piece of ledge that had saved Shelby from a sure fall to death and the road above.

"You two all right, Cody?" Jake called.

Cody looked up to see his assistant's craggy face peering over the ledge at him. A halo of gray hair crowned the older man's face and matched the bushy whiskers that grew in thick abundance over his upper lip.

"Yeah, we're okay, Jake," Cody said, letting

out the breath he'd been holding. He lowered his head to wipe his sweat-covered forehead across the rolled cuff of his shirt sleeve. "Shelby?"

She moaned softly.

"Darlin', you okay?"

"I'm . . . I'm scared, Cody," she whimpered.

"We're going to be all right. Just move your legs from around me." His voice was soft and gentle.

Her legs remained rigidly clasped around his.

Cody's patience abruptly dissipated. "Shelby, damn it. I can't walk us up this wall with you clinging to me like some damn monkey. Now, drop your legs!"

He felt her arms tighten around his chest. Then, slowly, one of her legs fell away from his, then the other.

"Good. Now just hang tight, darlin'." He regained his foothold against the wall and glanced upward. "Okay, bring us up, Jake."

The old man moved Soldier back; the rope grew taut and slowly began to move. Within seconds, Cody and Shelby appeared at the road's edge. Jake and several of the ranch hands rushed forward and grabbed Cody's arms, pulling him up and over the ledge, while two other wranglers grabbed Shelby. Cody lay sprawled for several seconds on the hard ground, drawing in large gulps of air and waiting for his body to calm. Shelby struggled to sit up, but the belt that still held them together prevented her movement. Seeing her intent, Jake stooped before Cody and quickly released the belt buckle, then helped her to a sitting position and shoved a canteen of water into her hands. A shout of joy filled the air as the Double K's guests swarmed forward, relief etched on every face, and on some, still a little fear.

Lance Murdock knelt beside Shelby as she tipped the canteen to her lips and took a long swallow of the cool water. "Are you all right, beautiful? You're not hurt, are you?" He wrapped a consoling arm around her shoulders and pulled her toward him. "I tried to help you, but they—" he threw a sneering glance at Jake and the other wranglers "—wouldn't let me."

Shelby couldn't answer. Her body was still trembling violently and she was on the verge of tears. She looked toward Cody, who was already getting to his feet.

"Hollywood, I'm sure you'll excuse us for a while, but I have to talk with Shelby," Cody said, his tone icier than an Alaskan glacier.

Shelby was certain he was going to tell her to go home again. Threatening tears burned her eyes and she blinked rapidly, desperately trying to stem their tide. Why did she always fail? Why couldn't she ever do anything right?

Lance stiffened, but made no move to leave Shelby's side. "Now, see here, Cody, I don't think Shelby's in any condition for an argument. Anyway, it wasn't her fault the horse reared. There was a snake in the road. I saw it."

Shelby jerked around to stare at Lance. A

60

snake? Then it hadn't been her fault the horse had thrown her? She hadn't done anything wrong? Relief swept over her.

"I didn't say it was her fault."

"Oh, well, whatever," Lance said haughtily, and shrugged. "I'll have Shelby ride double with me the rest of the way to the campsite and you two can talk later."

"We'll talk now," Cody said through clenched teeth.

Shelby wriggled out of Lance's embrace and struggled quickly to her feet, suddenly afraid the two men were going to start talking with their fists. That was about the last thing she wanted, though she felt flattered at the prospect of two men fighting over her. The thought surprised her and she instantly disregarded it. Cody and Lance would probably fight over anything; she was just a handy excuse. They didn't like each other; that was obvious. She put a hand on Lance's arm. "It's all right, Lance, really. Cody's right. I do need to talk to him now."

"Well, okay, beautiful. But we still have a date for dinner and moonlight." He dropped his arm from around her shoulder, threw Cody a look that was a blatant challenge, and gave her a quick peck on the cheek.

Surprised and flattered, Shelby watched the handsome movie star walk away and remount his horse. She turned back to Cody. "I want to tha—"

He held up a hand. "Wait a minute." He

61

scanned the group until he caught sight of Jake. "Hey, Jake. Take them on into camp and get quartered down. I want to talk to Shelby. We'll catch up with you in a bit."

"Sure thing, boss," Jake called back. "Okay, folks, the excitement's over. Let's go on in and get our grub." The old wrangler began urging both guests and cowhands back onto their mounts and down the road.

Minutes later, Cody and Shelby were alone on the trail.

A conflicting storm of emotions raged within Cody. Part of him wanted to grab her by the shoulders and shake the living daylights out of her, make her listen to reason, force her to stop being stubborn and admit she was out of her element. Another part of him wanted to wrap her in his arms and hold her close, relieved and overjoyed that she was safe. Still another part of him burned with fury at himself for caring for her in the first place. He took refuge in the one emotion he felt safe with, the one that would protect him from her . . . anger.

"So, you falling for Hollywood?" he asked bluntly, hooking his thumbs in the front pockets of his jeans and looking down at her with a challenging glare.

Taken back by the question and his sniping tone, Shelby could only stare at him. After a few long seconds she finally found the power of speech again, but decided to ignore his question. "I want to thank you for rescuing me, Cody. You risked your life to save mine and I won't forget it."

Cody clenched his jaw tightly. That was not the response he'd wanted, and it certainly was no answer to his question.

Shelby noticed a small vein pulsing in the side of his neck. She had an insane urge to reach out and run her finger lightly down the trail of that thin blue line, but kept her hands stiffly at her sides. "It was a very brave thing to do."

"Shelby—" his voice was little more than a guttural drawl "—are you falling for Hollywood?"

"You mean Lance?" She smiled. "No, he's a . . ."

"Snake."

Shelby laughed. "Oh, come on, Cody. Lance is a nice guy . . . for a movie star, that is."

"Do you know many movie stars?"

"No. I didn't know any before I met him."

"Good."

Cody slipped his arms around her waist and pulled her to him. Before she knew what was happening, she was drawn up against his lean form. His mouth descended on hers. The touch of his lips was like the searing stamp of hot steel to flesh, burning into her, branding her his, and sparking flames of passion deep within her that she could not and had no desire to resist.

Her lips parted in surprise and he took instant advantage, his tongue darting forward to explore the dark, sweet cavern of her mouth.

Shelby's senses reeled under a storm of pleasure so intense that it left her unable to think, to move, to breathe. She had been kissed before, but never like this, never with such mind-shattering effect. She wanted it to go on forever.

He pressed his hands against her back, molding her pliant body to his as his lips ravished hers in a kiss both tender in its caress and savage in its demand. Time lost its meaning, and the world spun crazily, teetered, and threatened to slip away. Shelby lost all awareness of her surroundings—the soft chirping of the birds in the trees, the warm caress of the sun, the fragrant aroma of mountain freshness and clean air. She was cognizant only of Cody, of the virile, tantalizing scent of leather and horseflesh that enveloped him, the iron-hard arms that held her to him, and the crazy, racing thump of his heart as it beat in unison with hers.

She slid her hands over his arms, feeling the rigid, taut muscles beneath the thin chambray shirt. She tangled her fingers in the soft curls of golden hair at his nape and pressed closer to him, her body telling him what she could never put into words.

A soft moan escaped her throat and a shiver of pleasure shook her body. Cody's hands slipped to her waist; his lips left hers. He stared down at her, and as their eyes met, Shelby saw the passion she felt, the intense desire and need, mirrored in Cody's blue eyes, etched on the soft, smiling curve of his lips.

She felt languorous and unsteady on her feet

and, at the same time, seized by more energy than she'd ever experienced. She yearned for more of the sweet-torture of his lips on hers, and pressing her hands to the back of his neck, she pulled his head down toward her.

His lips brushed hers. "I want you, Shelby," he said huskily.

"I . . . I want you, too." She heard her own words and felt a thrill of shock. Never had she been so bold, so open.

Desire boiled within him, stronger than he'd ever felt, his need for her eliminating all thought of caution or resistance. Suddenly he bent down and swooped her into his arms, cradling her against his chest. His mouth covered hers in a brief but passionate kiss that left her breathless and yearning for more. "There's a little patch of meadow not far from here that I always knew was a special place — I just didn't know why." He paused and captured her lips again, then looked long and deep into her eyes when he pulled away from her. "Now I do."

She wrapped her arms around his neck, her body throbbing with need, her heart bursting with joy.

"It was meant for us, darlin'. Our own private place, with a view of the valley, a small, freshwater stream, and at night a ceiling of blackness sprinkled with a thousand diamonds, all just for you."

He carried her to where Soldier stood grazing and lifted her easily up onto his saddle. He swung up behind her and slipped one arm securely around her waist while lifting the reins in his other hand. His body was pressed against hers, his warmth invading her, drawing her. She felt the swell of his need against her and the heat of his breath on her neck as he bent forward and nuzzled the curve of her neck.

Soldier started to move forward at a slow, steady walk. Shelby's horse, Lady, lifted her head from the patch of grass she'd been grazing. As Soldier passed, Cody reached out and grabbed Lady's reins, which were looped over a low-hanging tree branch. The mare fell into step with the gelding.

As they rode, Cody's hand moved up the front of Shelby's shirt and cupped her breast. Flames of need swept through her and she arched forward into the touch of his fingers, the circling, rhythmic caress of his thumb on her tight nipple. She moaned, an unbidden sound that erupted from the deepest part of her. Lifting her arms over her head and behind her, she reached for him as he kissed the column of her neck, his lips turning her flesh to flame.

At a nudge from Cody's left heel, Soldier left the trail where the cliff turned into a sloping hill, and they moved onto a narrower path that wove its way through the thick growth of trees covering the hill.

Cody thought he was about to go mad. Every cell in his body was pulsating with need; every muscle was taut with wanting her. With each step

Soldier took, Shelby's body swayed, her buttocks rubbing against Cody, teasing, heightening his desire, inflaming the passion that threatened to consume him.

Lost in a fog of desire, Shelby was only half-aware of the sound of voices, faint and at a distance. Her eyes fluttered open, just for a second, and she saw a small clearing several hundred feet to their left; in its center the Double K group was setting up camp.

Small tents were being raised and staked to the ground; a campfire had already been lit. Tom was busily unloading the chuck truck, while another wrangler was setting up the tables and benches for dinner. Shelby spotted another flat-bed truck parked next to Tom's; it carried a huge tarp-covered square. Curiosity pricked at her, and just as quickly left.

Cody's tongue flicked the inside of her ear, sending a surge of pleasure through her. She felt his breath on her cheek, the accelerated beat of his heart against her back, the hard swell of his need pressed to her buttocks, and the mind-reeling, ravishing caress of his hand on her breast. The world once again slipped into oblivion, leaving only Cody and his sensuous, tormenting, sweet touch.

Soldier moved away from the Double K group and continued his descent down the sloping hillside.

"We're almost there, darlin'," Cody whispered raggedly.

He raised his head and guided Soldier to the clearing he sought.

Shelby felt deserted, the flesh that had thrilled to the touch of his lips suddenly cold and in need of his warmth. She leaned back and pressed against him, only half-aware of the passing landscape.

Within minutes the thick pine forest gave way to a small meadow of knee-high golden grass. A sudden movement drew Soldier's attention and his alert ears swiveled as a jackrabbit, startled by their approach, bounded into the air and disappeared back within the tall reeds. They left the meadow and entered a shallow copse of cottonwoods. The white trunks had turned a soft pink beneath the rays of the setting sun, and the usually brilliant gold leaves were dark amber. Cody pulled Soldier to a halt just as the forest ended and soft meadow grass gave way to bare earth and the odd cluster of wildflowers.

A wide creek cut jaggedly through the land before her, its slowly moving water glistening in reflection of the setting sun. Small ripples of pink, gold, and silver broke the blue-green surface to create a rainbow of nature.

Swinging his right leg over Soldier's rump, Cody slid from the saddle and reached up for Shelby. He drew her from the gelding's back, and even after her feet touched the ground, he held on to her, as if afraid to let her go.

Shelby moved her hands upward over his chest. She felt the hard surface of rippling muscle beneath her fingers and then slid her arms around his neck. It was all the encouragement Cody needed.

When Cody finally pulled his lips from hers again, Shelby knew her world would never be the same. Without her even being aware of it, Cody Farlowe had stolen her heart, and she knew she would never get it back. But she didn't care.

Holding her tightly against him, with one arm around her waist, Cody reached up to loosen the leather thongs at the rear of the saddle with his other hand. He tucked the bedroll under his arm, and shrugged his saddlebags over his left shoulder. Soldier and Lady were left to graze while Cody guided Shelby toward the small creek and to the fallen and leafless trunk of a tree that had given up life long ago.

"Now, you sit here a minute," he said huskily, "and enjoy the scenery."

But scenery was the last thing on Shelby's mind at the moment, unless she thought of Cody as scenery. She watched him move to stand in the shadows created by the branches of a tall pine tree and her heart did a little flip-flop. She was forced to wrap her arms around her knees and entwine her fingers to keep herself from jumping up and running over to Cody. She wanted nothing more than to be in his arms.

He dropped his saddlebags near the base of the pine, flapped his bedroll out, and spread it on the ground.

As if feeling her intent gaze on him, Cody

looked up. His eyes met hers, and a slow, seductive smile curved his lips.

Shelby felt herself warm, and a shiver of excitement swept through her.

Cody bent to scoop up a few dry branches and, pulling a pack of matches from his shirt pocket, set fire to the dry tinder. He rose and walked to stand before Shelby.

She stood and placed her hands in his, and he drew her toward the blanket. "You're beautiful, Shelby," he whispered as his lips moved over hers with feather-light tenderness. He pulled her into his embrace.

She stood on tiptoe to press against him, thrilling at his words, at his touch.

"I've wanted to tell you that since the first moment I saw you," he said. "And I've wanted to kiss you." His lips moved down the curve of her neck and left a trail of tingling, burning flesh behind. "And hold you." His arms crushed her to him. "And love you."

His lips covered hers, a demanding kiss that left no doubt about the hungry need that burned within him. His tongue filled her mouth, flicking fiery caresses that stoked her passion and her own growing need. A yearning hunger gnawed at the pit of her stomach, becoming stronger with each stroke of Cody's hands as they moved over her body. His hand slipped between her breasts, and one by one, he released the small pearl buttons that held her shirt closed. Brushing the fabric aside, he unhooked the front of her brassiere.

The sheer lace fabric fell away, baring her to his touch. Cody cupped her breast and brushed his thumb across the hardened peak of rosy flesh.

A soft gasp escaped Shelby's lips. Like lightning bolts, sizzling heat shot through her, charging every cell of her body, filling every nerve, fiber, and muscle with a tormenting ache.

His lips moved to the small hollow at the base of her throat, and his tongue caressed the tiny valley. "Let me love you, Shelby," he whispered raggedly, his voice husky with emotion and need.

Chapter Six

For Shelby, words were impossible, but her body gave Cody the answer he sought. Her arms tightened around his neck, she arched against him, and her lips sought his. For one fleeting second, doubt clouded her mind. Never had she been so bold, so wanton, but, then, she had never felt so sure of anything before. With un-wavering certainty, Shelby knew that Cody Farlowe was the man she wanted in her life for all time, the man she wanted to share her love with, raise a family with, and grow old with.

"Love me, Cody," she murmured. "Love me."

His lips sought hers again, capturing them in a kiss that turned her veins into searing rivers of fire, her body into a hungry inferno.

The hand on her breast moved slowly, strok-ing, petting, his thumb making a continuous cir-cle around the taut peak of her nipple, teasing, enticing, and pulling her into a realm of pleasure like none she had ever known. Then his hand was gone, and she felt suddenly abandoned, even as his lips ravished hers. His hands moved to her waist, and she felt herself being pulled downward.

Cody lowered himself to the ground, Shelby along with him. A little voice of warning called out from the back of his mind, but he ignored it, too lost in his desire to give thought to his earlier caution and misgivings.

He wanted to go slow with Shelby, to savor every touch and caress, to know her in every way a man can know a woman and to give her what no other man ever had, or ever would.

His fingers brushed across her rib cage and moved to the buckle at her waist, and all the while his lips wreaked sweet havoc on hers. She felt the loosening of denim as he released the metal button and zipper. She felt the cool chill of the early evening air on her hips as he slowly pushed her jeans downward. His lips moved to her breast, her stomach, her thigh . . . and then he was gone. Shelby wanted to cry out for him, for the intimate touch of his hands on her flesh.

Cody rose to his knees, pulled the boots from Shelby's feet, and tossed her jeans and then her panties aside.

Suddenly embarrassed, she moved to pull her shirt across her bared breasts, and bent one leg to hide the dark triangle at the apex of her thighs.

Cody reached out to touch her knee with his fingertips, and gently urged her leg back down.

"Don't hide from me, darlin'." His fingers slid lightly down the side of her calve. "You're too beautiful for that. Too perfect. Let me see all of you, Shelby. Let me know all of you."

In the shadowy light of dusk the crackling flames of the small campfire cast a yellowish glow on the area and turned Shelby's lightly tanned skin a shimmering gold. Her limbs were graceful and long, her body a tantalizing landscape of subtle curves and gracefully sweeping valleys and planes. Shadows danced upon her flesh, dueling with the wavering saffron light, and, to Cody, leaving Shelby appearing almost ethereal, a vision in the night too beautiful, too exquisite to be true. Long, silken tendrils of her auburn hair spread about her head in cascading waves and curls; here and there, deep within the swirling red tendrils, he saw sparks of gold.

"You're so beautiful, Shelby," Cody said, his deep drawl a velvety stroke to her senses, his words a reassuring caress to her faltering confidence. His gaze never wavering from her, he pulled at the front of his shirt. The silver-trimmed pearl snaps popped apart, and he shrugged free of the garment.

Shelby lay unmoving and stared up at him. Her fingers ached to roam through the golden curls that covered his wide chest and slide over the corded muscles of his shoulders. Still, she remained motionless, watching him, overwhelmed by his aura of masculinity, the virility, power, and strength.

74

He stood, kicked off his boots, and stripped the worn denims from his hips, allowing them to fall to the ground.

Moonlight bathed his body and transformed him into a bronzed effigy of male perfection, an Adonis who had been put on this earth especially for her. Shelby felt the breath catch in her throat, felt her heart pound against her breast like a caged animal frantic for escape. The aching hunger that had been building within her for the past hour threatened to consume her. She lifted her arms to him, and Cody lowered himself beside her. His lips once again claimed hers. His kiss swept her breath away, while his touch ignited the fires that smoldered deep within her and stoked them toward a raging conflagration whose consummation she welcomed.

A whimpering moan filled her throat as she felt his fingers brush the sensitive core of her need. Instinctively her body arched upward, hungry to know more of his touch, of the delicious sensations he was causing to erupt within her. She slid her hands over his shoulders and thrilled to the feel of his raw strength beneath her fingertips, the saten smooth skin that stretched taut over the powerful terrain. With growing confidence in herself, in his desire for her, she let her hands travel down his long torso, caressing, kneading his flesh, wanting to give him the same pleasure he was giving to her.

"Now, Cody," she said, her voice barely more than a soft gasp as his fingers stroked her again.

"Love me now, Cody, please, now,"

Waves of hot, molten pleasure swept over Shelby as Cody entered her, melding their bodies, and together they forged a trail of ecstasy like none she had traveled before, like none, she knew, she would ever travel with anyone else. She cried out his name, over and over, and finally, when she thought she could stand no more, when her body hungered for the delicious release his passion promised, she plummeted over the edge of euphoria on a cresting swell of rapture that shook her entire body.

She cried out her joy, and felt Cody thrust deeply, felt his arms tighten around her and his body tremble. After a long moment, he relaxed and shifted his weight so that he lay half beside her, half over her.

She felt the weight of him on her as comforting, and snuggled deeper into the warmth of his arms, her legs entwined with his. Cody's head lay at her shoulder, his deep breathing creating a gentle breeze upon the curve of her shoulder. She slid an arm across his chest, encircled his neck, and buried her fingers in the curls at his nape.

Feeling more content than she had in her entire life, a small smile curving her lips, Shelby closed her eyes and let the languorous tide of slumber wash over her.

As she lazed in the sanctuary of sleep's cocoon, a multitude of joyful dreams played across her mind, painting a haze over the trials of everyday life and softening the nightmare of reality that had brought her to this land, and into Cody Farlowe's arms.

An hour later she moved to nestle deeper within his embrace, wanting to feel closer to him, to be enveloped by him. Half-awake, she moved her hand to rest it on the fine hairs that covered his chest, and felt the smooth threads and wrinkled creases of denim material, instead.

Shelby's eyes shot open and she bolted to a sitting position, the thin blanket that had been draped over her naked form falling into folds at her hips. Her auburn hair fluffed about her head like a wild red mane, and her eyes were wide with alarm and fear.

"Whoa, there," Cody drawled, bending forward to brush his lips across hers. "What's the matter, darlin'? Have a bad dream?"

He sat with his back against the tree, whose wide limbs spread above them like a canopy. One of his legs was bent, his heel wedged into the soft ground as an anchor. One arm was draped over his knee, and he held a small metal cup filled with coffee in his hand. Though he had slipped back into his jeans while she'd slept, his shirt remained on the ground next to her own clothes. His wavy blond hair was tousled, several rebellious locks having fallen onto his forehead.

With a start of surprise, Shelby felt a coil of desire burn within her, and realized she wanted him to make love to her again, wanted to feel him inside her, uniting their bodies.

"I . . . I didn't realize I'd fallen asleep," she

77

muttered, pulling the blanket up to cover her breasts. She wondered how long he'd sat there watching her. The thought made her uncomfortable; she imagined he'd been able, somehow, to peer into her soul while she'd slept, and see things she didn't want him to see.

"We both did. I just woke up sooner than you." He leaned toward the still-smoldering fire, picked up a small pot, and filled another cup with hot water. He handed her the cup, its contents having turned a dark brown the moment the instant coffee crystals he'd poured in earlier were covered with water.

Shelby sniffed the fragrant aroma and took a careful sip of the steaming liquid.

Cody leaned back against the tree trunk and held an arm out toward her, his fingers brushing lightly over the curve of her shoulder.

A tremor of longing shook her.

"Come here, darlin'," he said softly, the words at once a plea and a command.

She moved into the circle of his arm, once again reveling in the feel of his embrace, the scent of leather and horseflesh that was uniquely Cody.

Shelby lay with her back against one side of his chest, her head nestled in the curve of his shoulder. She felt his arm slip around her waist in a proprietary embrace that she welcomed and relished.

With a deep sigh of contentment, Shelby let her gaze wander the endless sky, an ebony blanket of velvet sprinkled with a thousand sparkling diamonds and a thin crescent of pale gold. The sounds of night wafted on the still air: the haunting wail of a screech owl; the soft, gurgling whisper of the creek as its shallow water moved slowly and steadily past; and, in the distance, the faint sound of song coming from the camp of the Double K's guests and wranglers.

Shelby never knew she could feel such peace and happiness, such belonging.

Suddenly a hooting howl split the silence. Shelby stiffened and sat bolt upright, her eyes widening in alarm. "Cody, there's a wolf out there!"

His soft chuckle washed over her like a silken caress. He reached out and pulled her back against him, but she remained tense, ready to jump up and run if necessary.

"It's only a coyote, Shelby, and he's not going to hurt you."

The sound came again, this time followed a few seconds later by an answering howl.

"Are you sure, Cody? I mean, really sure they aren't dangerous?"

"Does a duck swim?"

She settled back against him, but still did not relax. "What else is out here?" she asked, her voice cracking slightly as she eyed the surrounding darkness. Suddenly the piny woods and rolling meadows didn't seem so beautiful and peaceful. "Bears? Cody, are there bears in Montana? I've read about bears attacking people, campers. And mountain lions—are there mountain lions in Montana?"

"They're here, but they don't normally attack people. It's usually people who attack them, or provoke them."

She swung around and looked at him, her face etched with fear. "Oh, Lord, do you have tarantulas here? I hate tarantulas. They scare me to death." She shivered and moved deeper into the curve of his arm.

He heard the anxiety that edged her tone, felt the tightness in her limbs that wouldn't quite slacken, even within the safety of his embrace. He damned himself for doing exactly what he'd known he should have avoided at all costs.

He'd been right all along. She didn't belong here, and this little episode of alarm over the possible presence of a few animals only convinced him further. He had let his guard down, let her slip behind the barrier that he'd built around his emotions, around his heart. It had been a mistake—he'd known it would be—yet he had let it happen.

She would never fit into his way of life. She didn't know how, and deep down inside her, whether she admitted it or not, Cody knew she didn't want to. She had been born in the city, had lived all her life in that hustle and bustle of crowded streets, concrete sidewalks, and sky-reaching buildings, and that's where she inevitably would return once the fantasized image of country life wore off and once the guilt over abandoning her sister's dream subsided.

Cody, on the other hand, would remain here in the wide-open countryside where he'd been born and that was so much a part of him. It was the only place he felt truly alive and free; he could never give that up again. Not for anything. Not even for Shelby Hill.

As the ache of loss began to envelop him, he touched his lips to her crown in a light kiss and swore silently to himself. Now he was going to have to expel her from his life, to rebuild the wall around his heart and leave her on the outside. It was the only way.

excited. Had what made their second day so less bring away than their first because her questions had been too close, that should have been that day, but the questions, that close...only day.

Chapter Seven

Cody stared out at the horizon. The tops of the pine trees on the rolling hills created a ragged silhouette against a sky turned pinkish gray by the coming of dawn.

His hand lay upon the plane of Shelby's stomach and her hand moved to cover it. She had fallen asleep again, but even so, she was reaching out to him. Her fingers moved over his, in an unconscious caress, her touch light and sensual.

Letting his head rest on the tree trunk at his back, Cody closed his eyes and damned himself again. He should have kept his distance from her. He should have maintained a tighter rein on his emotions, a leash on his desires. He should have ignored her.

He looked down at the sleeping woman who lay with her head against his chest, and knew there had been no way in hell he could have ignored her. No man in his right mind would not take notice of Shelby Hill. She was too beautiful and too spirited to pass without drawing attention to herself. And what made her even more special was her not being aware of how truly beautiful she was. He had been able to see that almost from the first day. She was completely without pretense, and that quality of innocence combined with her beauty drew men like a magnet.

It had attracted him. And Lance Murdock.

Cody frowned at memory of the movie star. He didn't like Lance, but he had to admit, that had nothing to do with the man himself. It was because Lance was obviously interested in Shelby, and though Cody knew he had no right, the mere thought of Shelby with Lance made him want to kill the guy.

He raised a hand and pinched the bridge of his nose, trying to rid himself of the headache brought on by a long, sleepless night and a powerful weight of guilt. He had to walk away from her; there was no other way. Eventually she'd tire of the ranch; of the lack of shopping malls, fancy restaurants, and movie theaters. The city, which only a few hours earlier she'd sworn not to miss, would begin to look better and better in her mind, and then the day would come when she would decide to leave.

Cody let his head fall back and rest against the trunk of the tree. It was better to break it off now. To end their relationship before it went any further. Hell, it had already gone too far, but he couldn't help that. He just couldn't let it go on.

They'd both be hurt, and it would only be worse if he waited.

Shelby stirred against him, drawing his attention again. He looked down at her and felt desire erupt, felt it coil hot and burning deep inside him, ready, anxious, hungry for her; he fought to control it.

"Cody?" Shelby pushed herself to a sitting position and ran a hand through her hair. She shivered slightly at the chill in the morning air and pulled the blanket up around her shoulders. "How long have you been awake?"

He shrugged. "A while. I'm an early riser."

She scooted forward on the blanket, lay her head on his shoulder and wrapped an arm around his waist. "Ummm. I never knew how wonderful a night under the stars with a handsome cowboy could be."

Cody struggled with himself to keep his arms from encircling her, his hands from touching her, his mouth from claiming hers. Already he could feel the gnawing hunger threaten to consume him, rendering him powerless to keep his resolve.

She pressed her lips to the curve of his neck, drew in a deep breath, and luxuriated in the scent of him. He smelled fresh and clean, like spring air and tangy spices. She snuggled against him, pressing her naked body against him.

All that separated them were his clothes, which he had put on while she slept. He swore silently, and struggled to maintain a grip on his emotions. "Shelby, we have to get going. It's almost dawn. Jake will be getting ready to breakfast and break camp."

"Okay," she said, pulling open the front of his shirt and pressing her lips into the soft golden hair that covered his chest. But she didn't move to rise. Instead her hands slid over his body, boldly caressing, exploring, igniting.

A faint groan escaped Cody's throat. He felt the inseam of his pants tighten as his desire for her grew. Cursing softly, knowing that if he didn't stop her they'd both be lost, he took hold of her shoulders and gently, but forcibly, moved her away from him. "You'd best get dressed, Shelby. I left a bar of soap and a towel down by the stream for you."

Shocked at his blatant rejection and suddenly embarrassed by her own boldness, Shelby scrambled to drag the blanket up around her naked form.

Cody rose to his feet, took a sip from the coffee cup he'd grabbed from beside the fire, and wrinkled his face in distaste. It was barely lukewarm. He tossed the liquid into a patch of nearby weeds and looked down at her. "We need to get back to the campsite before anyone realizes we didn't make it there last night. Gossip travels like a hot fire on a dry prairie in a place like the Double K." He began to kick at the smoldering wood of the fire, spreading the charred pieces about on the bare ground.

85

Shelby watched, stupefied. What the devil had gone wrong? He was obviously displeased. His tone even sounded a little angry. But why? Had she said something? Done something to turn him away from her?

Shelby remained on the blanket, watching him, trying to figure out why the man who was with her this morning was not the same man who'd made love to her the previous night.

He poured what coffee was left in the pot onto the wood and ashes of their campfire, then, shaking the utensils out, packed them back in his saddlebags.

She looked at her clothes, lying near her feet, and, suddenly unsure of herself, up at Cody. She'd made love to the man last night, yet she was loath to stand up and dress in front of him. Especially since he seemed so . . . she searched for a word to describe her feelings . . . so matter-of-fact.

Cody saw her hesitation, her glance at the clothes, and understood her reluctance. He nodded. "I'll go saddle Soldier while you wash up and dress."

She watched him turn and walk away, and frowned. Was this the same wonderfully gentle man who had made passionate love to her twice? The same man who had held her in his arms for hours while they'd talked, laughed, and snuggled together? The man she had shared her memories of Katie with, of their childhood

86

dreams and schemes?

Cody tightened the cinch around Soldier's belly and glanced over his shoulder to check on Shelby's progress. She hadn't budged. "We're going to miss breakfast if you don't get a move on, Shelby. Driving cattle is not something you want to do on an empty stomach."

His curt words jerked her from the reverie that had overcome her.

Holding the blanket tightly around her, she scrambled to her feet, frowning as pain gripped every muscle. A long day in the saddle and a plunge over a cliff were showing their effects. She hurried to the edge of the creek, ignoring the screaming of her stiff limbs. Kneeling on the ground, the blanket draped over her shoulders, she picked up the soap and plunged it and her hands into the rippling water. Goose bumps raced up her arms and down her back; the water was like ice. She thought of the hot tub that Jake had told her would be trucked to the campsite at the end of each day, and the barrels of water that would be heated so the guests could clean off the dirt of the trail. She sighed. Roughing it had never been her thing.

She forced herself to ignore the coldness as she lathered soap over her face, arms, and body, then splashed it off as best she could. She nearly rubbed herself raw with the towel in an effort to both dry and warm herself at the same time.

Cody was still fiddling with Soldier's packings

when she made her way back to the campsite. She struggled to keep the blanket around her as she pulled on her jeans. With her back to Cody, she slipped into her brassiere and blouse, then tugged on her socks and boots.

Before she was done buttoning her shirt, Cody rolled up the blanket she'd used to cover herself, and stood over her waiting for the one she sat on.

A dozen questions burned on her tongue, but she hesitated to voice them. What was the matter with him this morning? Why was he so all-fired intent on getting back to the camp before any one noticed their absence? She was sure they had already been missed the night before. And why was he acting as if he couldn't wait to get away from her? What had she done?

Shelby stood and stepped off the blanket they'd lain on. In the blink of an eye, Cody whipped it from the ground, shook it, folded it, and rolled it. "You ready?" he asked, moving toward Soldier. He tied the bedroll to the back of his saddle.

"Sure," she replied somewhat flippantly. Letting him see how much his aloofness hurt her was the last thing she wanted to do. She followed him to his horse, refusing to limp, even though her legs felt as though someone had been using them as battering rams. She looked around for her own mount. "Where's Lady?"

"A ways up the hill. She found herself a nice

green patch of grass up there to chew on last night, so I tied her there. Soldier always prefers to stay closer to camp. I'll grab her lead rope when we pass her on the way to camp."

Cody swung onto Soldier. After he'd settled onto the gelding's back, she took Cody's offered hand and mounted behind him. She nearly bit her tongue as every bruise and sore spot on her body protested. Her breasts were against his back and her thighs fitted snugly into the curve of his. She felt him shift his position and tried to scoot back to put space between them.

Cody's heels touched Soldier's sides and the horse instantly moved forward. Shelby, being foolishly stubborn, refused to hold on to Cody. Instead she tried to grip the sloping side of the cantle. With the horse's sudden motion, she was jerked backward and her legs flew up against the rear of Cody's calves. She slid from her precarious seat on the saddle's cantle, over the rolled saddle blankets and onto Soldier's slick rump.

She was going to fall off! The words screamed in her mind at precisely the same moment Cody, realizing what was about to happen, twisted around and grabbed the front of her shirt. He hauled her unceremoniously toward him.

"What the hell are you doing, Shelby?" he thundered. His gloved fist maintained its grip on her shirtfront even after she'd regained her seat.

"I . . . I guess I didn't have a good enough hold on the saddle when Soldier moved."

"When you ride double you don't hold on to the saddle, you hold on to me. I thought you knew something about riding. Now, put your arms around my waist before you fall off and break your neck."

She slipped her arms around his waist, but tried to balance herself as far up on the cantle as possible, leaving at least an inch of space between their bodies.

"Slide down onto the saddle, Shelby. You're not doing Soldier any good perching on his rump like that." His voice was a thunderous growl that left no room for argument and held no warmth whatsoever.

Shelby cringed, but only long enough for her anger to kick in. Just who did he think he was, anyway? Last night he had been the perfect lover. This morning he was a stranger, aloof and arrogant. Before today his curt words had always held a teasing note, but now they sounded cold and hard. Could she have said something to anger him? She tried to think over their conversations since last night, and could come up with nothing that would have turned his mood so sour. Could it be that this was merely the way Cody Farlowe acted with a woman after he got what he wanted?

No, she couldn't believe he was that type of man. But maybe last night had meant more to her than it had to him. Or maybe he didn't want it to mean anything. Shelby felt a hurtful stab at her heart. Well, she had never been one to throw herself at a man. If Cody didn't want a relationship between them, and it certainly seemed this morning that he didn't, then there wouldn't be one. They would simply be boss and employee. Tears hovered at the corners of her eyes and she blinked rapidly to stem their flow.

Seconds later they broke through the trees of the forest that surrounded the campsite of the Double K group, and Shelby heard Cody curse under his breath. She peered over his shoulder and saw that everyone was already up and Tom had breakfast well on its way to being cooked. The fragrant scent of bacon sizzling over an open fire; simmering fried potatoes, onions, and peppers; fresh pan biscuits; and scrambled eggs filled the air. She looked at the linen-covered redwood picnic tables that Tom's assistant had set up and saw bowls of freshly cut cantaloupe, musk melons, and strawberries, as well as several jars of preserves.

Shelby's stomach growled, and she flinched, hoping Cody hadn't heard.

"Hey, boss, we were about to send a search party after you," Tom said as Cody maneuvered Soldier up beside the chuck truck, then swung his right leg over the gelding's neck and slid easily to the ground. Tom smiled, rubbed his fingers over the seemingly permanent stub of gray whiskers that sprinkled his jaw and tipped his hat to Shelby. "Miss Shelby, you just grab yourself a plate from that stack there on the table and I'll serve you up a nice hot breakfast."

"Thanks, Tom." She grasped the saddle horn and made to dismount.

Cody's hands encircled her waist, holding her securely as she slid from the saddle. She tried to act nonchalant, despite the fact that her heart had begun a drumroll the moment she'd felt his hands on her. She wanted to turn in his arms and pull him toward her, capture his lips with hers. Instead she remembered his earlier rejection, smiled sweetly, and managed to maintain a calm facade, though she hadn't felt so empty inside since she'd gotten the news of Katie's death. He released her the moment her feet touched the earth.

"We'll break camp and start moving the herd right after breakfast."

Shelby wasn't sure if he was talking to her or to Tom, but the older man didn't seem about to answer, so she decided he'd been talking to her. "Where is the herd?" she asked, unable to hide her confusion. There wasn't a cow in sight, yet she knew they were supposed to have reached the herd by last night.

"If Jake did his job right, which I'm sure he did, they're right beyond this grove of trees." He grabbed two plates and held them out to Tom. "Fill 'em up, Tom. I'm starving."

She noticed the old trail cook watching them, his glance moving back and forth between her and Cody. "Just let me run a brush through my hair, Tom, and I'll be right back."

Tom nodded and began heaping food onto Cody's plate. Cody didn't seem to take any notice of her departure.

Shelby hurriedly walked toward the tree where one of the wranglers had tied Lady, and placed her saddle and the bags on the ground at the base of the tree trunk. She pulled her hairbrush and a small mirror from the saddlebag and began to draw the brush through her hair.

"Shelby, you can come in here to freshen up a bit, if you'd like," Eva Montalvo said, poking her head out from between the white flaps of a nearby tent. "I mean, you probably want to change clothes, and since you didn't put up a tent last night, well, I just thought . . ."

Shelby didn't miss the blonde's quick glance at Cody, or the suggestive wink she threw him. A surge of jealousy swelled in her breast and she instantly tamped it back down. It wouldn't do her any good, and it would only make her miserable. Cody had obviously decided that a relationship between them was a mistake. That, or he was a good, old-fashioned ladies' man and she'd just become another notch on the post of his bunk. Either way, the more she thought about it, the madder she got, her fury totally overriding the uncertainty and self-doubt she would normally have wallowed in.

Well, if that's the way he wants it, then fine!

she thought, clenching her jaw so tightly her teeth began to hurt. In a few days, when she felt able to confront him without the fear of bursting into tears, she'd talk to him, let him know that what had happened between them needn't interfere with their working relationship. Evidently that's how Cody wanted it, so that's how it would be. After all, she'd probably never be able to replace Cody on the ranch, and she didn't want to. The Double K needed him. Shelby felt a wave of longing. If truth be told, *she* needed him.

Ten minutes later, having changed into a fresh shirt, brushed her hair, and applied a touch of makeup, she felt presentable again and, despite the lump in her throat, eager to speak with Cody immediately. The feeling surprised her. Normally she'd just walk away and let things die between them, or put off a confrontation as long as possible. But there was no sense to that. They'd both feel better if they cleared the air now, and she couldn't take the chance that Cody would leave the ranch. She grabbed a plate and moved to stand before Tom, holding it out to him. "Where's Cody?" she asked, looking around and not seeing him anywhere.

"He rode out a few minutes ago." Tom slapped a giant spoonful of scrambled eggs onto her plate, followed by four or five lengthy strips of bacon and a mound of potatoes. "Said something about wanting to check the trail up ahead."

He gave a short chuckle and shook his head. "Too conscientious, that one. Makes work for himself. A couple of boys were up there just a few days ago. Don't know why Cody thinks he has to check it again."

She felt a blush warm her cheeks. Cody had felt the need to leave camp for a while. To put distance between them. Shelby saw Tom watching her and she straightened her shoulders. "Well, I guess he figures it's better to be safe than sorry."

"Hey, beautiful, you stood me up last night."

Shelby turned to see Lance Murdock approaching, an almost-comical expression of anguish creasing his handsome features. "Where'd you slip off to?" He wrapped an arm around her shoulders and steered her toward the table where he'd left his plate. "Or shouldn't I ask?"

"Oh, I just, uh . . ." Every eye at the table was turned toward her, every ear waiting for her answer. It was clear her absence had been well noted by one and all.

"Well, never mind, we'll make up for it tonight," Lance interjected. "We all tried to party last night, but we were too tired. After a half an hour in the hot tub, we were all more than ready to hit our sleeping bags. Tonight will be different, though. We'll be more used to a day in the saddle." He plucked a piece of bacon from her plate and took a bite out of it. "So, I'll bring the bottle—" he winked and kissed the tip of her nose "—and you bring that gorgeous bod of yours."

"Lance, I don't know if this is such a . . ."

Suddenly a thin wheezing sound cut through the quiet air, followed by a loud whap and a strangled cry from Lance as he jerked backward. He grabbed at his forehead, a slur of curses tumbling from his lips.

Shelby felt a stab of panic. She swung around to face him. "Lance, what's wrong? Are you all right?"

"Damn little monsters," he muttered. He dropped his hands from his forehead and looked up at her, outrage and a desire to murder reflected in his eyes.

Shelby, as well as all the other guests at the table, stared in astonishment at the plastic dart just below Lance's hairline.

Chapter Eight

Someone giggled.

Lance jumped from his seat and yanked the small dart from his forehead. The rubber suction cup released his skin with a soft sucking sound. A deep frown drew his dark brows together, and he exuded rage as he scanned the surrounding clearing, searching for the culprit. "Who the hell did that?" he demanded, brandishing the toy dart in the air. "Who shot me with this thing?"

Several children who had been playing nearby ran for cover behind thick tree trunks, their giggles echoing through the dense woods. Another dart zinged through the air and slammed into Lance's pant leg; then another barely missed his arm and went flying over the heads of the guests seated on the opposite side of the table.

Shelby clapped a hand over her mouth, but failed to hold back the laughter gurgling in her throat. A giggle burst forth, and a second later everyone else in the camp succumbed to hilarity. Tears streaked her cheeks and she quickly wiped them away. "I think you've just been bush-whacked."

"Little brats," Lance mumbled, throwing the dart to the ground and stepping on it with the heel of his boot. The plastic blade snapped. He glared down at Shelby. "Obviously your child-care wrangler isn't doing a very good job of controlling his charges."

Shelby bit down on her bottom lip and was just about to offer an apology, when she changed her mind. If she was going to run the Double K the way Katie had, she couldn't go buckling under every time there was a problem. She had to learn to start facing things head on, and now was as good a time as any.

She threw Lance what she hoped was a winning smile. "Come on, Lance, they're only kids. They were just having a little fun. You were one, too, once." She lifted her eyebrows. "Weren't you?" Before he could answer, she continued. "Of course—" she glanced at the children who were now peeking out from behind the trees "—they shouldn't go around ambushing their own men, or we won't have anyone left to protect the cattle against rustlers and Indians."

There was a soft hum of conversation as the four children who were on the drive huddled together in the shadows. Suddenly they all ran forward and gathered around Shelby. Bobby Rothman, the self-appointed leader of the group and clearly the oldest at eight or nine years of age, stepped forward, doing his best to imitate a John Wayne swagger, yet keeping a wary eye on Lance.

"We'll protect your cattle for you, Miss Shelby."

For a moment, Shelby looked at Bobby and was reminded of her own nephews, now lost to her forever, and the catch in her throat made her unable to respond. Before the tears could start, she managed to get control of her emotions.

"That makes me feel much safer, kids." Shelby crouched so that she was eye to eye with the children. "But you won't shoot any more of the good guys, now, will you?"

A snicker passed among the children as they looked at one another. Bobby pushed back his cowboy hat, ruffling the brown bangs that covered his forehead, then glanced over his shoulder and gave them a menacing glare. The group instantly quieted.

"Okay, run along, kids. We'll be leaving shortly," Shelby said, laughing at their whoops and hollers as they skipped back toward the trees.

She turned back to Lance. "I think you're safe now. At least from our own group."

"Very funny." He sat down at the table and stared into the depths of his coffee cup.

To several hundred thousand women who watched Lance every week on television, his pout would have melted their hearts. To Shelby, it seemed slightly ridiculous. And childish. But, then, he was a guest at the Double K and it was her job to make the guests happy.

"So, is that invitation for tonight still open?" she asked on impulse in an effort to cheer him up.

It worked. The pout disappeared and he turned to her with a smile, his eyes once again full of light and humor. "Just try to get out of it," he challenged. "I've been waiting all my life for a woman like you to come knocking at my door."

"Right," Shelby said with a laugh, moving away from the arm that was about to encircle her shoulders. "I'd better go and help Tom." She turned to the other guests. "Finish up, folks. We'll be moving out in half an hour."

An excited murmur filled the air, punctuated occasionally by loud grumbles or groans. By the time Shelby approached Tom, he had the barbecue pit disassembled, the pots and pans stowed in their crates, and the chuck truck almost completely packed up. All he was waiting for were the guests' dirty dishes, which would be transported back to the ranch house for washing, and the picnic tables.

"So, I guess we'll see you at lunch in a few hours," Shelby said.

"Nope."

She started, surprised. "No?"

"That's what I said."

"But what about lunch? The guests have to eat."

"They'll eat."

She was starting to dislike Tom's habit of making short, abrupt answers. "How? What?"

"Brought in a couple of pack horses this morning. They got your lunch packed on 'em. Picnic-style. Couple more of the boys will meet you at the campsite tonight with your fixings for dinner."

"Fixings? You won't be there with the chuck truck for dinner, either?"

"Nope."

Shelby sighed in exasperation. "Why not?"

"Tonight's your 'cowboy cookout.' Your guests gotta help you do it all—gather the wood, make a campfire, cook the food, and do the dishes."

"What? These—" She looked over her shoulder at the group of guests just rising from the breakfast table. "These wealthy people are paying to go on this cattle drive . . . to stay on a dude ranch, and we expect them to build their own fires and cook their own food?"

"Yep. That's part of what a real cattle drive's all about. Didn't have no chuck truck back in the 1800s."

"No, but they had a chuck wagon and a cook," Shelby argued, remembering all the cowboy movies she'd endured while Katie had hogged the television set every Saturday morning.

Tom turned toward Shelby, a look of infinite

patience in his aged brown eyes. "Miss Shelby, you're the new owner here, and I'll do whatever you say. Katie always saved the second night of the cattle drive for the guests to experience a real cookout. She said they liked it, and it always proved one of the most successful nights of the drive. But I'll do whatever you want. You tell me you want the chuck truck out there tonight, I'll be there with the truck."

Shelby stared at him, suddenly unsure of herself. She didn't know the first thing about cooking in the outdoors over an open fire, but, then, if this was something Katie had integrated into the routine of the drive with success, who was she to tamper with it? Anyway, Jake and Cody would be there, and they'd help. "Uh, no, that's okay, Tom. Let's leave things as they are. At least for now."

She turned and walked toward the horses; they were tied to a rope looped between two trees at one end of the camp. Several of the wranglers had just finished placing the saddles and bridles on the animals and were rechecking the cinches. She walked up to Lady and patted her on the neck.

"Good morning, girl. Hope you've had a better start on the day than I've had."

The horse nickered softly and turned to rub her forehead against Shelby's thigh.

Within minutes the tents were down and packed, the chuck truck and hot-tub truck on their way back to the ranch, camp broken, and all the guests on their horses. Cody still hadn't returned.

"Fine," Shelby muttered. "If that's the way he wants it, okay, that's the way it will be. You'd think I'd ordered the man to marry me or something." She pressed her heels to Lady's ribs and the horse broke into a trot. A small shriek broke from her lips and she grabbed the saddle horn.

Her rear end bounced into the air, along with the rest of her. The hat that shaded her eyes toppled off and down her back, to dangle by the leather thong around her neck, and her hair flew about her shoulders in a wild spray. Her rear came back down on the saddle with a thud, only to be tossed up again. Over and over she bounced in rhythm with Lady's steps until finally she managed to pull on the mare's reins and force her back into a walk . . . a smooth walk.

She wiped a hand over her forehead and brushed several strands of hair from her face. "Lord, girl, let's not try that again," she mumbled, shifting her seat on the saddle. "Trotting is not one of my favorite speeds."

Jake rode up beside her. "Lean forward and put a little pressure on your stirrups when you get Lady into a trot, Shelby. It'll be a mite easier on your . . . uh, backside."

"Thanks, Jake. My brain remembers what to do, but unfortunately, its instructions to my body are a bit slow."

103

"You ride point with me this morning. Keep the dust out of your face."

"What about the guests?" She knew from all Katie's cowboy movies that riding point meant riding in front of the herd and ahead of the dust kicked up by the animals' hooves. She smiled. At least she wasn't a total novice, thanks to her sister's obsession with *Bonanza, The Virginian, Wagon Train,* and half a dozen other old series and movies that replayed on Saturday mornings.

"Getting dirt kicked up in their faces is half the fun they pay to come here for."

She was about to ask him another question, when she noticed they'd crested a small hill and the herd had come into view. The cattle were spread over a wide area of sloping hillside, their reddish brown bodies blending well with the rugged terrain and fall foliage. At that moment, Shelby could have sworn she'd never seen so many cows.

"We're going to move all those?" one of the guests said, riding up beside Jake.

Shelby looked past Jake to see Bobby's mother, Ruth Rothman, pull her horse up on the opposite side of the wrangler. The plump brunette was staring in awe at the sea of animals in front of them.

Jake smiled at the woman. "Yep. But don't worry, ma'am, it ain't hard. Main thing you gotta remember is just to keep your eyes out for strays. Sometimes the young ones wander off away from

104

their mamas. Kinda exploring, you know? Then they get kinda turned around and confused. Just like kids."

"But what if they stampede?" Mrs. Rothman persisted. "Wouldn't it be dangerous?"

Shelby looked at the middle-aged woman, whose face remained creased with worry, and frowned herself. Those were just the kind of questions she didn't need to hear. She was already nervous enough about this drive without someone bringing her own fears and concerns out into the open for her to think about some more.

"They won't, unless someone starts playing with a gun, or the sky shoots lightning bolts down at them, or some such. All you gotta remember is, don't get in their way and don't try to stop them if they start going."

"Oh, great," Shelby mumbled, conjuring up an image of her guests lying trampled in the Montana wilderness by the hooves of two hundred panicked cows. What in heaven's name was she doing out here playing cattle baroness to a bunch of rich jet-setters?

Guilt swept over her and she practically cringed at its assault. She was out here because Katie had asked her to be, that's why. At least that's how she'd interpreted Katie's leaving her the ranch, instead of stipulating in her will that it be sold and the monies given to Shelby. And of course, there was the letter, leaving no question. Katie had wanted the ranch to go on, and that's exactly what Shelby was going to do, come hell or high water.

Within seconds, the group was heading down the hillside toward the herd and Jake was shouting orders, telling everyone what position to take up and what to do.

Suddenly Shelby's fear subsided, to be replaced by excitement. She was on a real cattle drive . . . an honest-to-goodness cattle drive. This wasn't some trumped-up movie stunt or amusement park pretense, but a real live cattle drive.

She watched the Double K wranglers gallop around the herd and start urging the cows into a tighter group, lifting their coiled lassos or hats high over their heads and then smacking them against their chap-covered thighs. The guests took up their assigned positions and began emulating the ranch hands, while the child-care wrangler and his kids took their place at the rear of the herd. Whoops and whistles from cowhands, guests, and children filled the air, along with a lot of excited and enthusiastic laughter.

Shelby rode up beside Jake. She was surprised at how quickly her body was adapting to being in the saddle again, though she had no illusions that she would be anything but a knotted pretzel of flesh at the end of the day. Again she wished she'd had the foresight to tell Tom to bring the masseuse out on his next trip to the herd. "Give me a few more riding lessons today, Jake?"

The older man smiled and nodded.

Shelby smiled back. "Do I do anything now besides ride?"

"Yeah," he shouted. "Stay on the trail and make sure it's clear, keep an eye out for strays, and watch for Cody."

She stiffened. She'd watch the trail and keep an eye out for strays, but that was all. Cody Farlowe could watch out for himself, and she was sure that's exactly the way he wanted it.

Chapter Nine

Cody hooked his leg over the saddle horn, leaned a forearm on his bent knee, and gazed down at the activity that had broken out on the hillside below. Jake had the Double K wranglers and guests well situated around the herd and they in turn had the animals on the move. He knew the trail up ahead was clear—he'd covered it thoroughly that morning; and the campfire site in the meadow where they'd stop for lunch was ready—he'd seen to it himself. Now he had no excuse for not rejoining the group, yet he hesitated.

He wiped a thin film of sweat from his forehead with the back of his hand and pulled the black brim of his hat lower so it sat just barely above his eyebrows. The sun seemed merciless for this time of year, and it wasn't even noon yet. Even in the shade of the pine tree Cody was under, he could feel the intense rays filtering through the branches and penetrating his shirt.

He'd ridden hard that morning, trying to rid

himself of memory of the previous night, stopping only when he realized Soldier was tiring. But no matter how hard he rode or how much he told himself to forget her, Shelby wouldn't leave his mind. Everywhere he looked, he was reminded of her. The rich, red Montana earth was the lustrous hue of her hair, the fertile greenness of the trees was the exact shade of her eyes, and the rolling hills made him recall the subtle curves that had fitted so well against his body. The warm touch of the sun was like the soft caress of her hands, and he heard her voice on the wind.

He heard children's laughter, and looked down to see the tail end of the herd passing through the valley below, the kids bringing up the rear. Suddenly he realized how much he missed Katie and Ken's boys. Every day after they'd come home from school, Katie had let them run out to wherever he and Ken were, to "lend a helping hand," as she'd put it. The ranch was a good place for kids. A happy place. Cody sighed and a gnawing emptiness swelled inside him as he continued to think of Josh and Joey, and that he'd never see them again. The image of Katie that had naturally come to mind when he thought of the boys, reminded him of Shelby. Involuntarily he sought her out.

She wasn't hard to locate, in spite of the distance between them. Her long auburn hair was like a spot of fire against the landscape. Even half-covered and shaded by the brim of her hat, her hair drew the sun's rays and glistened brilliantly. She was riding toward the front and off to one side of the herd, and Lance Murdock was riding beside her.

Cody felt a quiver of jealousy. She might not belong here, on the Double K with him, but she didn't belong with that phony Hollywood ladies' man, either. Cody had seen his type before. He'd seduce Shelby and then break her heart when another beautiful woman caught his eye. Fury fired Cody's blood. Shelby deserved better than that.

He dropped his leg from the saddle horn, slipped his foot into the stirrup, and nudged Soldier into action. The horse bolted forward, moving over the sloping ground as effortlessly and swiftly as the wind. Cody rode up behind the herd, passing the wranglers and guests, and moved into position beside Shelby. On her opposite side was Lance Murdock.

Shelby turned at his approach, shot him a very cool glance, then caught herself, hoping no one had noticed. She changed her expression to a smile.

Lance glared. Cody ignored him.

"Well, where have you been?" Shelby said, her tone of voice holding a lot more cheerfulness than the frosty gleam in her eyes.

"Scouting the trail. Making sure it was clear and our noon campsite was ready. Don't want to have any more accidents. Everything okay?" He eyed Lance, then looked pointedly back at Shelby.

One reddish eyebrow arched. "Everything's just

wonderful. Lance was telling me how the guests had a little party last night, which we missed. They've planned another for tonight, though, and definitely expect us to be there. They figure tonight's will be better, anyway, since they're all confident they'll be much more used to a day in the saddle than they were yesterday."

Cody grinned. "I wouldn't be too sure about that. Driving a herd is a little harder than just riding across the range. Especially if you do your share." He stared past her at Lance.

His dark brows arched haughtily. "I guess when you're paying rather than working, there's a little more leeway in the regiment."

"Not on this drive," Cody answered.

Lance sniffed and Cody felt an urge to drive his fist into the movie star's nose. Instead he flexed the hand that rested on his chap-covered thigh and glared. "That's the thing about signing on to accompany a 'real' cattle drive, Hollywood," he said through clenched teeth. "It's work. Hard work. And everyone is expected to pull their own weight. Guest and wrangler alike."

Lance shifted in his saddle and began to look uncomfortable. "Uh, Shelby, I guess I'll see you at lunch," he said. "I'd better get back to my position and make sure we haven't lost any calves."

"You do that, Hollywood," Cody said, tipping the brim of his hat at the man as he began to turn his horse away.

Lance reined in and glowered at Cody. "In case

111

you've forgotten, the name's Murdock. *Mr.* Murdock."

Cody smiled. "Whatever you say, Hollywood."

Lance jabbed his heels into his horse's side and the animal took off at a gallop.

As soon as Lance was out of earshot, Shelby whirled on Cody, anger blazing from her eyes. "Cody Farlowe, that was no way to treat a guest."

"Sorry."

"You are not."

"True, but I figured I'd better say it, anyway."

"Well, maybe you ought to say it to him."

"Yeah, when cows jump over the moon," he mumbled.

"What did you say?"

"Nothing."

They rode side by side, each staring straight ahead at the horizon or off into the surrounding landscape. It was more than fifteen minutes before either spoke again.

"Look," Cody said suddenly, turning toward Shelby. "This is no good between us. What happened last night, it was wrong. I'm sorry. I should have had more control over myself. Things went too far and it's my fault."

Shelby's mouth went dry and tears stung the back of her eyes. She'd never had a man say he was sorry he'd made love to her before. They might have thought it, but good Lord, she'd never heard them say it.

Of course, there hadn't been that many men in

112

her life. Maybe this was some cowboy code of the West to protect the little lady from feeling like a . . . a . . . What was the word? Trollop? And what was she supposed to say? Oh, that's all right, Cody, no big deal? Or, yeah, it was nice, but I guess we shouldn't have?

"You probably want me off the ranch. Can't say as I blame you. I'll pack up and leave when the drive's over. I guess it's best that way, anyhow."

She swallowed hard and searched for her voice. "No, that's not what I want, Cody. There's no reason for you to leave." She felt her eyes filling with tears and blinked rapidly to hold them back. "What's done is . . . done. Let's just forget it." The words almost stung her tongue, but she forced herself to go on. "The Double K needs you." *I need you,* she added silently.

Copdy looked at her, saw the hurt his words had caused, the sheen of unshed tears in her eyes, and knew she was battling desperately to control her emotions and remain calm. He felt like a heel. No. Worse than that. He felt like the lowest form of life on the earth, though he wasn't exactly sure what that was. He turned away and glanced at the cattle. It was better this way, he told himself. Maybe she was hurt for the moment, but it would pass. Someday she'd probably even thank him for ending their relationship before it got too involved. He sniffed softly and shook his head at the time-worn cliché. Thank him? Hell, he was probably lucky she didn't fire him, then blackball him right out of Montana.

Shelby turned her face away. A tear escaped the corner of her eye and ran down the side of her cheek. She brushed at it quickly, hoping he wouldn't notice. She should have known Cody didn't really care for her that way. Hadn't he made it painfully clear ever since her arrival at the Double K that he thought she was inept? A "city girl" who ought to go back where she belonged, that's what he'd told her countless times in the past few days. Obviously a man like Cody Farlowe wanted a woman who could share the life he loved, who could ride a horse as if she had been born on it, drive cattle as well as or better than she drove a car, cook over an open fire, and make love in the wilds of the countryside beneath a starry sky.

Shelby took a deep breath. Well, she'd proven she could at least do one of those things.

"Hey, Cody, we got us a problem back here."

Cody and Shelby turned to see Jake ride up behind them.

They reined in and waited for him to catch up. "What's the matter?" Cody asked, removing his hat and wiping his forehead with his sleeve. He replaced the hat and waited for Jake's answer.

"We got a cow down about a half mile back, stuck in a ravine."

"So? Pull her out."

"She's in labor."

"Oh, wonderful," Cody snarled, yanking on the reins and pulling Soldier's head around.

"Who's with her now?"

"Jamie and that blond woman, Eva something-or-other. They're trying to keep the cow down."

Jake had been forced to yell his last sentence as Cody galloped away.

"Eva Montalvo?" Shelby asked, surprised. The New York socialite hadn't impressed her as the sort to get her hands quite *that* dirty.

Jake shrugged. "The dame with all them fancy strings hanging off her shirt."

Shelby laughed. "That's Eva." She swung Lady around. "I'll come, too. Maybe I can help."

Jake shrugged and nudged his horse into a lope. Shelby made to follow and was instantly assaulted by pain as her sore muscles reacted to the accelerated motion. She pulled desperately on the reins.

Jake turned around to look at her when she didn't appear beside him, but she waved him on and kept Lady moving at a brisk, but smooth walk.

Shelby clung to the saddle horn, stood in the stirrups, and tried to keep her rear end from making contact with the saddle too often. She hung on and prayed her legs wouldn't turn to jelly and land her on the ground. Spending the next few months in a body cast was not in her plans.

When she reached the spot where the ground disappeared abruptly before her, Shelby reined in. Jake had already descended into the narrow ravine where the cow, Jamie, Cody, and Eva were already gathered. A glistening stream of water snaked its way through the center of the ravine, only a few feet from the small group.

The animal let out a loud, groaning moo and made a feeble effort to get to her feet. Her tail swished and slapped against Cody's thigh.

"Hold her head down!" Cody yelled. "If she thrashes around in here, she'll kill herself, the calf, and most likely us, too." He knelt at the rear of the animal, jerked his gloves off, and pushed up his sleeves.

Jamie moved to straddle the cow's neck and hold down her front legs, while Jake held her rear legs, preventing her from kicking out. Eva grabbed the animal's head.

"We've got her," Eva said.

Shelby stood at the edge of the ravine, watching anxiously and feeling helpless. She didn't know what she could do, if anything, to assist. She glanced at Eva Montalvo, surprised at the woman's mettle. Obviously getting bruised and dirty weren't as offensive to the socialite as Shelby would have thought.

The cow thrashed again. "Looks like baby needs a little help," Cody said. He pushed the hat from his head. "Hold her down, guys."

Jake pulled the cow's hind legs forward, and Cody's hands and forearms disappeared into the cow.

Shelby stared, awestruck.

"I got him," Cody yelled. He braced his heels in the dirt and pulled backward with his entire body, a grimace creasing his handsome face. "Come on, fella, give me a little help here," Cody mumbled, straining to pull the calf from its mother's womb.

Suddenly the calf's two front hooves came into view, followed immediately by its legs and Cody's blood-covered arms and hands. "Front legs are out," Cody yelled. His hands delved back into the mother cow. A second later, the calf's small head popped out.

Shelby stared at the blood, thin rivers of red that covered Cody's arms, the calf's head and legs, and dripped to form a small pool on the ground. Her stomach twisted into a knot and began to churn, rolling end over end. Nausea swelled to close her throat; the horizon blurred and began to swirl around her. She clenched her hands into fists, digging her nails into the flesh of her palms in an effort to regain her composure.

I can't faint, she told herself. *I can't. Please, God, don't let me faint now.* But her prayer fell on deaf ears. Her heart began a slamming beat, its frantic acceleration sending the blood in her veins racing madly. Her limbs began to tremble, and her legs suddenly felt like two thin sticks of rubber that were quickly softening, melting beneath her weight. She shook her head to clear it, but the movement only made the dizziness worse. The horizon turned to a sea of brown and green waves beneath a soft blue blanket. She blinked rapidly, and in that same instant the world disappeared. Blackness rose up to engulf her, enveloping her in its infinite darkness, drawing her into its cold, icy void. She felt herself falling forward, spiraling into a deep, endless chasm, and knew there was nothing she could do to save herself.

Out of the corner of his eye, Cody caught a sudden movement on the ledge of the crevice. His attention was torn between the calf, which was still struggling its way into the world, and the flash of blue and white that, in his peripheral vision, he had noticed suddenly slip from view. The calf wriggled, made a final forward lunge, and was abruptly free of its mother's womb. The animal got immediately to his feet, and Cody threw a quick glance over his shoulder to where Shelby had been standing only seconds earlier.

"Damn. Wouldn't you know it?" he cursed. "Jamie, get back here. Now!"

Startled at Cody's unusually rough tone, the wrangler scurried to obey the order.

"Take over for me here. They seem to be doing okay on their own, but keep an eye on things. If the calf needs help — help him. Give Mama a hand in cleaning the little fella off and then get them moving. I'll meet you back at the camp. Billy's kept everyone on the trail, I hope."

"Sure thing, boss," Jamie said, his rugged face breaking into a grin.

Cody noticed the wrangler glance up to make sure Eva Montalvo was watching, and shook his head in disgust. Women! What the hell was it that brought citified women out to the country and allowed them to turn normally intelligent, sensible wranglers into lovesick puppies?

He moved to kneel beside the shallow stream and plunged his arms into the cool water, quickly washing himself off. A minute later, he jammed his hat back on his head, hoisted himself up the waist-high ledge of the ravine, and knelt beside Shelby's unconscious form. He felt her pulse, satisfied himself that she had merely fainted, as he'd suspected, cursed again, and slipped one arm around her shoulders and the other under her knees. Rising to his feet, he drew her against his chest and carried her toward a sparse grove of cottonwoods. The trees offered all the shade to be had in the immediate area, which wasn't a whole lot.

Shelby's warm body against his brought forth memories of what it had been like to make love to her the previous night, to claim her lips with his, while his hands explored her luscious curves. He felt the burning heat of desire begin to simmer within him, and cursed beneath his breath. He'd spent the better part of the morning trying to forget how good it had been with her and how much he wanted to know that feeling again.

Having her this close, crushed against him, was almost more than he could bear. All he had to do was look down, bend his head just a little, and he would be able to brush his lips against the taut peak of her breast. Every fiber in his body throbbed with need, and he tried to steel his mind to it, blotting out the messages from his body. "It's wrong, damn it," he grumbled. "She doesn't belong here. In a few weeks she'll realize that and be gone, so save yourself a lot of grief and stay away from her."

He knelt slowly and laid Shelby down on the sun-warmed ground, then rose back to his full height. "Great. Now I'm talking to myself." Propping his hands on his hips, the dark brim of his hat pulled low on his forehead, Cody stared down at her and wished for the hundredth time that she had never come to the Double K. Wasn't one hoof-stomping blow to his heart enough? Did he have to go through it again?

The question, he knew, was rhetorical. But at least he hadn't fallen in love with her yet. He liked her well enough, and his body ached for her, but that was all. It wasn't love. And if he could convince her to leave, as he knew she would eventually, anyway, his feelings wouldn't have time to turn into love. Angry with himself, he let his gaze fall on the horizon, and stared at it without really seeing it. He felt like a man trying to straddle a picket fence that had cactus on one side and angry bulls on the other. No matter which way he fell or jumped, he was doomed.

Cody kicked a heel at the dirt. "Ah, hell. Who am I trying to kid, anyhow?" Shelby Hill had already stolen a substantial part of his heart, and he knew damn well he'd probably never get it back.

On the other hand, if he used what smarts he'd been born with, combined with the lesson he'd already learned about getting involved with a city girl — he glanced at Shelby's prone figure and amended his last thought — city woman, he would continue to do what he'd set out to do that morning. He'd stay as far away from her as he could get.

Shelby moaned softly, the sound disturbing Cody's reflection. Against his will and his better judgment, he allowed his gaze to roam over her body, devouring it, much as a starving man does his first offer of food. The desire for her was constantly with him, growing stronger all the time, overwhelming his logic and his stubborn determination to deny what he wanted so much to possess. His fingers ached to touch the red-gold strands of hair, spread out on the ground around her head. His lips longed to know her warm caresses and the intimacy just beyond them. His body hungered to once again experience the cresting waves of pleasure that their union had brought.

Cody dropped his hands to his sides and clenched them into fists. Suddenly, instead of Shelby, he saw another woman lying on the ground before him. She had wavy earth-brown hair that cascaded about her ivory shoulders, brown eyes so dark they were nearly black, and a long, thin body that was almost the exact length of his own. Lisa. Her exotic looks had captivated him at once, and he'd been able to think of little else. He certainly hadn't considered how insane a relationship between them actually was—a wealthy New Yorker and a cowboy. He shook his head at his past naïveté.

Every muscle in his body stiffened at the painful memories, but with them came the discipline he needed to control his runaway yearnings for the beautiful and rich new owner of the Double K.

Shelby's eyelids fluttered open and she stared up past the branches of the cottonwood tree into the bright sun. Her head instantly began to throb with a piercing pain that seemed to volley back and forth between her temples. She rose on her elbows, and the pain grew worse. She moaned, closed her eyes for a second, then opened them again. Slightly better. She looked around and finally noticed the dark silhouette of a man standing over her.

Alarm jolted her, momentarily stopping her heart and bringing it almost into her throat.

He moved, just slightly, but enough so that the light fell onto the side of his face.

Shelby sighed and chided herself for being so foolish. "Cody."

He knelt beside her, balancing on the balls of his feet and resting his arms on top of his thighs. "Yeah, it's me. You all right?"

Shelby moved to sit up and the world did an instant spin out of control. She snapped her eyes closed and put a hand to her forehead. "Ummm, only if the world slows down a bit." She sat still for a long moment and then tried to look up at him again. This time his image didn't whirl into a blur, though the pounding in her head hadn't lessened any. "What happened?"

"You fainted."

"Fainted? I've never fainted in my life. Not once. Anyway, why would I faint?"

"A lot of women faint at the sight of blood. Or birthing."

"That's ridiculous. I've seen blood before."

"Seen birthing?"

She hesitated. "Well, no, but . . ." She straightened her shoulders. "Why should that make me faint? It's a natural thing. And besides, it was only a cow."

"Bull."

"What?"

He smiled. "It was a boy, so it's not a cow, it's a bull."

Shelby threw up her hands, and cringed at the pain in her head that was aggravated by the movement. "Whatever," she grumbled, dropping her head between her hands and massaging her temples.

"Got a headache?"

Her reply was barely more than a mumble of acknowledgment; she didn't dare speak louder. The cymbals in her head had begun to crash again.

Cody assumed her muttered response meant yes and stood, saying, "I'll get my canteen. A little cool water on your forehead might help you feel better."

She groaned again, but didn't look up. She heard the scuff of his boots on the ground as he turned and walked to where Soldier stood contentedly grazing on a small clump of wildflowers. Shelby shifted her sitting position and almost cried out at the ache that filled both her hip and her right knee. She wiped a hand across her eyes, ridding herself of the telltale tears that would alert him to the fact that more than her ego had been bruised when she'd fainted. Cody Farlowe had decided, all by himself, that she didn't belong on the Double K, that she was totally inept when it came to running the ranch, and that she would run back to the city at the first chance of things getting a little rough.

Though she hated to admit it even to herself, for a while—during the first few days she'd been at the ranch—she'd almost done just that. But she hadn't, and now she found herself wondering, again, if he wasn't right. Maybe she should put the ranch up for sale. If she had half a brain, which sometimes she doubted, she'd be on the next plane back to California. Cody had made it painfully clear that's where he thought she belonged. Yet last night his kiss, his body, had said otherwise.

Remembering their lovemaking, the gentle but passionate man who had taken her to heights of ecstasy that she had never imagined possible, Shelby felt a surge of longing. Instantly the longing was followed by an overpowering wave of stubbornness, an unusual trait for her, but one that had been surfacing regularly since she'd met Cody. He might know just about everything there was to know about riding, roping, and running the Double K, but he didn't know about women. At least not about Shelby Hill. She was through with wandering and searching for a life that fitted her. What she'd left behind hadn't been very fulfilling, anyway. In losing her sister, she had been handed a chance to settle down, to do something worthwhile, to keep Katie's dream alive and make it her own, and damn it to hell, that's what she was going to do. She'd show him, she thought. And then maybe he'd . . . She balked at the direction her thoughts were flying and she tried to deny them, but it didn't work. Maybe he'd let himself love her? The words echoed in her mind, like a shout in a deep canyon, repeating themselves over and over.

"You okay?" Cody asked, staring down at her and frowning. His tone had softened, taking on a note of warmth.

Shelby looked up at him, surprised. She'd been so deep into her daydream that she hadn't even been aware of his approach. "I . . . I'm fine. It's just the headache."

Cody tipped the spout of his canteen to the neckerchief he'd taken off, soaked it, then squeezed some of the excess water from the fabric. He hunkered down in front of her and pressed the cool cloth to her forehead. "This'll help."

125

She leaned into his touch, finding his gentleness and concern more soothing than the wet cloth. "Mmmm. Thanks."

"How about the rest of you? Everything okay?"

She saw his gaze travel over her legs, and squirmed slightly, nervous under his scrutiny. Fainting at the sight of a calf being born was bad enough. She did not want him to realize that she'd hurt herself in the process. By the time they made camp that evening, she felt sure that both her hip and her leg would be covered by ugly yellow and purple bruises to accompany those she'd gotten when she'd fallen over the cliff.

She averted her gaze from him and hid behind the rag. "Yes, I'm fine. No broken bones."

"You took a nasty drop, Shelby. You sure nothing hurts?"

She wanted to scream, *Yes, it hurts. It hurts like hell*. But she didn't. Instead she peeked around the drooping corner of his neckerchief and smiled. Any other time she'd want nothing more than his attention, but not now, not when she'd so foolishly hurt herself again. "I'm fine, Cody. Really. Maybe you'd better go back and check on the calf and its mother."

"They're fine."

She grimaced inwardly. The way her hip had begun to throb, and judging by the stinging pain on the side of her knee, she was not going to be too graceful in rising to her feet. And walking back to where Lady was standing was going to seem like the death march to Bataan. This she definitely did not want Cody to witness. An attempt at subterfuge was called for. She jerked upright and turned to look in the direction of the ravine. "Was that Jamie calling you?"

Cody glanced over his shoulder. "I didn't hear anything. Anyway, I think I'd better help you."

"Oh, I know I heard him, and I'm sure he was calling out your name. I'll be fine, Cody, really." She took the damp rag from him. "You'd better go check and see what he needs. Maybe something's wrong with the calf."

Cody looked at her for a long moment. "You sure you're okay?"

"Fine," she lied. "Fine."

Cody nodded, though he did not look at all convinced, and left her to walk back to the edge of the ravine. Shelby scrambled to her feet and nearly cried out at the stab of pain that shot through her hip and leg. She hobbled toward Lady, hurrying to reach the horse before Cody heard her movement and turned around. Struggling to control the tears the piercing pain had brought to her eyes, she practically fell against the mare's side. She grabbed the saddle horn with one hand, the flap of the saddlebag with the other, and released a long, relief-filled sigh. At least she hadn't fallen on her face.

The horse turned her head to look back at Shelby.

"It's okay, girl," Shelby whispered. "It's only

127

me, Miss Klutz of the Year."

Lady shook her head, sending her mane flying, and went back to munching on a clump of grass.

Shelby tightened her grip, trying to pull herself up with her arms, and raised her left leg to place her foot in the stirrup. She didn't get her foot more than a few inches off the ground than her other leg buckled beneath her.

"Ohhh." The fingers of her left hand turned white from the pressure of maintaining her grip on the saddle horn. Lady, startled by Shelby's clumsiness, shied, and took a step sideways.

"No, girl, stay put," Shelby urged, panicked at the thought that the horse might actually walk away from her. "Don't move, Lady, please."

Cody watched out of the corner of his eye. He'd figured she'd hurt herself when she'd fallen to the ground. Now he was certain. But he also understood the need to save a little pride. He waited until she'd managed to mount the small mare, before finally turning around again. He stood still as Shelby urged Lady up beside him.

"I'll ride on ahead and make sure everything's okay," she said. "Jake's probably already back and stopped for lunch."

Before he could respond, she was gone.

Chapter Ten

Only a few minutes after Shelby's arrival at the camp Jake had set up for the lunch break, Jamie and Eva Montalvo rode in. Cody, however, had taken over the job of prodding the new mother cow and her calf back to the herd, and he didn't arrive for almost another hour.

Shelby looked up from the grill full of sizzling hamburger patties and hot dogs she was tending and watched him slide from the saddle and remove Soldier's bridle, replacing it with a light halter. "Go on and graze, boy," Cody said, taking off the saddle and giving the animal an affectionate slap on the rump. The big horse immediately ambled toward the open pasture beyond the campsite, and Cody veered toward a cooler full of ice and beer, beside which Jake stood talking to one of the other wranglers.

Shelby poked at the grilling patties with her spatula, her gaze never wavering from Cody. In the confusion and excitement of the new calf's birth, she'd almost forgotten about their conversation of only moments earlier, when Cody had apologized for making love to her. But on the twenty-minute ride to where Jake had made the noonday camp, while trying to ignore her throbbing body, she'd had plenty of quiet time to remember, and her temper had risen steadily. With each step Lady had taken, Shelby's anger had soared a degree higher, until now she was so mad at Cody and herself that she could barely keep from marching over to him and telling him what a chauvinistic, pigheaded, insensitive clod he was. Imagine, making passionate love to a woman, being warm and caring, then the next morning acting as if she were Medusa. And to top it off, if that wasn't bad enough, the cad had the nerve to say he should never have done it.

Every time she remembered his words of apology, Shelby's temper jumped up another notch on her invisible temperature gauge. Could a person explode from rage? she wondered, glaring at Cody. Well, maybe she wasn't drop-dead gorgeous, and maybe she wasn't an expert at riding a horse, roping a cow, or running a ranch, but she had feelings just like everyone else.

She flipped a patty and the dripping juice that fell onto the fire sizzled loudly. A few hours earlier she'd had a lot of self-doubt, an excess of uncertainty about whether she really should stay at the Double K. She'd been thinking maybe it would be better for everyone concerned if she just put the place in the hands of a real-estate agent, packed her bags, and left as Cody wanted. But anger had given her a new outlook. A bit of self-confidence. Or stubbornness. She wasn't sure which, and she didn't care. The self-doubt hadn't completely disappeared, but she'd made up her mind to ignore it. She was staying . . . at least until the cattle drive was over. She'd take it one day at a time, one minute at a time, if necessary, and see what happened.

Shelby smiled to herself, feeling pleasantly surprised. Normally she would have capitulated, accepted everyone's opinion that this wasn't right for her, and moved on. She felt a warm glow of satisfaction.

A chorus of giggles broke out from behind the large mound of rocks, off to one side of the camp area and just behind Shelby. She turned to look, found her attention drawn upward, and was startled to see two small objects, like colored cigarettes, soaring through the air toward her, sparks of fire flying from their tips.

Shelby stared at the approaching entities, mesmerized.

The tiny missiles hit the ground and exploded with a loud double bang. Eva Montalvo screamed; Jamie whirled around, as if ready to draw a nonexistent gun from his hip; Cody looked ready to murder someone; and Shelby practically jumped out of her skin.

Her knee crashed against the raised grill and her spatula caught the edge of one of the hamburger patties, sending it and several wieners flying. The spatula bounced off the toppling grill and into the fire, along with the rest of the meat. The flames went wild, spurting up and out. Within seconds, the grass that was a good two feet away from the campfire, sparked into crackling orange flame.

Confusion reigned as people ran in different directions. The guests dashed for cover, not knowing what had happened; several of the wranglers moved toward the herd to make sure the cattle hadn't been scared enough to start moving; and several other ranch hands darted toward the rocks from where the firecracker had come. The children, peeking out from their hiding place, were hysterical with laughter, until they saw the men bearing down on them, their eyes blazing displeasure. In a flash the kids broke and ran, each heading in a different direction.

Shelby jumped up and tried to stamp out the grass fire caused by her flying grill, but it had gotten too good a hold on the dry reeds. On the verge of panic, she looked around helplessly, and groaned. Cody was running toward her, a large blanket dripping with water held in front of him.

"Watch out, Shelby." He pushed her brusquely aside and threw the wet blanket on top of the flames. They instantly disappeared and thin curls of white steam rose from the tightly woven gray wool blanket.

Forgetting his earlier promise to himself to stay

132

away from her, forgetting that he'd also sworn to remain calm, cool, and collected around her no matter what, but most of all forgetting that she was his boss, Cody spun on his heel and glared at Shelby. "What the hell were *you* doing cooking?"

She had been on the verge of thanking him for yet another rescue, but his tone halted the grateful words. Instead she bristled. "I was helping. Isn't that what this picnic lunch and this drive are all about? Everybody doing something? Or did I misinterpret your comment to Lance earlier?" Her words dripped with such sarcasm she almost winced herself at their bitterness.

But Cody didn't. "Only what they know they can handle, and evidently — " he looked at the toppled grill, burning hamburger and wieners, and smoldering blanket " — this is not up your alley."

Shelby opened her mouth, a defensive retort on her tongue, when suddenly she realized how quiet and motionless the rest of the camp had gotten. Long seconds before she turned to look, she felt herself flush, felt the warmth of embarrassment flood her cheeks, and knew she'd turned as red as an apple. Damn. Why was it that every time she got near Cody Farlowe, one of two things happened: either she wanted to fall into his arms or bash him over the head with a frying pan? At the moment, neither option was open to her.

She pulled herself up straight, tossed her head so that her hair fell back over her shoulders, and looked up at him with as much dignity as she could muster. "Cody, I doubt our arguing is making the guests feel comfortable. Perhaps we should discuss this later—in my office back at the ranch."

Cody looked as if she'd slapped him across the face. His features seemed to turn to stone, but his voice when he spoke was filled with anguish, not the anger she'd expected.

"It's wrong, Shelby," he said, only loud enough for her to hear. "All of it's wrong. You here at the Double K, trying to lead a life you don't want. Us, you and me, falling into a relationship that can't work." He shook his head and reached up toward her face, gently brushing his fingers over her cheek. "Much as I wish it wasn't, it's wrong." He turned away and strode to where Soldier stood grazing. A second later he was gone, riding away from the camp as if fleeing hades itself.

Shelby stared after him in shock, resisting the urge to follow him. Finally, ignoring the others staring at her, she bent down and began to clean up the spilled grill and ruined blanket. The hamburgers were a lost cause. Maybe Cody *was* right, she thought. Maybe she didn't belong here. All she'd done since coming on this drive was get herself into one mess after another. And that included being seduced by the ranch's foreman.

Dumb move, Shelby, she told herself. *Real dumb move.*

The more she tried to convince herself that she should leave, that the relationship between Cody and her had been a mistake and better ended here and now, the more her heart rebelled at the idea. At both ideas! She was really coming to enjoy the ranch, even if she did have to be rescued from it now and then. As for Cody, well, she was pretty sure she knew how she felt about him, she just wasn't sure how he felt about her. Then again, maybe there wasn't anything to find out.

She kicked dirt onto the smoldering fire and walked toward the guests, most of whom were sitting on picnic blankets in the shadows of a few scrub pines. "Sorry, folks, I guess I ruined lunch. Is there enough other stuff to hold us over?"

"Hey, beautiful. Smile," Lance said. "We've already got a feast here."

Shelby turned to see Lance rise to his feet and move to stand beside her. She smiled appreciatively at his support, and, he assuming the smile was an invitation, wrapped an arm around her shoulder and drew her to his side.

"Look, those picnic baskets your cook sent out were full to the brim with a dozen different goodies," he hastened to add.

"Yeah, Shelby, look at this." Eva Montalvo held up a plate of sliced cheeses, which Shelby noticed included Brie and strawberry cream, and in her other hand Eva lifted a relish tray complete with caviar and stuffed anchovies.

Shelby laughed and shrugged. "Well, with a spread like this, I agree, who needs hamburgers and hot dogs?" She threw a glance over her shoulder, saw that Cody was still gone, and pushed away the remorse she felt at his absence.

An hour later, after promising Lance that she'd join him at the party the guests planned for that evening, Shelby left the group of guests and went in search of Jake. She found him by the string of horses, checking over each one to make sure they were all still in good shape.

"Jake," she said, moving to stand beside him. "I need to talk to you."

The old man grunted in what she'd come to realize was his way of acknowledging someone.

"Jake, is there something I don't know about that's bothering Cody?" she asked, wanting to add *such as me,* but refrained.

The cowboy shrugged. "Best ask him."

"I would, except he always seems to be angry with me." She pushed aside her memory of their lovemaking, one of the few times he hadn't acted mad at her, and continued. "Look, Jake, I really want to make a go of it here on the Double K. I want things to stay the way they were when Katie was here, but—" Her voice caught and she was forced to pause when tears filled her eyes.

Jake heard the catch of emotion, released the buckle of the bridle he was checking, and straightened, turning toward her.

"I don't like to carry tales about other people's business, Miss Shelby."

She didn't answer, she just looked at him, and that was enough. The old wrangler's face softened and he shook his head.

"Look, I'd tell you if I could, but I can't. I don't know what's eating Cody. But I will tell you this—he ain't been the same since he got back."

"Back?" she echoed, puzzled. "Back from where?"

"Ah, I don't know. One of them big cities back East. New York, I think."

"But why'd he go to New York? He loves it here. What could have possibly made him leave Montana?" She had a hunch even as she asked the questions what Jake was going to say, and did not look forward to hearing his answer.

Jake pushed his hat back, turned away from her, and began to fiddle with the cinch. "I think you'd best talk to Cody."

Shelby reached out and touched Jake's arm. "Please, Jake, if you know, please tell me. The way things are going, I'm afraid Cody will leave the Double K." *And me,* a little voice cried deep within her.

At her last remark, Jake paused and looked back at her for a long moment. Then he sighed. "A woman. He went to the city to be with a woman."

That was the answer she'd both hoped for and

dreaded. But at least now she felt pretty certain she knew why Cody was so dead set against "city girls." She felt a surge of resolve.

"A woman from the city . . . like me." It wasn't a question but a statement.

Jake answered, anyway. "Yeah, kinda. But not as nice as you. Leastways, I didn't think so."

Shelby smiled at the older man's compliment. "Thanks, Jake. Now, I need you to do something else. Will you help me?"

Jake shuffled uneasily. "Whaddya want me to do?"

"Help me finish the drive the way it's supposed to be. Help me get the cows to the west ridge and the guests back to the ranch in one piece."

He nodded. "What about Cody? He's the boss. Uh, I mean the trail boss."

"I just need you to help *me,* Jake. Whether Cody's around or not." She smiled. "I want to learn how to do things for myself, the way Katie did, and I figure you'd be the best teacher I could ask for."

Jake nodded once more. "Okay, I guess I can do that."

Shelby had to clasp her hands together to keep from reaching out and hugging him, something she sensed would embarrass him. "Great. What do we do now?"

"We get the gear packed back on the saddle horses, get mounted, and start moving the cows. As it is, we're going to be a mite late pulling into

138

our campsite tonight."

"Okay, I'll get our guests on their feet." Shelby hurried off toward where the group of "dudes," as the wranglers called them, were sitting. At least, she tried to hurry, but her aching limbs forced her to move slower than she would have liked. "Come on everyone, time to hit the trail."

Half an hour later, the jokes and laughter had been put aside and the kids rounded up. Everyone had taken his or her assigned positions around the herd, and they were on the trail again. But there was no sign of Cody.

As the sun hung low in the sky, just on the verge of sinking down behind the tree-capped mountainous horizon, Shelby rode up beside Jake at the head of the herd. "How much farther till we make camp?"

"About another mile. We got a small stream to cross up ahead, then we'll just about be there."

"Is it deep?"

Jake chuckled. "It's a stream, Miss Shelby, not a river. Hell, it ain't even a creek. Just a piddle bit of water sliding across the top of the land, that's all."

Shelby relaxed and let her gaze scan the horizon. It really was beautiful country: wide, open spaces; endless meadows; majestic mountains; and all beneath a brilliant blue sky that held not one hint of smog. "How could a person ever want to live anywhere else?" she said softly.

Jake looked at her and smiled. "Sounds like you been put under the spell."

"If you mean the spell of this country, you're right. I was only here once before, when Katie first bought the ranch, but I stayed just a few days. I couldn't wait to get back to Los Angeles. That's where I was living then, before I moved to San Francisco." She looked around at the surrounding landscape again. "I must have been crazy."

"Most folks are. That's why we got so many cities."

"Well, I'm not. At least not anymore. And I'm never going back." Not until the moment she said the words and heard them with her own ears did she realize how much she meant them. She wasn't going back to the city. This was where she belonged now. She was sure that somehow Katie had known she would stay on the Double K, that given half a chance she would fall in love with the country that had been her sister's home. "I only wish you were still here, Katie," Shelby whispered, blinking rapidly to hold back the tears that came to her eyes.

"Well, I'm glad to hear you're staying," Jake said.

Shelby stared at the old cowboy. "You are?"

"Sure. The boys have been a mite nervous about what was going to happen with the ranch. Didn't know if you would sell it off to some city dude who'd look at it more as an investment or a tax deduction, or what. Most figure that . . ." he paused and ran a hand over his grizzled chin.

"Figured what?" Shelby prompted, realizing he wasn't sure if he should continue.

"Well, most of us figured that if you'd wanted to live up here on the ranch, you would have been here before. You know, long vacations and such."

Shelby nodded. "I should have come, but, well, I just never thought it was me, you know? Katie was always the one crazy about horses, and the Old West. Not me. I guess I just didn't know what it was really like."

"There's the stream, Miss Shelby," Jake said, raising up in his stirrups and pointing straight ahead.

Shelby stood up and looked toward where Jake pointed. She didn't see the stream, but she knew if he said it was there, then it was there. Once again her gaze roamed the quickly shadowing landscape, and once again she saw absolutely no sign of Cody.

Chapter Eleven

Cody threw another branch onto his campfire and watched as the hungry, crackling flames licked at the dried wood, sending sparks flying up into the darkness.

He broke off a piece of the twig he held in his hands and threw it into the fire. Then another piece. And another. The gesture didn't relieve his anger, and it didn't give release to his frustration.

"Damn it all to hell." He threw the last bit of twig into the flames. "Why should I care what she does? If she wants to stay at the Double K until she proves to herself and everyone else she can't make it, what skin is it off my nose? And if she breaks her pretty neck because of her stubbornness, what business is it of mine?"

The crooning wail of a coyote in the distance was his only answer. He remembered Shelby's fright of that same sound only the night before. For a few hours he'd fooled himself, had forgotten that she was only there temporarily, that within a few days or weeks she'd get tired of the country, start to feel the lure of the city lights, chuck it all, and leave.

"I knew she was like Lisa. I knew it," he swore. "So why didn't I stay away from her?"

He slouched against the tree at his back, picked up another twig, and threw it into the fire. Memory of his ordeal in New York filled his mind. Love, or what he'd thought was love, had made him blind. And crazy. He'd been disappointed when Lisa had said she couldn't stay in Montana. She'd explained that it just wasn't "her," that she had her career to think about, her professional future. But he hadn't really heard her words. Instead he'd heard only bits and pieces, his mind registering only what it wanted to accept. He'd believed that after a few years of working, Lisa would tire of the daily grind and the bustle of the city, that she'd want to settle down in a little house far from the concrete and noise and raise a family.

Cody sniffed. What an idiot he'd been. Like a lovesick calf, he'd followed her to New York, tried to fit into her world, tried to like her friends. It hadn't worked, but he should have known. Lisa's family was blue-blooded, and in the social register. He was fourth-generation Montana-born and his only claim to fame was that his great-great-grandmother had been an Indian who'd walked the Trail of Tears with the Nez Perce chief, Joseph. Lisa's family was old

143

money. Cody's bank account wouldn't even pay for the car Lisa had driven.

Money, or rather his lack of it, had finally done in their relationship. He'd been unable to find a job in New York, and after a while, he had begun to feel like a kept man.

Now here was Shelby. Another city girl with a lot of money who was making his passion boil. It was history repeating itself, and there was absolutely nothing he could do about it.

"Like hell there's not," he swore. "I can stay away from this one." But even as he said it, he was rising to his feet and kicking out the fire. Staying away from Shelby might be what his mind told him was the right thing to do, but the rest of him wasn't going along with the idea, and it was the rest of him that was in control. At least for the moment.

Cody whistled for Soldier and the huge gelding sauntered from the darkness toward him.

"Come on, boy, we've got some miles to cover," Cody said, swinging up into the saddle. He nudged Soldier and the horse broke into a trot. Another nudge and the trot turned to a gallop that had them flying over the night-shrouded prairie as easy as the wind.

She didn't belong here, but he wanted her to stay, even if it would only be for a while. She wasn't the type of woman he wanted in his life, yet he did want her in it, for as long as possible. She was everything he had sworn to stay away from, to avoid, and she drew him to her. He felt like a helpless fly caught in a spider's silvery web. His mind should be on the drive, on getting the cows and the guests to their destination safely, without any problems, but it wasn't. Shelby's image filled his thoughts, haunted him, teased him, and refused to let him think of anything else.

He urged Soldier to a faster pace, cutting across the flat, dark meadows that sprawled between forests. He wove his way through the trees of a thick copse', jumped small gullies and mounds of rocks left by settlers years earlier to mark their paths.

Finally he saw the soft glow of a campfire in the distance beyond the trees. He reined Soldier in, forcing the huge gelding to a walk. They moved through the trees quietly, like a gray specter. Cody heard music, a lively country tune, floating on the still night air. As he drew closer, he heard laughter and singing voices accompanying a song playing on Tom's portable radio.

He dismounted and slung Soldier's reins loosely over a low-growing limb of a pine tree, allowing the gelding enough slack to graze. Then he approached the Double K campsite on foot, slowly, quietly, hesitating, for some reason even he was unsure of, to be seen just yet.

He heard the gurgling sound of bubbling water and recognized it instantly. The hot tub. Cody had forgotten about Katie's latest luxury acquisition. With everything that had happened in the past few months, that little detail had completely slipped his mind, but evidently Tom had remembered.

Who would ever have thought of trucking a hot tub out into the middle of nowhere for a bunch of pampered jet-setters playing cowboy, except Katie? She'd been one in a million, Cody thought. Exactly the type of woman he dreamed about sharing his life with. Ken had been a lucky man.

Cody moved closer to the clearing, but remained in the shadows. He looked around the fire-lit site, searching for Shelby. Most of the Double K's wranglers were already bedded down for the night, knowing they had a hard day of riding and driving the cattle ahead of them in the morning. He spotted Jamie behind an outcrop of rocks, with Eva Montalvo snuggled securely in his arms.

Cody shook his head in disbelief. On the surface Jamie seemed the epitome of the innocent, naïve cowboy, a real throwback to the old days. In reality, Cody knew, Jamie had more notches on his bedpost than most men alive could even dream about.

He spotted Jake sitting on the ground by the truck that had brought up the hot tub. He had his back against the rear wheel and his hat pulled down so that it almost rested on the bridge of his nose. He was obviously trying to get a little sleep and still be alert to any problems.

Most of the guests had retired to their bedrolls, or tents, for those that had wanted them, but a few were still huddled around the crackling campfire, raising their glasses high and singing along to the music. He didn't see Shelby.

He took a step nearer the clearing, his gaze scanning the terrain again, moving over each figure, each shadow. Then he heard her laughter, soft and melodic, a musical chime that blended with yet rose above the other sounds. He moved closer, spotted her, and stopped, sudden anger replacing the desire that had driven him to return to the campsite.

Shelby let her head rest against the ledge of the hot tub. The churning water felt so good, especially on her bruised hip and knee. She hadn't realized just how weary her body was until she'd stepped into the tub and let the heated, swirling water envelop her. Now she felt so languid, so relaxed, she wanted nothing more than to stay there all night. The brandy had helped, too, coiling through her insides like a soothing fire, dulling the edges of her frazzled nerves and leaving her mildly content to just enjoy the evening and the company of the cheerful guests, and Lance.

Most of the others had long ago left the tub

and slipped into their bedrolls or were sitting around the campfire. She was thinking what a great idea this was—trucking a hot tub to the middle of nowhere to greet the guests after a long day in the saddle. Now that was innovative thinking . . . the kind that made the Double K one of the best dude ranches in the country. On the next trail drive, she decided, she was going to add her own contribution: a masseuse.

Shelby looked up at the wide star-specked sky, but her thoughts were not on the scenery. Could she maintain the excellence of the Double K? She was so different from Katie.

She felt Lance Murdock shift position; he seemed to have glued himself to her side for the evening. Though his attention was nice, and a definite ego booster, she was beginning to tire of his continuous presence. She couldn't even turn around without finding him at her heels or elbow, a seductive gleam in his eye, a sensual innuendo on his lips.

She smiled to herself. She must be getting cynical in her old age. Six months earlier she most likely would have drooled at his feet if he'd even looked at her, and here she was wishing he'd direct some of his attention to a few of the other females on the drive. Eva would probably love it. Shelby opened her eyes and glanced in the direction she'd seen the woman walk after departing the hot tub. She saw the blond socialite ensconced in Jamie's arms and changed her mind about Lance. Eva evidently had captured the attentions she'd sought.

"Hi, beautiful. I thought maybe you'd turned into Sleeping Beauty and I was going to have to wake you with a kiss. Not that I would mind."

Shelby turned to smile at Lance. "It's just so comfy in here. I could stay like this forever," she said.

"Here, have a little more of this." He tipped the flask he held in his hand over her glass and a stream of amber liquid poured forth.

"I really shouldn't," Shelby said. "I already feel relaxed enough to sleep for a month."

"So what? You're the boss around here. If you want to sleep for a month, then do it." He capped the flask and set it on the ledge of the hot tub, then turned back toward Shelby. "After all, isn't that the privilege of being the boss? You do what you want, when you want?"

Shelby laughed softly. "Not around here."

"Hmm, I see there're a few things you need to learn, my beautiful Shelby Hill," Lance said, his voice barely above a whisper. He moved his head between Shelby's and her upraised glass.

Before she knew quite what was happening, his lips had covered hers and she felt herself being pulled into his arms. Though she knew she should resist, she didn't. Instead she returned his kiss. She wanted to know what it felt like to be kissed by a movie star. But more important, she wanted to know if she would feel any of the

149

same stirrings she had when Cody had kissed her, held her, loved her.

She slipped an arm around Lance's neck, a subtle gesture that invited the deepening of his kiss, the tightening of his embrace. Shelby felt his chest crush against her breasts, his hands press against her back, pulling her to him, molding her body to his. And that was all she felt. No tingles. No music. No stars. And no hot, sparking fires of passion. Nothing. Only the desire to escape from his embrace and crawl into her own sleeping bag. Alone.

Feeling her hesitation, her lack of response, Lance pulled away. But his words were a surprise. "I knew it would be perfect between us," he said, still holding her to him. "And when you visit my place in Malibu . . ."

She knew he said more, but she didn't hear him. A movement at the edge of the clearing, in the black shadows of the surrounding trees, drew her attention. She squinted into the darkness, trying to discern exactly what it was that was out there. Was a bear about to wander into the camp? Jake had said that sometimes, when they were especially hungry, they roved into the campsites. Should she scream for Jake? Warn everyone? She stiffened and tried to push Lance away. His arms tightened around her.

"Hey, what's the matter, beautiful? We were just getting to know each other."

"Something's out there," Shelby whispered urgently, her gaze glued to the edge of the forest.

Lance whipped around, the drowsy look of passion that had been on his face instantly replaced by one of combined fear and uncertainty. He stared in the same direction as Shelby. "What is it? Did you see?"

"Not really. It was in the shadows, but it was big." She shivered despite the heat of the water. "Jake said there were bears out here."

Lance jumped from the hot tub, leaving Shelby in the center of the bubbling water by herself. On bare feet, ignoring the piercing stones and pebbles that littered the ground, he ran toward Jake, who was now snoring loudly from his position against the truck's rear wheel. Water flew from Lance's body and in the moonlight his Day Glo bikini bathing suit shone dazzling yellow. He bent down and grabbed Jake's arm, shaking it roughly.

"Get up, man, get up!" he shouted, jerking on the old wrangler's arm again. "There's a bear in the camp."

The five guests sitting around the campfire jumped to their feet, startled by Lance's announcement. They looked about in fear and confusion.

Jake pulled his arm free of Lance, grumbled a few curses, which he normally would not have uttered in mixed company, and scrambled to his feet. "What the hell's all this talk about bears?" he growled loudly.

151

"Over there." Lance pointed in the direction Shelby had been staring. "Shelby saw it. Didn't you?" He looked back at her for confirmation.

She glanced at the guests and the wranglers, who had sprung up from their bedrolls upon hearing Jake. "Well, I . . . ah . . ." All of a sudden, with everyone staring at her, ready to panic, she wasn't so sure she'd seen anything. Maybe the drinks and the relaxing heat of the tub had made her mind fuzzy, or maybe the shadows the campfire created on the trees had played tricks on her eyes.

Jake grabbed his shotgun from the cab of the flatbed pickup truck and walked to stand in front of the hot tub. He stared down at Shelby. "Well, Miss Shelby, what did you see? Was it a bear?"

Shelby grimaced, and wished she could just slip beneath the water's surface and hide. "Jake, I . . . ah, well, I don't really know what it was. I mean, I saw *something*. A shadow, a big shadow, moving over there by the trees." She pointed to the edge of the clearing.

Jake turned away from her and, with the shotgun cradled in both hands, walked cautiously toward the area Shelby had indicated. Raising the gun to a half-ready position, he inched forward. He heard the other wranglers scurrying for their guns and moving up behind him.

Suddenly the sound of dry leaves crackling under the heavy feet was accompanied by a rustling noise within the dark forest.

Jake stopped abruptly, drew the butt of the shotgun up to his shoulder, and pointed it toward the thick growth of trees. The other wranglers emulated his move.

Shelby stood frozen, watching the scene, her heart in her throat.

A soft whinny broke the night's silence, deepened now by everyone's fear. Soldier's head burst from the shadows and into the moonlight at the campsite's edge.

One of the women guests screamed. Jake cocked the trigger on his rifle, and Shelby jumped a good three inches off the bottom of the hot tub.

Seeing the reception he'd drawn, Cody reined in, took a quick look around, then stared down at Jake. "You getting ready to shoot me with that thing, old man?"

"God almighty, Cody," Jake said, his whole body crumpling with relief. "Where you been? Shelby thought she saw a bear and that dang movie star got just about everyone in a snort, including me and the boys."

Cody smiled. "Well, if there was a bear out there, I didn't pass it on my way in. Must've taken off at hearing all the ruckus you guys were making. I heard you half a mile away." He threw a brief glance at Shelby, who was now standing up in the middle of the hot tub. Her ivory-colored bathing suit left little to the imagination, but, then, Cody thought with a smile, he didn't have to imagine what lay beneath those two tiny pieces of material. He knew. He felt a hungry yearning coil in the pit of his stomach, and was helpless to pull his gaze away.

Water glistened on her tanned body, moonlight turned her skin a burnished gold, and the beads of water on her flesh were shimmering teardrops of silver. He watched as a droplet trickled in a jagged line from her shoulder, over the soft mound of her breast, and disappeared within the deep cleavage of her bosom. Her auburn hair had fallen from its careless topknot to fan about her shoulders in cascading waves of red, and her eyes, so brilliantly green in the daylight, were now dark fathomless pools that returned his stare.

Desire swept over him like a tidal wave. He wanted her. Damn, he wanted her more than he had the night before. More than he'd ever wanted any woman.

"I'll get you something to dry off with, Shelby," Lance said, hurrying back up to the side of the hot tub. He grabbed a towel and held it out to her. "Come on, beautiful, let me help you out of there."

Cody watched as Shelby pulled her gaze from his and turned toward Lance. She stepped from the tub and allowed the movie star to wrap the huge square of terry cloth around her. Lance kept an arm around her shoulder and guided her toward the campfire.

Cody's eyes never wavered, never left Shelby's. He knew Jake was staring at him, knew the other wranglers and guests were watching him, but he didn't care. He was unable to tear his gaze away, unable to move, to think, to feel anything except the fury that was growing in his gut, a fiery rage and all-consuming jealousy that made him want to lash out at the handsome guest whose advances Shelby was obviously accepting, and enjoying.

Drawing in the leash on his self-control until it was as tight as a stretched rubber band, Cody spun on his heel and walked to where Soldier stood. Taking hold of the reins, he prepared to mount, then paused. Running away wasn't the answer. Nothing would be solved that way. And it wasn't his style. But, then, what was there to solve? Hadn't he already determined that her leaving was for the best. It wouldn't work any other way. She'd go back to the city where she belonged, probably with Hollywood, and he'd stay here on the ranch, where he belonged. That's the way it had to be. And that's just the way he wanted it.

He led Soldier to the edge of the clearing. "Jake, I'm bedding down. Make sure everyone's up at dawn and ready to move. We've got a lot of riding to do tomorrow."

Shelby watched Cody walk away and a little part of her heart died. She wanted to go after him, but her feet were rooted to the ground and her pride seemed to suddenly swell up and freeze her limbs. Last night had been a dream, a wonderful, beautiful, dream. But now she knew that's all it had been. That's all Cody would allow it to be.

"Here, beautiful, take a sip of this. It'll help calm your nerves," Lance said, holding a glass out to her and urging her to sit down beside the fire.

Shelby looked at the glass, looked at Lance, then around the campsite. The other guests and wranglers had returned to their bedrolls. Even the few guests who had been singing only moments earlier were now snuggling into their sleeping bags.

She glanced in the direction Cody had walked and narrowed her eyes to scan the darkness for his form, but saw only the deep, empty blackness of night.

Chapter Twelve

It took another hour for Shelby to politely untangle herself from Lance's solicitous attentions. No matter how much concern he showed for her or how much charm he poured on, she could not seem to rid her mind of Cody. And that was beginning to make her mad. He'd obviously had no problem ridding himself of any thought of her.

Shelby snuggled deeper into her sleeping bag and closed her eyes, willing sleep to come, demanding it to overtake her so that she would not have to think any longer. She punched the jacket she'd rolled into a ball to act as a pillow and shifted her position, moving slightly to the left and coming up against the thin canvas of the tent. She pulled her knees up and pushed her chin down.

She heard a soft rustling noise.

Shelby froze. Her eyes shot open and she stared into the black gloom that surrounded her.

It came again, this time like a sort of scratching sound.

Shelby's heart began to hammer. Something

was in the tent with her. Something a lot bigger than a spider. She bit down on her bottom lip to keep from screaming and lifted her head an inch away from the rolled jacket.

A dark shape moved at her feet.

Her breath lodged in her throat and her head dropped back down. Oh, dear God, please make it go away, she prayed. She inched her hand away from the bedroll and toward the side of the tent. Maybe she could lift the canvas and roll out. Her fingers sought the edge of fabric that met the ground and couldn't find it. She was lying on it! Panic threatened to overtake her.

The thing bumped against her foot.

Shelby flinched and felt her heart jump. What was she going to do? She was in the tiny tent with some kind of wild animal, and it was at the end that had the entry flap. There was no way for her to get away.

She felt tears of fear sting her eyes, felt the bubble of hysteria churn within her breast, and fought desperately to control both.

Her mind raced for some way out, some escape. Maybe if she could unzip the sleeping bag she could throw the flap down on top of whatever it was at her feet and catch the animal, or at least scare it away. Holding her breath, she moved her hand to the zipper, felt for the inside pull, and grasped it between her fingers. Slowly, cautiously, she began to inch it downward, one tooth at a time.

The thing moved.

Shelby jumped, barely able to stop the scream that gurgled in her throat from escaping her lips. Trying to maintain some shred of calmness to see her through, she lay still and listened, hardly daring to breathe.

She inched the zipper down again. It moved a half an inch, caught, and would not budge any farther. She tried to pull it upward. It refused to move. She pushed it downward. Again it refused to move. She felt around the pull with the tip of her fingers.

Oh, God, it was caught on her nightgown. She tried to tug on the fabric, but couldn't free it.

The thing moved against her foot.

A soft sob of terror escaped her lips and she nearly bit down on her tongue. She yanked at the zipper. Nothing.

A small squeak echoed within the dark tent. Shelby peeked over the edge of her sleeping bag. The silhouette of a tiny, dark head popped up into view. Shelby cringed.

Suddenly the thing jumped onto her sleeping bag and on top of her!

With a loud shriek of terror, Shelby jerked her nightgown free, oblivious to the sound of ripping fabric, scrambled from the bedroll, and dove for the flap of the tent. She accidentally rammed a shoulder against the tent's support pole as she flew past it and out into the night. The pole jerked free of its wedged spot in the ground and one end of the single-person tent collapsed. Shelby fell face first in the dirt, jumped to her feet, and whirled to stare at the crumpled mass of white canvas, as if waiting for a monster to emerge and attack.

Her heart pounded madly within her chest. She breathed in ragged gulps of air and took several steps back away from the lopsided tent.

"Shelby, are you all right?" Cody ran up beside her, gripping his rifle in one hand. His gaze swept over her half-naked form. The lacy pink baby-dolls she had on did little to conceal the subtle curves of the body beneath the sheer fabric, and the soft rays of the moon shining on the delicate silk threads only proved to intensify the seductiveness of the image. Her breasts moved against the pink silk, rising and lowering with the heaving raggedness of her breath. Though Cody's gaze longed to linger, he forced himself to look away, to scan the same direction as she continued to stare.

Several other wranglers had also jumped to their feet and run up behind Cody and Shelby, their guns at the ready, while most of the guests merely peeked from their tents or remained huddled in their bedrolls.

"Shelby? Shelby, what's the matter?" Lance called. He hurriedly tried to zip up his pants as he ran toward her.

She turned toward Cody. "There . . . there was

something in my tent. It jumped on my sleeping bag and attacked me."

"Stay here." He lifted the barrel of the rifle toward the tent and cautiously moved forward, his gaze never wavering from the crumpled canvas. Reaching it, he poked the muzzle of the gun into the thick fabric several times.

A squeak erupted, and the material moved.

Cody smiled, bent down, and reached out a hand to lift up the canvas.

"Cody, watch out!" Shelby yelled.

A small, fur-covered head poked out from the folds of canvas, its tiny ears swiveling in alertness, its beady eyes blinking rapidly in fear. Suddenly it dropped its front paws to the ground and darted from the tent, past Shelby and Lance, who both jumped back.

"What was that?" Shelby squeaked, her voice barely audible.

"A rat," Lance said.

"A prairie dog," Cody corrected.

Shelby felt her body sag in relief. A prairie dog. She'd panicked half out of her mind because a harmless little prairie dog had entered her tent. She glanced at Cody and, from the heat searing her cheeks, knew she was blushing profusely. Thank heavens it was dark, the campsite lit only by the yellow glow of the moon overhead.

Lance wrapped an arm around Shelby's shoulders. "Are you all right, beautiful? That must have been horrible. Cooped up in a tent with that thing."

She looked up at Lance and struggled not to laugh at his expression of disgust. "I'm fine, Lance, thank you." That thing, as he'd called the little animal, had probably been more frightened of her than she had been of it. Unfortunately she hadn't realized that when she'd screamed and woken the entire camp, including Cody.

A silent groan filled her throat. Cody. She'd made a fool of herself in front of him again. Were the heavens against her, or what? She shrugged away from Lance's arm and, seeing that the others were all retiring back to their bedrolls, walked up to Cody. "I guess I owe you thanks for another rescue."

"You wouldn't if you'd take my advice and go back where you belong," he said gruffly, shouldering the rifle. Several of the wranglers nearby were still gawking at Shelby's ill-concealed form, but a quick glare from Cody sent them on their way.

Unaware of the others, Shelby stared at Cody in shock. What was with this guy, anyway? "I am where I belong."

"No, you're not. And if you were smart, you'd admit it."

Lance stepped forward. "Now, see here, Cody . . ."

"Stuff it, Hollywood," Cody growled. He turned back to Shelby. "And get some clothes

162

on before you start a damn riot."

Shelby wrapped her arms around herself, suddenly aware of the flimsiness of her nightgown. Before she could respond, Cody turned on his heel and strode across camp and back to where he'd spread out his own bedroll.

Too enraged even to think about what she was doing, Shelby pushed past Lance and stalked after Cody. By the time she'd reached his bedroll, he'd lain down, his hands behind his head, his hat pulled low over his eyes. He was using his saddle as a pillow.

Straight out of a cowboy movie, Shelby thought through her rage. At the foot of his bedroll she stopped, clenched hands propped on her hips, and glowered down at him. "Cody, I think we need to talk."

"Nothing more to say," he mumbled, not bothering to look up. The fact was, he *couldn't* look up. If he did, he knew he'd lose what little self-control he still had and pull her into his arms, and that made him angry.

"I'm not leaving the Double K."

"You will in time. City girls always go back to the bright lights."

"Not me."

"Uh-huh."

She wanted to reach out and smack the hat from over his face, to wipe away the confident gleam she knew was in his eyes. Instead she counted to ten, turned, and marched back to the

163

crumpled remains of her own tent. Tossing aside the canvas, she pulled her sleeping bag free and snuggled down into it. The man was impossible. Totally, frustratingly, impossible. And all she wanted to do was feel his arms around her, his lips over her own, his body entwined with hers.

Dawn came before she was ready for it. In fact, judging by her body, she might never be ready. She was tired, saddle sore, bruised sore, and still very weary. Given half the chance, she could sleep for a week. But not on this hard ground. She wanted a bed, a nice, soft, feather-stuffed bed, with huge pillows and a down comforter. Shelby tried to roll over, found it impossible within the confines of the sleeping bag, and buried her head deeper into its folds, blocking out the pink rays of the morning sun that had swept over the campsite.

She heard the rustling movement of those who'd already risen, identified a soft clanging sound as that of frying pans being settled over open fires, and smelled the tangy aroma of sizzling bacon, accompanied by that of baking biscuits. It still wasn't enough to make her want to rise. She flipped back the top of her bedroll, anyway. She was determined to prove Cody Farlowe wrong, and that meant getting herself up and into the day. She'd show him she could run the Double K, that underneath all her citified ways, she had just as much mettle as Katie had had. She just had to find it. She was already coming to love the open countryside, the clean air, the craggy mountains, and the wild, lush growth that sprinkled Montana. All she had to do now was stop getting herself into situations that Cody had to rescue her from. Shelby sighed. At the rate she was going, that might be easier said than done.

Holding the top flap of the sleeping bag against her breast, Shelby struggled to sit up. She looked around the camp and was mortified to see that just about everyone, except her, was up, dressed, and bustling about with purpose. Great, she thought. Put another big black mark next to her name. She reached around behind her and grabbed the jeans and shirt she'd left folded on top of her saddlebags, and dragged them into the bag beside her. No way was she coming out of this sleeping bag in her nightie. She remembered the leering stares she received only hours earlier when she'd dashed unthinkingly from her tent.

Shelby stuffed her pants down inside the bag and poked her toes around until she managed to get them into the legs, then struggled to pull them up. At her hips she discovered a problem: she wasn't a contortionist. Lying down, she snaked back into the bag and into her jeans, then sat up again and hastily slipped on her shirt. She turned and reached for her boots.

A large hand clamped down on top of hers. "I

wouldn't do that if I were you."

Shelby whirled around to stare at Cody. "I was only going to put my boots on," she said, totally confused.

"I know, but out here you don't put them on without first finding out who slept in them last night."

"Huh?"

Cody picked up one of her boots, turned it upside down, and shook it. Nothing happened. He handed it to Shelby, picked up the other, and turned it upside down.

Something small and brown plopped onto the ground when he shook the boot. Shelby jumped and shifted away from the insect as it scurried toward a cluster of rocks nearby.

"What was that?" she gasped, thankful she hadn't put her foot into the boot. The spider might not be tarantula size, but it was big enough to have taken a good bite of her toe.

"Brown recluse."

"A what? Brown recluse? Aren't they poisonous? Don't people die if they get bitten by one of those?" Shelby felt suddenly both faint and nauseous.

"Some people have been known to die from their bites." He met her gaze, but where she had expected warmth, she found only hard self-righteousness. "Still think it's beautiful out here?" he goaded.

Shelby grabbed her boot and tugged it onto

her foot. Another rescue. Exactly what she'd hoped to avoid. Why was Cody always there when she needed deliverance? What was he? Clairvoyant? If she had to be rescued, why couldn't Lance, America's Saturday Night Cowboy Hero, come to her aid once in a while? She didn't give a damn what *he* thought. She felt Cody watching her and glanced up at him. "Thank you, Cody. I'll make sure to evict any other tenants who decide to rent out my boots for the night." Scrambling out of the bedroll, Shelby got to her feet and busied herself rolling up the sleeping bag and tying it securely so that it would fit on the back of her saddle.

"Just tuck them down in the bottom of your bag and you won't have to worry about tenants," he said, and chuckled in spite of himself. Pushing the brim of his hat back, Cody turned and walked to where Jake had several pans of bacon cooking over the campfire.

Suddenly a young boy, whooping and yollering and shooting off a cap gun, darted out from behind one of the guest tents and collided with Cody. They both fell to the ground in a tangle of arms and legs.

Shelby watched in horror, waiting for Cody to reprimand the youngster. In the mood he was in, she knew his rebuke would be severe.

"Whoa, there cowboy, what's your hurry?" Cody said, laughing as he stood and helped the boy to his feet.

The boy looked up at Cody and, realizing he wasn't going to get scolded, relaxed. "They were going to scalp me, Cody," he said, pointing back at the other children, who cowered behind the tent.

Cody smiled and motioned for the kids to come forward. They gathered around him and he knelt down. "Listen, guys," he said softly, "I need to ask for your help."

They all stared at him in astonishment, including Shelby. This was not the reaction any of them had expected.

"The cattle are a bit jumpy this morning, probably didn't get a good night's sleep, you know?"

The kids nodded.

"Well, loud noises scare them, and if they get scared, they'll start to run. You've seen cowboy movies on TV, right? With stampedes?"

The kids nodded again.

"That can be pretty dangerous. Getting run over by a cow isn't any fun, let me tell you."

"You been run over by a cow, Mr. Cody?" Bobby asked.

Cody laughed. "A few times, Bobby, but only one cow. A whole herd would leave me flat as a pancake, and that's what we want to avoid. So, as a favor to me, would you guys mind not shooting off those irons of yours, or yelling too loud until we get back to the ranch?"

Within minutes the kids were off playing another game, without their cap guns, and Cody proceeded on his way toward Jake.

Shelby watched him walk away out of the corner of her eye. *He's really good with kids,* she mused, the thought making her feel warm inside. He might be all steel and brick wall about some things, but underneath, there was definitely a very soft, very tender heart.

Cody hunkered down beside Jake and shot a glance back toward Shelby. "Damn woman, just won't say uncle."

"Maybe she's got more grit than you give her credit for," Jake answered, poking at the bacon with a long fork.

"Gonna get herself killed or crippled, and everyone else around her, too. That's where her grit will get her." Cody snatched a piece of bacon from the frying pan and bit down on one end. It crunched loudly. "She doesn't belong here, Jake. You know it, I know it, and she knows it."

"Katie thought she did. Otherwise, why'd she leave her the place?"

" 'Cause they were sisters. And she didn't have anyone else to leave it to. You know that as well as I do. Ken's folks were dead, Katie's folks were dead, and there weren't any other brothers or sisters. On either side. That left Shelby. Miss City Girl."

"You're being too hard on her, Cody. Give her a little slack. The kid's been trying. You had to learn once, too, remember?"

169

"People raised in the city ought to stay in the city."

Jake stirred the mound of scrambled eggs cooking in the pan beside the bacon. "If that was so, Katie would never have been here. And if Katie had never been here, there wouldn't be no Double K."

Cody snatched another piece of bacon and a biscuit from a nearby pan and stood. "Have them ready to pull out in an hour, Jake. I'm going to check the horses and ride out to tell the boys on watch to come in and get their grub." He walked to the spot where he'd slept, slung his saddlebags over one shoulder, picked up his saddle, then crossed the camp to where Soldier had been tethered for the night. "Come on, boy. A little fresh air in the face and some open countryside will do us both some good."

Minutes later, Shelby stood beside Jake and watched Cody ride out of camp. "Where's he going this time?" she asked.

Jake chuckled and shook his head. "To chaw on his figuring, most likely."

Puzzled at Jake's words, Shelby continued to stare at Cody as he passed within a few yards of where she stood and headed toward the herd.

He kept his gaze carefully averted from hers. Damn old man, he swore to himself. Always has an answer for everything.

Chapter Thirteen

Cody slouched in his saddle and stared out at the sea of cattle spread out in the valley before him. They were grazing contentedly, seemingly without a care in the world, unlike him.

Before the tragic auto accident that had taken Ken's life and Katie's, along with their children's, Cody had had his life all planned out. He'd work on the Double K for about five more years. Then he and Ken were going to buy another spread, as equal partners, and operate it as a working cattle ranch, with Cody in charge. He'd also decided that if or when there was to be another woman in his life, she'd have to be a country girl, born and bred. He'd had enough of city women after his escapade with Lisa. If he had ever had a lesson drilled into him, it was that one. And he didn't need a repeat of it.

But all those plans had been shattered with Ken's death. It would take him twice as long now, or longer, to save up the money he needed to finance a spread like that on his own. If he ever could. He stared out at the herd, their red hued hides reminding him of the color of Shelby's long hair, and how soft and silky it had felt sliding through his fingers like strands of satin. He moved his gaze to the mountainous horizon and saw the color of her eyes in the rich green of the forests that covered the craggy peaks. He'd never felt hair quite so soft, or seen eyes such a lustrous, exotic color. He remembered how, when she got angry or excited, the little specks of gold within those pools of green sparked to life and turned to bright, flashing slivers of fire. Like the time he'd held her clothes away from her at the river. She'd risen out of the shallow stream, rivulets of water, turned silver by the gleam of the hot afternoon sun, sliding down the long length of her legs. He'd almost gone crazy with want right there in front of her and everyone.

Cody scanned the horizon without really seeing it. He cursed under his breath and pulled the brim of his hat lower onto his forehead to block out the morning sun, which was quickly warming the air. It was impossible to focus on anything without seeing Shelby, remembering how good she felt beneath him, her body entwined with his, welcoming him into her.

She was beautiful, he knew, but more than that drew him to her. There was an innocence about Shelby Hill, a freshness that he hadn't seen in a woman in a long time. Most of the women who came to the Double K had left that quality behind them long ago, if they'd ever had it in the first place. The female guests at the ranch mainly consisted of the wealthy wives of celebrities and jet-setters who wanted a little fun, a little sun, and a lot of extra attention and pampering; or hardcore businesswomen from the big cities who were out for a little rest and relaxation, preferably with someone who reminded them of their childhood cowboy hero. Eva Montalvo and Jamie came to mind. He hoped Jamie wouldn't make the same mistake he himself had, and go following Eva back to the big city.

Cody thought he had found someone different when he'd fallen for Lisa, someone who shared all the same values and wanted out of life what he did, even if she couldn't be talked into living in Montana. It had taken him six long months in New York City to lose his rose-colored glasses and find out just how wrong he'd been.

But Shelby wasn't like those other women. She was softer, still sweet, still innocent and open. His mind drifted back to the night when she'd lain next to him, giving all of herself to him and asking for nothing in return.

"Nothing but my damn heart," he said aloud into the quietness that surrounded him. Cold resolution swept through him and he shook his head. "Not again," he mumbled, his voice harsh with determination. "I won't go through that again!"

He heard the Double K group approaching long before they came into view. Their laughter sprinkled the air and drew the attentions of several cows, who lifted their heads in curiosity, immediately decided there was no threat, and went back to grazing. Soldier, too, heard them. His ears swiveled and twitched continuously, and his right front hoof pawed the ground in nervous anticipation of their arrival. The big gelding hated being still and the sound of the others signified imminent movement to him.

Cody twisted around in his saddle and looked back down the sloping trail. He spotted Shelby instantly. She was riding in the lead beside Jake, and directly behind her on the narrow path was Lance Murdock, his snow-white, black-buttoned, cord-trimmed cotton shirt gleaming in the sunlight like a patch of newly fallen snow.

"Couldn't lose track of him up here this time of year if I tried," Cody grumbled. He stared a second longer at Shelby, and felt his blood start to warm and longing settle in the back of his throat like a hard knot. Damning himself for the umpteenth time that morning, he sunk back in his saddle and waited for them to rein up beside him.

Maybe Jake was right, he decided as the group neared. When Shelby reined in next to him and flashed a smile that would have lit up the darkest of nights, Cody sighed and tried to reposition his seat, his denims suddenly feeling as if they'd shrunk. Yeah, the old wrangler *was* right. At least about the fact that Shelby was trying. But it wouldn't do her any good. Eventually she'd go back to the bright lights. Cody felt certain of that. Maybe not today. Maybe not tomorrow. But sooner or later she'd want the luxuries the big cities had to offer. After all, you can't spend too much money in the country, and with her inheritance from Katie and Ken, Shelby Hill had a lot of money to spend.

But that wasn't her fault; none of this was. He was the one who'd let things get out of control. He'd saved her life, and she'd been grateful. And in her vulnerable state, he had taken advantage of her. So he'd be a good guy for the rest of her stay. Why make her miserable just because he felt as though the world had thrown him another lousy curve? He'd rescue her when she needed it again, smile at her when she smiled, make polite conversation when it was necessary. He'd even be nice to Lance Murdock for her, though that was going to be a little much to stomach. But he'd manage, because Shelby deserved that much. It wasn't her fault she was from the city and he was country bred, or that she was rolling in money and he was little better than rock-hard poor.

Same as with Lisa, he thought again. After six months in New York with her, he'd still been unable to find a decent job. She'd paid for everything, and after a while he'd begun to feel like a kept man. Remembering the feeling still left a sour taste in his mouth. It just wasn't meant to be for Shelby and him, that's all. It wasn't her fault. It wasn't his fault. Hell, it wasn't anybody's fault. Just the way things were.

But to keep his sanity, he'd try like hell to stay away from her whenever the occasion wasn't business.

Shelby reined up and held her mount next to Cody's. The urge to lean over and brush her lips across his was almost overpowering, but she managed to control herself. "Well, good morning again, cowboy. Beautiful day, isn't it?" She looked around at the valley below, the cattle spread across the meadow and the jagged mountains off to their right. Closing her eyes, she took a deep breath, released it, and looked back at him. "Boy, it feels good to breath clean air. Back in L.A. you'd end up in a coughing spasm if you tried that, and San Francisco isn't a whole lot better."

Cody nodded, but remained silent and a bit puzzled. He looked at her, tried to avert his gaze, found it impossible, and gave up the struggle. What had happened to the little spitfire who'd snapped at him earlier this morning after he'd saved her foot from a nasty spider bite?

"So, boss, where do you want me today? Point? Tail? What?" She stared at him and waited for an answer. She'd made a few decisions of her own in the past few hours. Now her only problem was how to prove to Cody that they be-

176

longed together, for she definitely believed that. No one had ever made her feel the way Cody did. Once, long ago, she'd thought she had been in love. Now Shelby knew she had been wrong. What she felt for Cody was like nothing she had ever experienced before, and it was wonderful. Of course, she mused, it would be much better if she knew for certain he felt the same way.

Insecurity niggled at her, but she quickly shrugged it away. No more of that. She had to be strong, to prove to both Cody and herself that she belonged here, that she could run the Double K, and that she could be the kind of woman he wanted in his life. And she wanted to be that woman. Lord, please, she desperately wanted that with all her heart.

He had the urge to tell her that the only place he wanted her was in his arms. Instead he said, "Take the point again, Shelby, but remember to stay off to one side of the herd. We haven't had a stampede around here for years, but you never know, and I don't want you—" he paused and tugged on the cuff of his leather gloves, refusing to look at her now "—or anyone else to be hurt if something should spook the cattle."

"Okay, boss," Shelby said agreeably. She'd noticed Cody's aloofness, the way he'd pulled his gaze from hers and refused to look back. It was going to take time to make him come around, she knew that. She hoped she wouldn't have a head full of gray hair and be walking with a cane when that time finally arrived. She nudged Lady and started down the trail.

Lance Murdock steered his mount past Cody and made to follow Shelby.

"Hold on, Hollywood," Cody said gruffly. He caught Jake's frowning glance and suddenly remembered his vow to be nice to the actor. He swallowed the bitter taste in his mouth and tried to smile, but he could practically feel his lips curving into a sneer rather than a smile, and his cheeks felt as if they were pushing against a granite wall.

Lance reined in and turned in his saddle to look back at Cody. His eyes flashed in anger at what he obviously assumed was going to be an order for him not to follow Shelby.

"Take the point with Shelby, Murdock," Cody said, his voice calm but sullen. "But stay to the side of the cattle. I can't afford some bigshot Hollywood producer or whatever getting all bent out of shape at me and taking it out on the Double K 'cause his star got himself trampled by a runaway herd of cows."

Surprised, Lance smiled. "Don't concern yourself, cowboy. I'm not about to get trampled. I know my way around horses, among other things."

"Yeah, it's those 'other things' that I'm worried about," Cody mumbled after the actor nudged his horse and proceeded down the trail toward Shelby.

He looked past Lance to where Shelby and her horse were still traversing the slope toward the valley and the grazing herd. Her hips swayed seductively with each step of her mount. Cody's jealousy and resentment flared to life when he realized that Lance Murdock's view of Shelby was the same as his.

"What's the holdup, Cody?" Jake asked, riding up beside him. "I got some antsy guests back there who want to get moving." He followed Cody's gaze, and smiled to himself. "Getting to you, huh?"

Cody turned. "Assign them their spots, old man. I'm riding point today." He put his heels to Soldier's side, a little harder than necessary, and the gelding broke into a trot.

"Kinda grumpy this morning, ain't ya, boss?" Jake called after him, and chuckled softly.

For the rest of the day Cody busied himself moving about the herd, checking on each guest and each wrangler, but most of his time was spent riding only a few yards behind Shelby and Lance Murdock. Torture had never been so sweet and so cruel at the same time. He loved watching her, and loathed himself for it. Normally on these rides it was the surrounding countryside that called to him, that caressed him with its warmth and intoxicated him with its tangy scents and wild beauty. But not this time. This time it

179

was Shelby who unwittingly played within his every thought, who held his gaze and attention, who refused to let him think or be aware of anything else.

By midafternoon, frustrated beyond all reason, Cody spurred Soldier and the big horse bolted forward. When they were beside Shelby, he reined in and forced the gelding to match Lady's easy stride.

Shelby turned to him. "Lance was just telling me what a wonderful time he's having. He's going to recommend the Double K to all of his friends back in Hollywood. Isn't that wonderful, Cody?"

Cody pushed up the brim of his hat with the tip of his thumb and leaned forward to look past Shelby at Lance. "Yeah, that's real nice of you, Hollywood. Real nice. But if you don't mind, there's something I need to talk to Shelby about." Without waiting for a reply, Cody reached out and grabbed one of Lady's reins, pulling both horse and rider with him as he turned Soldier away from the herd.

Suddenly Shelby got a severe case of nerves. This is what she'd been waiting for, and she was scared silly. What if he said something she didn't want to hear . . . again?

Cody released Lady's reins and the two horses fell into a slow walk beside each other. "Uh, Shelby, I've been thinking. Maybe you—"

It was going to be bad—she just knew it.

"Cody, there's something I've been meaning to talk to you about, too. I have a great idea." The words tumbled forth in a rush, but she couldn't help it. She just couldn't bear to hear him tell her to go back to the city again. "Tonight, when we make camp, let's have a good, old-fashioned marshmallow roast over the fire and do a sing-along. I remember Katie used to watch some old cowboy shows on television and they used to sing. I thought it was hokey then, but now it sounds like fun." She glanced over her shoulder at Lance and then turned back to Cody. "What do you think? Jamie has a guitar, and he told me Jake plays the harmonica, and I'm sure the guests would love it."

Cody shrugged. This was not the conversation he'd had in mind. Actually, he didn't know what he'd had in mind. He just hadn't been able to stand watching her with Lance Murdock any longer.

"Oh, look, a calf's wandered away," Shelby said, pointing to a young heifer that had sauntered halfway up a small knoll to the right of the slowly moving herd. "I'll go get him."

Before Cody could respond, Shelby pressed her heels to Lady's side and the small mare took off at a lope. They were in front of the wandering calf within seconds, and Shelby positioned Lady so that they could cut the exploring youngster off from his intended path and steer him back toward the herd.

He balked, sidestepped, and let out a long wail.

"Don't let him get by you, Shelby," Jake called, watching from his position on an outcrop of large rocks to her right. "Keep him in front of you."

Remembering the lessons Jake had given her that first day out and had repeated to her every day since, Shelby braced her feet against the stirrups, held on to the saddle horn with one hand, and pulled on Lady's reins with the other. The mare lunged to the left at the same time that the little calf made to dash past on that side.

The calf stopped, wailed again, and scrambled in the other direction. Shelby moved the reins to the opposite side of Lady's neck and again the mare cut the calf off from its chosen path of escape.

The calf made one more lunge, found Lady and Shelby again in his way, and, as if sensing the futility of its efforts, turned and headed back toward the herd. Shelby and Lady followed closely behind and kept a wary eye on the little fellow, both ready to head off another charge for freedom if the calf took a mind to it.

Jake rode up beside Cody, and caught the younger man's surprised gaze. "Told you so," he said, and chuckled softly.

Chapter Fourteen

Cody sat with his crossed arms resting on the saddle horn, Soldier's reins dangling loosely in the fingers of his right hand. "You been teaching her some of your tricks, old man?" Cody asked, eyeing Jake suspiciously.

"Who me?" Jake smiled slyly. "Now, why would I want to go do a fool thing like that?"

"So she'd stay, that's why."

"And we'd have us a city girl for a boss?" Jake shook his head. "Don't sound like such a good idea to me. No, sir. I'm surprised you think I'd do such a thing, Cody." He paused and lifted a gnarled, work-roughened hand to scratch the gray whiskers that covered his chin. "Then again, from what I just seen, maybe there's more country in her than we been giving her credit for." He watched Cody out of the corner of his eye. "She is Katie's sister, after all."

"Katie was different."

Jake shrugged. "Maybe."

Shelby rode back up to the two men, a wide smile of self-satisfaction curving her lips. "Well, how'd I do?" she asked brightly, looking at Jake.

"Couldn't have done better myself," Jake said, tipping his hat to her. "You learn quick, missy."

Shelby laughed, a deep, throaty sound that sent desire snaking through Cody. In that instant he wanted nothing more than to reach out, drag her up against him, and claim her lips with his.

"Hah! I bet you say that to all the girls." She looked at Cody inquiringly, waiting for his approval, needing to hear it. "How about you, Cody? Did I do all right?"

His eyes were shaded by the low-riding brim of his Stetson, concealing them for her, yet she could feel his penetrating gaze, the magnetism of those brilliant blue orbs. He smiled then, a slight movement of his lips that caused the skin above his cheeks to crinkle and the laugh lines bracketing his mouth to deepen. Yet somehow, Shelby knew, the warmth of the gesture had not reached his eyes. What did she have to do to win a little praise from him? Or was that even possible?

"Mama wouldn't have let the calf stray too far," Cody said finally, almost wincing at his own callous words. He shouldn't be so hard on her, but damn it, he couldn't help it. It was either that, or he'd most likely kidnap her into the woods and make love to her, and to do that again, he was certain, would be emotional suicide, for himself if not for her.

Shelby bristled. "Well, perhaps, like some people I know, he would have been too stubborn to listen."

Cody tried to ignore the barb. Pushing the brim of his hat back with his thumb, he stared down at her. An angry sparkle lit his eyes, the smile disappeared, and the handsome face she had thought about all morning turned suddenly hard. "I know a few people like that myself," he said.

Shaken by his cold response, Shelby felt herself pale. She opened her mouth to speak, and found her voice gone and her thoughts in a confused jumble. She was furious with him for treating her this way. She wanted to lash out at him, scream at him that he was being unfair, and at the same time she wanted to burst out crying and find a place to hide.

She jerked Lady's reins and sent the horse into a spin away from the two men. Kicking the mare harder than necessary, she urged her into a gallop. Lady took off instantly, her legs stretching out to cover the ground, her mane and tail whipping about in the breeze created by the flight. Shelby's hat flew off, to hang down her back. Her long hair flailed about her head and shoulders, a tangled halo of red. Tears of frustration and indignation coursed down her cheeks in a steady stream, while yet more filled her eyes, blinding her. But she didn't care. It wasn't important where she went, or even in what direction she was headed, as long as it was away from Cody Farlowe. Far, far away.

"Now you've done it," Jake said, looking at Cody much as a father does a disobedient son. "You've got no call to treat her like that, Cody. No, sir, none at all. And you damn well know it."

"She doesn't belong here, Jake."

"Hogwash. That ain't the all of it. Something else about her is eating at you, Cody Farlowe, and I'll tell you, it ain't making you a real well-liked guy around here." Jake shook his head. "No, sir, not real liked at all."

Cody stared out at the horizon, his expression hard and unreadable.

"Way I figure it, either you got a terrible deep hankering for that little beauty, or a real bad dislike. Either way, you've got to fix it, Cody. Fix it before it ruins both of you, and maybe the ranch, too."

"The ranch will be fine," Cody said.

Jake nodded, watching Cody carefully. "Yeah, I guess it probably will be, but I don't know about you." He looked back at Shelby's retreating figure. "Or her," he added softly.

Lance saw Shelby race past him and nudged

his horse into a gallop to follow. Within minutes his larger gelding had caught up with Lady. Lance reined him in and set his pace to match the mare's.

Shelby kept her face averted. She didn't want to look at Lance, didn't want him to see the tears that still filled her eyes. And she didn't want to have to explain her actions, or admit to what a fool she'd been to think Cody Farlowe could care for her.

Lance reached over and gently pulled back on Lady's reins, forcing the horse to slow her gait to a walk. Shelby still refused to look at him.

"What's the matter, beautiful?" he asked softly.

She shook her head, not trusting her voice to be steady.

"Shelby, I may not know you as well as I'd like to, but I suspect that you wouldn't normally go spurring your horse into a mad run if something wasn't wrong. Especially since you've already admitted to me you haven't been on a horse in years and never were much of a rider."

She took a deep, ragged breath and wiped a hand over her wet cheek, brushing away the moisture that clung there.

"Shelby?"

She blinked rapidly, stemming the tide of tears, at least for the time being, and turned to Lance. A weak and hesitant smile curved her lips. "I . . . I just had an altercation with Cody, that's all. It really isn't important."

"Not important." He nodded thoughtfully, but didn't veer his gaze from hers. "But it was enough to send you flying over this meadow like the hounds of hell were after you."

Shelby laughed, unable to help herself despite her blue mood. "You make it sound much worse than it really was."

"Not from my vantage point."

His horse and Lady had settled into a slow, comfortable walk.

Lance reached over and touched Shelby's shoulder, a touch that was both comforting and intimate. "Come on, tell me what's wrong."

Suddenly embarrassed, she winced. "It's really nothing. You'd just be bored."

"Let me be the judge of that. Now, come on, tell me what's wrong?"

She took the handkerchief he offered and wiped her eyes. "Well, ever since I got here Cody's been trying to convince me that I don't belong on the Double K. That because I was raised in the city I belong in that environment and should go back to it."

"Is that what you want?"

Shelby smiled, remembering her arrival on the ranch and her first feelings of total confusion. She'd been overwhelmed by the details and responsibilities she'd suddenly faced at being the new owner of the Double K. "If you had asked me that during my first two or three days here,

I'd probably have shouted a resounding *yes* from the rooftop of the ranch house."

"But not now?"

Shelby's smile widened. "No, not now. I love it here. Everything's so clean, so fresh, so . . . alive. I never knew what my sister saw in living out here. We talked on the phone every week, and I used to tell her she was living out in the middle of nowhere, the end of the earth. I couldn't understand how anyone could get along without everything the city has to offer—theaters, stores, malls, parties, people."

"And now you do."

It wasn't a question, but Shelby answered it, anyway. "Yes, now I do. She used to laugh at me and tell me I was the one who lived in the middle of nowhere. Katie was always trying to get me to move here and work on the ranch with her, but I couldn't see it. I visited once, for about four days, and couldn't wait to get back to Los Angeles."

"So what's changed, Shelby? The ranch is still the same. No closer to the big city. It still has no shops to speak of, no theaters, malls, or scores of people, no paved roads or freeways, and very little in the way of easy convenience. And I doubt that there are very many parties around here, at least not the kind you'd find in L.A."

"I have," she said softly, suddenly realizing just how very true that was. She had changed.

She was no longer the same Shelby Hill who, for the past few years, had wandered from town to town, job to job, trying to find herself. She'd always felt so out of place, so unconnected with the world. Now she knew why. For so many years, Shelby had thought she and her sister were different in every way, and now, finally, she'd come to realize how very alike they truly were. But it was too late to share that with Katie.

Shelby looked up at the sky for several long moments, then smiled. But that was okay, too, she thought suddenly. Katie had already known. Somehow she'd known that if she could ever get Shelby to the ranch for more than a couple of days, she'd fall in love with it.

Had Katie also suspected she'd fall in love with Cody? Shelby wondered. A slight frown creased her brow at the thought of the handsome foreman who seemed to want nothing more than for his new boss to go away.

But Cody is not going to get his wish, Shelby vowed. *He's just going to have to get used to the idea of having me around, and maybe someday—*

"You could make this a part-time deal," Lance said, interrupting her thoughts, and reaching over to lay his hand on top of hers. "Live in California for part of the year and here the other part. I hear they have pretty bad winters up here, anyway. You'd probably get snowed in. And I doubt there're be many guests during the winter months."

"Oh, no, that's not true," Shelby said, remembering one of the letters Katie had written her the previous year. "My sister said there are a lot of cross-country skiers who come to the dude ranches in the winter. And the pond by the house freezes over thick enough for ice skating, and we've got a sleigh in the barn for sleigh rides, and . . ."

Lance laughed and held up his other hand. "Enough, I get the picture. This is a year-round venture. But that still doesn't mean *you* have to be here year-round." His fingers exerted a soft pressure around hers, and the timbre of his voice dropped slightly "Shelby, have you ever thought about living on the beach? In Malibu? Sunsets are beautiful there."

She reined up and stared at him in surprise and more than a little disbelief. This couldn't be what it sounded like. He couldn't be proposing to her.

Lance realized instantly how this question had sounded and hurried to clarify his words. "Uh, I just meant, well, there're some great places for sale down by my beach house."

She released the breath she had been holding. "I'll bet there are, with some great price tags attached to them."

"From what I hear, that wouldn't be a problem for you."

191

Shelby suddenly remembered that with her sister's passing, she no longer had any financial worries. And that was an understatement. It was also something she hadn't given much thought to.

Cody watched Lance Murdock ride up beside Shelby, saw the man reach over and take her hand in his, and his blood boiled. He had no right to be jealous, no right at all. Nevertheless, he was. And the feeling was tearing his insides to shreds.

Jake was right. He had to do something. But what? Take what she was offering, then live every day on pins and needles waiting for her to come and tell him she'd finally decided to go back to the city? Or keep acting like an ogre until she, and everyone else on the ranch, ended up hating him? Neither one sounded like a very good choice, but he'd been thinking on it for hours—no, days—and had come up with no alternatives except one, and maybe that was the one he should go with, after all.

"One day at a time, Cody, one day at a time," he mumbled as he urged Soldier down the slope toward the moving herd. He rode up behind Jamie and Eva Montalvo.

"Jamie, ride on ahead and make sure our camp's set up for tonight and Tom's there with the chuck truck," Cody growled, taking his frustrations out on the cowhand.

Eva turned a sharp eye on Cody, one finely arched blond brow soaring skyward at the foreman's gruff tone. "What's with him?" she murmured to Jamie.

The wrangler shrugged and looked at his boss. "Billy was just up there a couple of hours ago, Cody. Said the campsite was clear and everything was ready."

"So check it again, Jamie," Cody thundered. The angry glint in his eyes, reinforcing his tone, left no room for argument.

The wrangler and the blonde took off, more than happy to get away from the obviously disgruntled foreman.

Cody took up Jamie's position beside the herd. After a few minutes he looked across the wide expanse of moving cattle and spotted Shelby almost directly opposite him. His gaze locked with hers, and no matter how hard he tried, he couldn't force himself to look away.

Chapter Fifteen

It was the third afternoon of the roundup, and though everyone had pretty much gotten used to being on horseback most of the day, they were still more than ready to make camp for the night and jump into the hot tub Tom's assistant trucked out. It was going on five o'clock when the group rode into camp, all nearly falling from their saddles and tripping over one another in their haste to stow their gear away and get to the food tables. The tantalizing aromas wafting toward them from Tom's barbecue pit had begun to tease their taste buds a good half mile back on the trail.

One of the wranglers took over brushing down Lady for Shelby. Even though she maintained that she could finish the job herself, he insisted it would be his privilege. She'd finally given in to him, secretly thankful for his offer. Deciding she must look as tired as she felt, she sidled away from the string of horses to stand beside Tom.

"Hi. We missed you yesterday," she said. Her gaze took in the two-dozen foil-wrapped potatoes that sat to one side of the grill. She'd never seen potatoes so big. They looked like small metal boulders. Enormous steaks a good two-inches thick and slathered with sauce sizzled on the grill.

She had a healthy appetite, but this was almost ridiculous. No one could eat a steak that big, especially not accompanied by one of those monster potatoes. On another grill, spare ribs, also covered with the tangy sauce, were cooking. Beside them, in a huge pot of boiling water, long cobs of fresh, golden corn floated.

Shelby's mouth had been watering since the moment she'd ridden into camp. Now she felt like drooling.

The smell of homemade biscuits floated up from another grill to tease her senses, and for one brief second she had the urge to attack the grill, grab some food, and run. Then Cody walked into the camp, caught her attention, and suddenly all thought and desire for food were swept from her mind.

What was it about him that made her senses reel? It certainly wasn't his smooth talk or polished charm, she thought derisively. He was stubborn, chauvinistic, unreasonable, opinionated, and damnably irresistible . . . at least to her. She couldn't deny what she felt for him — the powerful attraction that nearly consumed

195

her every time she saw him wouldn't let her. She dragged a heel in the dirt and stared down at her boot. Why not admit it? She'd fallen in love with Cody Farlowe, for all the good it was going to do her. Maybe she should leave the Double K and go back to California. At least there she wouldn't have to see him every day, and then, maybe, she'd get over him, in time.

Cody reached up, swept the black Stetson from his head and wiped a shirt sleeve across his forehead as he continued to walk toward Shelby and Tom. This wasn't going to be easy, he knew, but he'd made his decision and he needed to tell her. To get it understood between them. A quick glance around the campsite told him most of the others were still brushing down their mounts and stashing their gear for the night. Except Tom, who was busy cooking; his assistant, who was setting up the hot tub; and Jake, who was sitting on a rock at the edge of the campsite, smoking a cigarette and staring a hole through Cody.

He waved a hand at Jake, more of a dismissal for the old man to do something else beside stare at him than a gesture of acknowledgment.

Jake continued to watch him.

Cody paused before Shelby. "I need to talk to you," he said, his voice low, his tone serious.

Shelby felt suddenly nervous and apprehensive. From the look on his face and in his eyes, she didn't think she was going to like whatever it was Cody intended to say. But she'd run away earlier when he'd wanted to talk; she couldn't do that again. It wasn't fair to either of them.

"Hey, beautiful, you're not trying to get out of our dinner date, are you?" Lance asked cheerfully, coming up behind Shelby and slipping a proprietary arm around her waist. Though he'd been riding beside the herd all day and beneath a blazing sun, he looked as fresh, crisp, and clean as he had that morning before they'd started.

Shelby glanced from Lance back to Cody, uncertain what to do. She saw the rage in Cody's eyes, like a dark, volatile storm sweeping over a clear blue sky, threatening, ready to erupt, to unleash its fury, and her apprehension grew. "Lance, Cody and I were just about to talk."

"Well, you can do that later. Looks like dinner's ready and all it's going to do is burn or get cold if we don't eat it now." Without removing his arm from around her waist, Lance reached out with his other hand, grabbed two plates from a stack on a nearby table, and steered Shelby around to the front of the grill. His shoulder brushed against Cody as they passed him.

Lance paused and looked back. "Sorry, but you two can talk later, I'm sure. Anyway, it's only business, right?"

Lance smiled, and Cody was reminded of the Cheshire cat in Alice in Wonderland. He'd never liked that cat.

Shelby accepted a plate from Lance and allowed him to pile it high with food as they stood before the grill, then he maneuvered her toward a picnic table set up a few yards away. She felt a bit guilty at deserting Cody, but, if truth be told, she didn't think she wanted to hear what he had to say. At least not right now. One cry for the day was enough. She didn't want to chance another.

A huge bowl of green salad was set in the center of the table they approached, along with jars of preserves, slabs of real butter, and a plate of sliced apples and cheeses. If she didn't gain at least five pounds from this little excursion she'd be surprised. Somehow she was going to have to find a way to enjoy the food on the ranch without gaining weight.

She noticed a huge chocolate cake sitting on another table and groaned in defeat. She was going to have to buy an exercise bike, though she hated the things. In fact, she hated exercise, but she'd have to do it if she didn't want to end up looking like a blimp.

She sat down beside Lance and, as if feeling his gaze riveted to her back, peeked over her shoulder at Cody. He caught her glance and Shelby wished instantly she hadn't looked. The murderous glint in his eyes made her uncomfortable. What in heaven's name could he have wanted to talk to her about that Lance's arrival and the need to postpone their chat had gotten him so upset?

"Bobby! Where's Bobby?"

The loud shout drew everyone's attention. Shelby turned in her seat to see Ruth Rothman, one of the guests, run into the center of the campsite. The woman's entire body seemed to tremble as she scanned the area repeatedly, not finding what she sought.

"Bobby? Oh, my God, where's Bobby?" she muttered over and over.

She ran to where Tom had set up the barbecue pits next to the chuck truck, circling about them, searching. Her husband followed close on her heels, more sedate, but his own fear for his son was etched in every line of his face.

Shelby stood up and stepped away from the table, apprehensive. She looked at the table where the children were seated. All had stopped eating, talking, laughing, and were now staring, like little frozen statues, at Bobby's mother.

Ruth rushed up to Shelby and grabbed her by the upper arms, her fingers digging into her flesh, crushing her shoulders. "Where's my son?" she screamed, shaking Shelby. "Where is he? Your man was supposed to be watching him. You said this was a safe trip. That it was okay for children."

Henry Rothman tried to pull his wife away from Shelby, mumbling words of comfort. She struck out at him with one hand and jerked her arm out of his grasp. "Get away from me, Hank. I want my son!" She turned back to Shelby, who had tried to pull free of the woman's grip and failed. "Where is he? Where?"

Cody walked quietly up behind Ruth Rothman and gripped her shoulders, forcing her to turn and face him. He kept his voice soft and calm as he spoke, but there was a steely strength in his tone that seemed instantly to soothe the woman and draw her confidence. "It'll be all right, Mrs. Rothman. We'll find him. He's probably just on the outskirts of camp. Maybe playing around."

She turned to him, tears in her eyes, fear quivering on her lips. "He's my baby, Cody. We came here because of him, because of how much he loves cowboys. If anything's happened to him . . ."

Cody had continued to grip her shoulders, but now his hold softened. "Nothing's happened to him, Mrs. Rothman, believe me. We'll find him, I promise."

The woman nodded, momentarily reassured by Cody's words and confident tone. She began to cry softly, tears streaming down her cheeks in a constant flood, and her shoulders shook. "He's afraid of the dark, Cody. I always have to leave a night-light on in his bedroom."

Her husband, who had been standing nearby, unsure what to do, pulled his wife into his arms when Cody released her. "Bobby's all right,

Ruth. He probably just wandered off to the outskirts of camp, playing, that's all. Like Cody said, boys do that."

Ruth shuddered, took a deep breath, and looked up at him. "But it'll be getting dark in another couple of hours, Hank. What if they don't find him before it gets dark? He'll be out there alone, and you know how afraid he is of the dark."

"We'll find him, Mrs. Rothman," Shelby said. She glanced at Cody for reassurance, and saw her own worry and uncertainty mirrored in his eyes. But she saw something else, too. Strength and determination, and realized that if it hadn't been for that, something she sensed Bobby's worried mother also saw in Cody, Ruth Rothman would most likely be hysterical.

He turned and called for the wrangler who had been put in charge of the children at the beginning of the drive.

"Ben, when's the last time you saw the Rothman boy?"

The young wrangler ran up to stand before Cody. He appeared no more than a boy himself, his brown hair hanging over his forehead, a blanket of freckles sprinkling the bridge of his nose and lean cheeks. "Gosh, Cody, uh, 'bout a mile back from camp. I took a head count then cause we were kinda spread out behind the herd. They were all with me then."

"But nobody saw him ride into camp?" Cody

looked around at the other guests and wranglers who'd gathered around them in a tight circle.

No one spoke up. A few shook their heads.

"All right, then. We search. Get your mounts resaddled, boys. Each of you take a canteen, an extra blanket, and some bandages from Tom's first-aid kit."

"Oh, my God," Ruth Rothman wailed.

Cody whirled around. "It's only a precaution, Mrs. Rothman. In case he fell or something." A dozen curses ran through his mind. Why in the hell hadn't he waited until she was out of ear-shot before saying that? Damn it all. A lost kid was bad enough, but he wasn't really that worried. It had happened before, and it would happen again. They usually found the kid not far from camp or the herd, exploring or chasing some small animal. But a hysterial woman was worse. They didn't calm easy, got the whole group upset, and usually harped on the incident for the rest of their stay at the Double K.

Shelby lay a hand on Cody's arm. "Where do we start?"

He looked down at her as if she were daft. "*We* don't start anywhere. You stay here and calm down Mrs. Rothman and the rest of the group. The boys and I will go out and find Bobby." He started to turn way.

Shelby grasped the fabric of his shirt sleeve and held him in place. "Hold on, Cody. This is just as much my responsibility as it is yours.

202

More so, in fact. I want to help."

"You will be helping by keeping that woman from going completely hysterical on us." He pulled his arm free and started to walk where the wranglers were already mounting. He was still several feet from his destination, when Lance stepped in front of him.

"I want to go along and help, Cody."

Cody hooked his thumbs over his belt and glared at Lance. "Hollywood, one missing *kid* is more than enough. Stay here and help Shelby keep everyone calm." He'd ground out that last sentence through clenched teeth. Pushing past the actor, he walked to his horse.

One of the wranglers had saddled Soldier for him. Cody swung himself up into the saddle and turned to the ranch hands. "All right, boys, you know what to do. The kid can't be that far away." He lowered his voice so that only the wranglers could hear him. "I want each and every one of you back here by dark, no matter what. Understood?"

The men nodded and turned their mounts from camp. Within seconds they were gone.

Shelby marched up to Jake, who hadn't joined the rescue. Someone had to stay behind besides Tom and Billy, and Cody had ordered Jake to keep the guests reassured and in line.

"That man is insufferable," she stormed, glowering in the direction in which Cody had ridden.

"Yep, he can be that," Jake agreed.

She turned to the old man. "Fill me a canteen, Jake, and get me an extra blanket and some bandages."

"You going to follow them after Cody told you not to?"

"I'm the boss around here, Jake, not Cody. But, then, he seems to have forgotten that."

Jake chuckled and rose from his seat. "I think that just might be the one thing he ain't forgot."

Shelby stared at him in confusion. What in blazes did that remark mean? She shrugged it aside to think about later. Right now there was a missing boy to find, and she was going to try to do just that. Whether Cody Farlowe liked it or not.

Minutes later, Jake had Lady saddled, the extra blanket secured to the back of her saddle, a full canteen slung over the saddle horn, and several swaths of bandages tucked into her saddlebags. He stared up at her after she mounted.

"Missy, you make sure you get back here before dark, you hear? And you be careful out there. I shouldn't really let you go, but—" he turned away and spit a wad of tobacco juice into the nearby brush, then looked back up at Shelby "—don't see's how I can stop you. Like you said, you're the boss."

"I'll be fine, Jake."

"You'd better be. Anything happens to you

and Cody'll have my head, that's for sure."

Shelby laughed. "He'd probably thank you."

"Don't bet on it, missy. Don't bet on it."

Shelby pulled up on the reins and turned Lady back in the direction they'd ridden in from. "See you in a couple of hours, Jake," she called over her shoulder.

The old man watched her leave, and smiled.

Several yards away, Lance Murdock quietly slipped his horse away from the campsite, mounted, and also rode out.

Chapter Sixteen

Shelby headed in the same direction as Cody and the wranglers. According to Jake, the men were going to ride about a mile back up the trail, to where the child-care wrangler had last seen Bobby, then fan out, turn around, and make their way back to camp. They hoped to run across the boy somewhere en route. She wasn't going to backtrack that far, she decided.

Something small and shiny, reflecting a ray from the quickly sinking sun, glinted in the grass off to her left. Shelby reined in, curious. She nudged Lady from the trail and into the narrow field that, after a few dozen yards, sloped upward and disappeared within a dense forest of cottonwoods. Once in the area where she'd seen the reflection, Shelby dismounted and began searching the ankle-high grass. In a clump of weeds, she found a cheap replica of a silver concho. Shelby bent to pick it up, and stared at it. Bobby had conchos on his cowboy hat. They were also on the pair of dime-store chaps he'd worn.

Excited, she remounted Lady and headed into the cottonwoods.

The sun was hanging low on the horizon, turning the sky a soft, hazy, very pale blue. The shadows among the trees had deepened making the woods seem dark, cool, and slightly foreboding. She knew that soon, when the sun sank below the trees and mountains in the distance, the entire area would be engulfed in darkness.

Shelby shivered at the thought, but refused to dwell on it. She searched for any sign that someone had passed this way before her, and found none. But, then, she wasn't exactly sure what to look for, and whether she'd recognize a sign even if she saw one. Nevertheless she felt that the concho was a pretty good indication the child had come this way.

"Bobby?" she called, loud enough for the boy to hear if he was anywhere near but soft enough so that she wouldn't attract the attention of Cody and the other wranglers. She was out here to help find the boy, not get reprimanded by Cody.

There was no response.

She kept trying. Every few feet she'd call out again, wait for a response, and feel a stab of disappointment when none came. She lost track of time, forgetting to check the watch on her wrist, paying no attention to the weakening rays of the sun as it sank lower and lower in the sky and the darkness of the grove as it grew deeper and deeper.

Shelby had only one thing on her mind: finding Bobby Rothman. Well, maybe two things: finding Bobby and proving to Cody that she wasn't some helpless city ninny who couldn't take care of herself. Even if she didn't find Bobby, at least she'd tried, and Cody would know it.

The copse of cottonwoods eventually gave way to a small meadow where the tall grass had been turned a golden orange by the rays of the setting sun. She urged Lady up the slope of a gentle knoll and paused on its crest. She knew she should give up the search and head back to camp. It was getting late and there was very little daylight left. She called again and twisted around in her saddle, looking in every direction, trying to see within the trees, through the thick growths of shrubs, past the high grasses of the meadow. There was no sign of the child, no sign of anyone or anything.

A screech filled the air. Shelby jumped, startled. A shadow passed over her, and she looked up to see an eagle, its wings spread wide, soar across the sky and disappear beyond the jagged tips of the trees in the distance.

Shelby proceeded into a thick growth of pine trees that bordered the meadow. What little sunlight still blanketed the earth suddenly disappeared beneath the sprawling limbs of the tall pines. Here and there thin, faint sunbeams filtered through, like streaming rays of a rainbow, a brilliance of color lighting up one tiny spot of earth now and then

She shivered and pulled back on the reins, bringing Lady to a halt. The air had turned chilly, but whether from the passing of time or the onslaught of shadowy darkness when she'd entered the forest, she was unsure. She raised her arm, pulled back the cuff of her shirt, and squinted at her watch. The tiny gold hands were nearly invisible. She moved her wrist around, trying to catch the light, and squinted again. Both hands seemed to be pointing downward.

"I couldn't have been out here for more than an hour," she muttered, lowering her arm. When she'd left camp it hadn't yet been five o'clock, so now, she guessed, unable to read her watch clearly, it was five-thirty. It didn't get dark until seven. Shelby glanced around at her dim surroundings. It was just the thickness of the trees, she told herself, making it seem much later than it was. She lifted the canteen, unscrewed its top, and took a long swallow of the cold water. It sent a chill through her, but quenched her thirst. She replaced the canteen and urged Lady forward. "Come on, girl, just a little farther. If we don't come across some sign of him soon, we'll turn back and head for camp. Maybe Cody or some of the guys have had better luck."

She prayed that was so. The mere thought of spending a night out in this country alone sent a shudder of dread and fear through her: a small boy would be absolutely terror stricken.

She moved deeper into the woods. The only sound she heard, besides her own voice calling out for Bobby, was the soft crunch of dried twigs breaking beneath Lady's hooves.

The trees grew thicker, closer together, and the light filtering through grew fainter, almost non-existent. Shelby reined in again. "I think maybe we'd best turn around, Lady," she said to the horse, and pulled on the reins to turn the mount back in the direction they'd come. Dark, looming shadows surrounded her; the light was so weak that she could no longer pick out any landmarks.

It suddenly dawned on her that she wasn't at all sure which way was "back." In the darkness, she'd totally lost her sense of direction, and every tree looked the same.

Stop it! she ordered herself, as panic threatened. Her nerves were going to have her conjuring up monsters and hobgoblins, when she was supposed to be out there looking for a child who was probably a lot more scared than she.

Don't bet on it, a little voice at the back of her mind whispered.

She tried to ignore the fact that her heartbeat had accelerated with her anxiety.

Suddenly the sound of a child crying met her ears. It was so soft she wasn't sure, at first, that she'd really heard it. She yanked back on the reins, jerking Lady's head upward. Startled, the horse reared, raising her front legs from the ground and flailing at the air wildly.

Shelby grabbed the saddle horn and clenched the horse's side with her knees in an effort to keep her seat. "Whoa, girl, whoa," she cried, trying to soothe the frightened horse. Lady's hooves dropped back onto the ground with a loud *thump*. One instantly rose again to paw nervously at the ground as she shook her head, sending her mane flying. Shelby clung to the saddle horn for several long moments, too shook up to let go.

When she finally managed to find her composure again, and her courage, she straightened up in the saddle and leaned forward to pat Lady's neck as a gesture of reassurance, something she could have used a little of herself. Her hand stopped midway to its destination, frozen in space as her gaze fastened on the small boy standing in a faint beam of sunlight only a few feet away.

"Bobby?" she asked softly. "Bobby, is that you? Are you okay?" She felt an onslaught of joy at finding him, but from the frightened look on his face, she thought he might be about ready to bolt from her.

Tears coursed down his face and he reached up to wipe at them, smudging his already-dirt-marked cheeks. He took a deep breath, wiped his nose across the short sleeve of his T-shirt, and hiccuped. "I . . . I got lost, Miss Shelby," he said finally.

Shelby swung her right leg over the saddle and slid to the ground. Keeping Lady's reins in her hand, she walked over to stand before him. "It's okay, Bobby, really. What happened? Why'd you wander away from the others?"

"I saw a raccoon. We went on a camping trip once, me and my mom and dad, and there was a raccoon that came into our camp. I set out marshmallows and he ate them. I wanted to feed this one, too. I had a cookie in my pocket."

"Well, I'm just glad you're okay."

"Is my mom mad?"

Shelby wrapped an arm around the child's shoulder and hugged him to her, feeling a flood of relief. "Bobby, I think your mom's going to be so thrilled to see you she'll forget all about being mad."

"Bet my dad won't."

"One look at you and I'll bet all you have to fear from your parents is being hugged to death."

He gazed at her, his eyes wide with hope. "You really think so, Miss Shelby?"

Shelby laughed. "I'm sure of it, Bobby. But for now I think we'd best get back to camp. It's getting late." And dark, the little voice at the back of her mind added, stirring her fear like a poker in a fire. "Where's your horse, Bobby?"

"Right back there." He pointed into the forest. "When I got off him to try to feed the raccoon I tied him to a bush and he's eating it."

"Okay, come on. Let's get him and start back." She looked around the now almost completely dark grove of trees. If they didn't get moving soon, she wasn't sure she'd be able to find her way out of this forest, let alone back to the campsite.

For the first time since she'd left camp, she wished Cody were with her. She needed his strength, his confidence, his expertise . . . she needed *him*.

She took the boy's hand in hers and held Lady's reins in her other hand. "Okay, Bobby, lead the way."

They started in the direction the child claimed he'd left his horse, but before they had gone ten or twelve yards it had become too dark to see more than a few feet in front of them.

"Hold on, Bobby, I've got a flashlight in my saddlebag." *Thank heavens,* she thought. It was no more than a pen light really, and emitted only a thin beam, but it was better than nothing.

Shelby flicked on the light and pointed it at the ground in front of them. It lit up their path, but their surroundings remained in the gloomy shadows of darkness. They wove their way through the thick growth of trees, hearing the night animals of the forest all about, but unable to see them. Something skittered across the ground in front of them, a long, thin shadow bolting through the flashlight's weak beam.

213

Bobby stopped, Shelby jumped, and Lady's muzzle rammed into the center of her back. Shelby stumbled forward, swerving to the side to avoid trampling the boy, and dropped the flashlight. The beam clicked off and total, impenetrable blackness instantly closed around them.

"Oh, no," she wailed, dropping to her knees. She began to run her hands over the ground, through the thick layer of dry pine needles that covered the floor of the forest.

"Oh, where is that thing?" she grumbled.

"Miss Shelby, I'm scared," Bobby said, his voice barely more than a whisper.

She heard the fear in his tone and tried to think of something comforting to say, something to bolster his courage. Her mind was a blank. She was too frightened herself to give courage to anyone else.

Her searching became frantic, and several times dry, brittle pine needles punctured her skin. After the first yelp, which scared Bobby further, Shelby bit down on her bottom lip and refused to yell out.

An owl hooted, its haunting cry echoing eerily in the grove.

"Miss Shelby?" Bobby said.

"I'm right here, Bobby." Her hand bumped into the flashlight and she released a long sigh of relief. "Thank God." She picked it up and flicked the switch. The thin beam lit the path. "Okay, we've got light again. Let's go." She held out her hand to the boy and he took it instantly, his smaller fingers wrapping tightly around hers.

"Pete's right up here, I think. It's hard to tell in the dark."

She stopped dead in her tracks. "Pete?" Was there more than one child out here?

"My horse. His name's Pete."

"Oh." She felt foolish, but, then, who'd ever name a horse Pete? Animals should have dignified names. She remembered that when she and Katie had been little, it had always been Shelby who'd named their pets. The Irish setter their father had brought home one summer night as a puppy she'd dubbed Rebel; the dalmatian was Duchess; and their cat, a black mixed breed tom, she'd called Warrior. Shelby smiled to herself. He'd lived up to his name, too. Hardly a week had gone by that Shelby and her mother weren't doctoring the cuts and scratches on Warrior's head.

"There he is!" Bobby cried, jerking his hand away from Shelby's and running forward. The horse lifted his head from a small cluster of wildflowers he'd been munching on and watched the approaching boy.

Bobby untangled the reins from the bush he'd secured them to, then looked at Shelby expectantly. "I need a leg up, Miss Shelby."

"Oh, sure." She moved up beside him and entwined her fingers, then bent down so that he could place his foot in her cupped hands. "Ready?"

"Yep." Bobby bounced at the same time Shelby pushed, and he landed with a plop in the saddle.

Shelby turned back to Lady and mounted. For one brief instant she wondered if it wouldn't be better just to sit tight and let Cody or one of the wranglers find them. The idea rankled and she quickly discarded it. She'd find her way back to the camp. She had to. Otherwise, she'd never hear the end of it from Cody. She looked at Bobby. "You stay right behind me, okay? I don't want to lose you again." She turned Lady around and they began to make their way through the dark forest, only the faint beam of the flashlight, which Shelby suspected was getting weaker by the minute, to illuminate their path.

Her hands shook, and fear gnawed at the pit of her stomach. The shivers that raced through her body and left her flesh goose bumped weren't entirely due to the now-crisp air.

"How much farther, Miss Shelby?" Bobby called.

"Just a bit," she lied, thinking that they should have come to the edge of the trees by now. They should be in the meadow, with the copse of cottonwoods ahead of them. Why were they still weaving their way through this pine forest? Panic bubbled up within her breast and she fought to beat it back down. She couldn't let herself fall apart. She couldn't let Bobby see

216

that she was scared. Oh, where was Cody? She'd give anything now to run into him, to feel the warmth of his arms around her, the security of his embrace. Lord, she'd even welcome his angry words and harsh glare right now.

Half an hour later, the flashlight's beam had become so weak it was almost useless. Shelby struggled to control her steadily mounting fear. Her nerves felt as if they were exposed to the elements, jittery and frazzled, while her heart hammered crazily in her chest, reminding her with each beat that she was more frightened than she'd ever been in her entire life. They were lost. Oh, dear saints in heaven, they were lost out there in the middle of nowhere. She didn't have the faintest idea which way it was back to the camp. For all she knew, they were going in circles. She couldn't even see the moon overhead through the trees.

Why hadn't she listened to Cody and stayed in camp as he had told her to?

"Miss Shelby, I'm cold. And I'm getting hungry."

Shelby felt a wave of guilt. If she'd stayed in camp as Cody had told her to, Bobby would be out here all alone.

She took a deep breath and forced her voice to remain steady, infusing it with a cheery tone that she was far from feeling. "I have a couple of candy bars in my saddlebag, Bobby. Would you like one?"

She twisted around to look back at him, the

hand holding the flashlight moving to follow. Suddenly a screech permeated the air, a blood-curdling cry that filled the grove and sent terror racing up Shelby's spine and chilling her to the bone. At the same time, a huge black shadow swooped down, blocking out the light as it descended directly toward her.

Chapter Seventeen

Cody was the last one to return to the camp. He'd ridden farther back up the trail than the other wranglers, and had crisscrossed the track behind them. But he'd found no trace of Bobby Rothman.

He slid from the saddle, his feet hitting the ground seconds before Soldier managed to halt. Cody ran up to Jamie, who was standing with the other wranglers waiting for his return, unsure whether to unsaddle their mounts or go back out to search again.

"Find him?" Cody asked, looking directly at Jamie. Before the young cowhand could respond, Cody guessed his answer. His gaze jumped from one wrangler to the next, seeing the same response in each of their eyes. He had a sinking feeling in his heart and a heavy boulder of anxiety and fear sitting in his stomach.

Normally the drives were uneventful and safe. Once before a child had gotten lost, but they'd found her within ten minutes. But that had been in broad daylight. Spending a night out in this country alone was a tough experience even for someone who was used to it. For a young child from the city, it could be terrifying. And dangerous.

Cody cursed softly and walked toward one of the campfires. He hunkered down, grabbed the coffeepot that sat on the grill, and poured the hot, steaming liquid into a cup he took from a nearby stack. He sipped it slowly, letting the coffee warm his insides, the wisping steam his face, and the hot tin cup his hands. He didn't want to think of all the dangers, both real and imagined, that young Bobby Rothman might face out there alone. Cougars still roamed the Montana mountains, as well as mountain lions, bears, and wolves. There were more than a dozen hazards that could endanger the child, and not all of them were animals. There were men up in the mountains, people who wanted no reminder of the outside world and lived as their ancestors had one hundred years ago. Some were good men who wanted only to avoid the bustle and trouble of society, but there were the others, the troublemakers, the dangerous ones. They were the ones who worried Cody.

He poured himself another cup of coffee and rose to his feet. He spotted Jake talking to the wranglers and motioned the older man to join him.

"I'm going back out, Jake, and I want you

and Jamie out there as well. The rest of the boys are to stay here and take care of the guests. No sense risking anybody else. I think you'd better send Tom for the sheriff, too, just in case." He looked around the camp. "Where's Shelby? As the owner of the Double K, she needs to know what's going on."

Jake ground his teeth on a wad of tobacco and refused to meet Cody's eye. "She ain't come back yet."

Cody felt a stab of intense fear. He stared at Jake in disbelief. Uncontrollable fury seized him, and he threw down the cup of coffee. The dark liquid flew from the cup and splashed over the grill, sizzling loudly. Cody grabbed the lapels of Jake's leather vest and hauled the wiry assistant foreman up against his chest. "What do you mean *she hasn't come back yet?*"

Jake swallowed hard, gripped both of Cody's wrists, and forced the foreman to release him. "Just what I said. She took out after you when you and the boys went searching. I told her not to go, but she wasn't about to listen."

"You should have made her."

"Hell, Cody, she's the boss, and she wasn't too timid about reminding me of that, either."

Anger blazed in Cody's eyes. Anger at Jake for allowing Shelby to ride out of camp after he'd told her not to, at her for being so fool-hardy, but most of all at himself for not realizing that she'd do just that.

Ruth Rothman stepped from her tent, saw

Cody, and ran toward him. She grabbed his arm. "What are you doing? You have to send your men back out. You can't quit searching. You can't leave Bobby out there alone. Please, don't stop looking." Tears streamed down her face as she pleaded, and with each word the pitch of her voice grew higher.

Hank Rothman ran up behind his wife and tried to pull her away. "Come on, honey, this isn't doing any good," he crooned. "They'll find Bobby. He'll be okay."

She turned on her husband. "He's out there alone. How can you say he'll be okay?"

"Don't worry, Mrs. Rothman, Lance will find your boy."

Everyone turned toward the tall redhead who'd moved up to stand beside the distraught woman.

She raised an eyebrow haughtily. "Well, he will. He's done it lots of times. Didn't you see that episode where the woman got amnesia and wandered off and—"

"That was a television story. Fiction," Eva Montalvo announced, looking at the redhead as if she didn't have a single brain cell in her head.

"When did he leave?" Cody asked. The venom in his voice was unmistakable.

The woman turned her eyes heavenward and put an index finger to her chin. "Umm, let me think. Must be a couple of hours now." She smiled. "Maybe a teensy bit more."

"Great." Cody slammed one gloved fist into

his other palm. "Now we have three people lost out there."

"Lance isn't lost," the redhead shot back angrily. "It's probably just taking him longer to get back, what with a child and all."

"Yeah, right," Cody mumbled. He whirled back toward his horse. "Come on, Jake. Let's get going before someone else comes up missing," He walked to where he'd left Soldier. Luckily he hadn't ridden him hard that day, and the big gelding had more energy and heart than most horses. He'd run all day and all night if Cody asked him to.

Leaving Soldier behind when he'd gone to New York was one of the hardest things Cody had ever done in his life. He'd never forget the thrill of that first ride on the huge bay when he'd returned.

He swung up onto the saddle. "Jake, you ride half a mile out on the trail and then swing off to the north. Jamie, you swing off to the south. Take lanterns. And if you find them, signal with two shots."

Jake nodded and handed Cody a lantern. "Where will you be?"

"Everywhere I can," Cody called back.

Cody leaned forward in his saddle and peered down into the valley. From the small knoll where he stood he had a clear view of the Double K's campsite, the herd, and the trail they'd come in on that afternoon. A good mile to the southeast of the camp he spotted a light. Jamie, he thought. He watched for long minutes as it moved, veering through the trees, disappearing every now and then behind a large rock or a thick growth of brush. He spotted another light in the thicket of trees almost directly below him. That would be Jake. Obviously neither man had found anything.

He gazed on the landscape below, seeing no sign of any other light. A hundred questions buzzed through his mind and fed the anxiety and worry building within him. Would Shelby stay on Lady and continue to search for the camp? Or would she stop and try to settle in for the night? Make a camp? Did she have matches with her to build a fire? Had she found Bobby? Were they together? Or was the child still out there alone? And what about Hollywood? That egotistical, self-centered Casanova who just had to play hero. Was he still riding around out there in the dark, or had he perhaps fallen down some gully and broken his fool neck?

Cody turned his eyes toward the sky. The search party could have used a little more help from the moon. He reached behind him into his saddlebag and pulled out a small pair of binoculars. Lifting them to his eyes, he scanned the dark landscape. Nothing but blackness met his gaze.

"Damn it, Shelby. Where in the hell are you?"

A coyote howled in the distance. Remembering Shelby's fright of that same sound only a few nights earlier, Cody felt a wrenching twist in his gut. He could imagine her terror now, and it cut through him like a knife. He wanted to protect her, to find her and comfort her, to let her know that he would allow nothing and no one ever to hurt her. The coyote howled again, and another memory of that night flooded his mind. His body ached for her. Damn, how he wanted her. And the hunger to possess her had grown stronger with each passing minute since they'd made love that night. Even now, he could close his eyes and taste the sweetness of her kiss, feel the silkiness of her skin beneath his touch, her body molding to his and welcoming him in union. He burned with the need for her, and he cursed the heavens for sending Shelby Hill to entice him.

He looked back out at the black horizon. "Where the hell are you, Shelby?" he asked again. Several times he'd crisscrossed the trail the herd had traversed, covered the acreage on either side of it, and he'd found no one, come up with no clues, no trail. Nothing.

For the first time in his life Cody felt real fear, so deep, so intense, so all-consuming, that it gripped his heart in a vice, squeezing, crushing. He would never be able to forgive himself if anything happened to her.

"Damn it, Shelby. If this fool stunt of yours doesn't prove you belong back in the city, then I don't know what does."

He lifted the small lantern he carried and looked at the watch on his wrist. Twenty minutes after midnight. They had been searching for Bobby Rothman since about four-thirty. They'd gone back out to search for Shelby and Lance Murdock at eight. He nudged Soldier's ribs. The horse began a descent down the slope toward the two bobbing lights moving through the dark landscape of the valley below.

He reached Jake first. "Go on back to camp, old man," Cody called out, riding up to his assistant.

Jake looked up, surprised. "We ain't giving up?" His craggy old face appeared tired and drawn, his eyes full of concern.

"Go on back, Jake," Cody repeated. "I'll go tell Jamie."

"You coming?" Jake called after him as Cody started to ride away.

"Yeah, I'll be there." His tone held a note of resignation that was not lost on the older cowboy.

By the time Cody rounded up Jamie and both men returned to the camp, Jake was deep in conversation with several county deputies who had arrived only moments earlier. Ruth and Hank Rothman were huddled nearby, talking to the sheriff.

Jake broke away from the group and walked over to Cody, who was pulling the saddle from Soldier's back.

"They say they ain't gonna start a search till sunup."

Cody clenched his jaw. That wasn't what he'd wanted to hear. He didn't want to think about Shelby being out there all alone, cold and scared.

"Get me a fresh horse, Jake."

"What?" The older man looked at Cody as if he were crazy.

Cody threw his saddle down and led Soldier over to where a bale of alfalfa hay had been spread on the ground for the horses. "You heard me," he said over his shoulder. "Get me another horse. I'm going back out. And get someone over here to brush down Soldier."

"You crazy? We've been looking for hours and come up with nothing. What makes you think you can find them all by yourself?"

"Jake."

The old man ignored the warning note in Cody's voice. "Anyways, look at yourself," he continued. "You're so plumb tuckered out you're about to drop right there where you're standing."

Cody turned to look at Jake. The old man was more than his assistant; ever since Cody's father had died several years earlier, Jake had appointed himself Cody's guardian angel. It had almost broken his heart when Cody had followed Lisa to New York, but other than one simple warning that it wouldn't work, he had remained silent. "Jake, I've got to keep looking.

I've got to find her."

Jake put a hand on Cody's shoulder. "Son, you're not gonna find nothing out there this time of night except trouble. And you won't do Shelby or yourself any good by getting yourself hurt."

Cody sighed deeply. The old man was right, but he hated to admit it. Yet how could he sleep knowing she was out there half-crazed with fear? How could he warm himself by the fire, eat food, drink coffee, or even relax, knowing Shelby had none of those comforts, none of that security?

"Jake, she's probably scared half out of her mind. The other night a coyote howled and she—" His voice broke, and he couldn't continue.

"Cody, that girl's got a lot more grit than you give her credit for. Sure she's probably scared. Lots of things in the country to be scared of if you ain't used to them. Just like in the city. A good old country boy like me goes into the big city, he can get scared of lots of things. But that don't mean he couldn't cope with them if he had to. And Shelby will cope, Cody. She'll cope out there 'cause she has to."

Cody shook his head. "I wish I could be as sure of that as you are."

"It's only four hours till sunup. If she ain't come back on her own by then, we'll all be out searching. Now, get some rest so you don't fall down where you stand."

Cody walked toward the campfire and, bending down, poured himself a cup of coffee. He wanted to go back out, to search for her, to find her, but his body was too weary, too exhausted. He'd been up since five that morning, scouting the herd, spelling the wranglers that had pulled night watch, and riding out to make sure the trail was clear. Then, at the end of what had already seemed a long day, he'd pushed both himself and Soldier almost to the limits in search of Bobby Rothman, then again in the second search.

His mind wanted him to go on, his heart wanted him to go on, but his body refused. He could feel his legs shaking with fatigue, his muscles contracting into knots, his bones aching. He'd been in the saddle for almost nineteen hours. If he could, he would have climbed back on his horse and stayed there for another nineteen. Whatever it took to find Shelby.

…illed they'd have water enough for the remainder of the … and get some hot … Take cover …Bum … while we wait … they have been … and ready …

… scuttle
… there.
… a … as
… when …

Chapter Eighteen

Shelby screamed and threw herself down on top of Lady's neck. The owl swooped over her, its dangling, sharp-clawed feet only inches from her back. Within seconds it was gone.

Trembling violently, her heart doing somersaults within her breast, she clung to Lady's mane and fought to regain her composure, such as it was.

"I think he was after the flashlight," Bobby offered, watching her.

She took a deep breath and sat up. "Well, I hope he's figured out it's not his dinner. Those feet of his were a little too close for comfort."

They pushed on through the woods for another hour, weaving in and about the trees, skirting around bushes and fallen tree trunks, and, once, crossing a small stream that Shelby definitely did not remember from her entry into the thicket of pines.

Finally, training the flashlight on her watch, to discover that it was nearing midnight, she decided they'd best make camp for the remainder of the night and get some rest, if they could. Both she and Bobby were bone tired and ready to fall asleep in their saddles.

One tree looked much the same as another in the dark, so Shelby merely reined in and slid to the ground. "We're going to rest for a while Bobby. Come on and get down."

She handed Bobby the flashlight. The beam was so faint now that she knew they had only minutes of light left.

"I'm c-cold, Miss Shelby."

"I'll be just a minute, Bobby, then we can wrap up in the blankets."

"Can't we make a fire?"

Shelby sighed. "I don't have any matches."

She worked quickly, untying first her bedroll from the back of her saddle, then Bobby's, and spreading both on the ground; she lay the extra blanket she'd brought on top. Tucking the saddlebags up against the trunk of the tree under which they would sleep, she then rechecked the reins of the two horses to make sure they were securely tied. One thing she didn't need was for one or both of the horses to wander off during the night.

"Okay, Bobby, let's try to get some rest. Come on over here and sit close to me. That way we'll keep each other warm."

"Can we eat those candy bars you said you had?"

"Sure. Then we'll get some sleep and in the

morning we'll find our way back to the camp." Shelby listened to her own words, heard her calm voice. She wished she felt as steady and confident as she sounded. Instead her body felt like one quivering mass of terrorized jelly. Her pulse seemed to be set on breakneck speed, anxiety and fright keeping the race going. Her heart seemed to be lodged permanently in the middle of her throat.

She tried not to think of what was out there with them in the wild. Occasionally the howl of a coyote, the screech of a bird, or the rustling of a nearby bush forced her to remember that there were other living things in the woods beyond the dark, but as soon as the thought came to her, she tried to push it away. Fear could too easily turn into sheer, unadulterated panic with just the slightest slack on the leash of her self-control, and that leash was already stretched as tight as a rubber band.

Shelby moved around a bit on the blanket, trying to find a comfortable spot, then lifted her arm over the boy's head. "Come on, Bobby, snuggle up to me. We'll stay warmer that way."

The boy did as he was told and Shelby pulled the bedroll and blanket up and tucked it in around their legs. She tightened her arm around Bobby's shoulders, pulled him closer, and held up the two candy bars. She pointed the light at them. "Which one do you want? The chocolate with nuts or the chocolate with raisins?"

"Raisins."

Shelby moved to hand him the chosen bar and the light from the flashlight sputtered and went out, plunging them into total darkness.

"Miss Shelby?" Bobby cried, practically crawling onto her lap.

"It—it's okay, Bobby. Snuggle close to me and eat your candy bar, then try to get a little sleep. It'll be morning before you know it."

"I'm scared."

"There's nothing to be scared of." She looked around, trying to penetrate the blackness that enveloped them, and wished she could believe her own words. She remembered Cody's warning about things that crawled into a person's boots at night to keep warm. Well, she had no intention of taking her boots off, so she didn't have to worry about that. But would those same creatures crawl into a bedroll? Or a blanket?

A nearby bush rustled and Shelby jumped, barely keeping herself from screaming.

Bobby clung to her and whimpered.

The bush rustled again and Shelby wrapped both arms around the boy and began to rock back and forth, as much to comfort herself as him. "Hush, Bobby," she whispered, her lips close to his ear. "It's okay."

"But . . . but something's out there."

"It'll go away in a minute." She kept her voice low, not wanting to attract the animal any more than it already had been.

"But what if it's a bear? What if he's hungry?"

233

"Then he'll eat the berries off of the bush and go back to his cave." Oh, that sounded so logical. She prayed it was true. "It's probably just a deer," she added hopefully.

Half an hour later, Bobby lay asleep against her breast, his soft, steady breathing a comforting sound. Shelby sat with her back against the tree, staring into the darkness and seeing absolutely nothing. But she couldn't close her eyes. Every time she did, her imagination conjured up all types of scenarios that turned her blood cold and made her heart nearly stop beating. And she couldn't relax. Her muscles remained taut, ready at the slightest provocation to send her jumping upright.

Each small noise from the woods sent Shelby's nerves into reaction. Each time she'd turn to stare in the direction the noise had come from, peering into the darkness and trying to penetrate its gloom, to see whatever threat lay in wait for her.

Several times she nodded off, but the moment her chin came to rest against her chest, she'd wake and jerk her head upright, alert, frightened.

The night passed slowly, each minute a millennium, each hour an eternity. By the time the first rays of light fell onto the forest, weak pinkish rays filtering down through the thickly entwined limbs to warm the ground, exhaustion had overtaken her and Shelby had finally fallen asleep.

A caressing heat warmed her blood as dreams of Cody filled her mind. She snuggled deeper into his embrace, felt the security of his arms around her and the steely hardness of his broad chest beneath her touch. She breathed deeply of his scent, that virile male scent spiced with the smell of leather and horseflesh that to her was distinctly Cody, and slipped her fingers through the ragged ends of hair at his nape.

Something sharp pricked at the skin between her fingers. Shocked consciousness erupted within her brain and Shelby's eyes shot open in surprise. She sat up and looked about, hazy fragments of her dream still clinging to her mind to weave themselves into her present reality.

Frowning, she glanced down at where her hand still lay and, remembering her dream, suddenly smiled. Instead of Cody's hair, she'd been running her fingers through the blanket of pine needles that covered the ground, and the steely hard chest she'd imagined caressing was in truth a large, smooth round rock that was next to the saddlebags she'd used as a pillow. She moved to roll onto her back and sit up, but Bobby's arms around her waist stopped her.

The boy squirmed, but did not wake.

Shelby lay back down on the saddlebags and pulled the blanket over her chest. She stared up at the trees towering above her and the thin patches of pale blue sky that peeked between the thick boughs. She'd let Bobby sleep for just a while longer. He'd had a rough night, and she didn't know how long it would take to find their way back to the Double K's camp this morning.

Cody finished tying the leather thongs that held his bedroll to the back of his saddle and moved to tighten the cinch around Soldier's belly.

Jake walked up behind him. "Tom has breakfast ready."

"I'll pass." Cody jerked on the leather strap of the cinch.

"I don't think the sheriff's gonna like that."

Cody turned a puzzled and impatient eye on Jake. "What the hell does the sheriff care if I eat breakfast or not?"

"He's planning out his search while he eats. Says he wants you over there."

"Son of a . . ." Cody hooked an extra coil of rope over his saddlehorn and whirled around. "Whose lamebrain idea was it to call the sheriff in on this, anyway?"

"Yours," Jake answered smoothly, looking pointedly at Cody.

Cody brushed past him and stalked across the camp to where the sheriff was holding court around a picnic table laden with eggs, bacon, potatoes, muffins, and several pots of coffee. The sheriff and two deputies were eating heartily as they talked. The Double K's wranglers, who stood nearby, sipped at their cups of coffee and warily watched their boss charge into the small conference.

"All right, Sheriff, it's morning," Cody declared, ramming clenched fists onto his hips and glaring down at the man. "Shelby, Bobby, and Hollywood have been out there all night. And it was a damn cold night, too. Are you ready to search for them now?" His words dripped with sarcasm, but surprisingly the sheriff didn't seem to notice, though the two deputies looked up at him with obvious alarm.

The sheriff slowly wiped his mouth with a napkin and rose to his feet. He was a good five inches shorter than Cody, but at least fifty pounds heavier. "Calm yourself down, son. I'm not the one who let them get lost."

Cody's face hardened with rage, but the sheriff continued before he could respond.

"Now, my boys and I will search the southern side of the trail you folks took in here yesterday. I want several of your men to ride back an extra two miles and then fan out and return, and several more of your men to cover the northern side of the trail."

"Except for the extra two miles, we covered that whole area last night," Cody said. His patience was at the breaking point. He wanted to get going, not stand here and debate who was going to search where. He reached for a cup of coffee and took a swallow of the hot liquid, letting it embrace and warm his insides against the morning chill. "I think we need to widen our area of search. The Rothman boy must have covered more ground than we thought, and Shelby might have found something that led her to that conclusion, too, and she followed it."

The sheriff nodded. "Okay, sounds good. We'll widen out on all sides."

Jake handed Cody a plate laden with everything that was on the table. He looked at it and handed it back.

"Eat it," Jake ordered. "You didn't eat nothin' last night, and you were up until the wee hours of the morning. I don't want to have to come searchin' for you because you got light in the head and fell off your horse."

Cody gave the older man a glowering look and accepted the plate. With one hand he managed to fork a towering mass of the fluffy scrambled eggs onto a slab of toasted bread, cover it with five long strips of bacon, and top it with another slab of toasted bread. He scooped it up into his hand, shoved the plate back into Jake's hands, and started back across the camp toward where Soldier was tied.

"Satisfied, old man?" he called over his shoulder, holding up the sandwich. He swung up into the saddle.

"I ain't gonna be satisfied till you find that girl and get that burr out from under your britches," Jake mumbled as he watched Cody ride out of camp.

Cody turned toward the wranglers, who were

scurrying to their own mounts. "Jamie, you ride with me." He pointed to two of the other wranglers. "And you boys, too." He glanced back at Jake. "Take care of things here, Jake, and make sure the Rothmans don't turn hysterical on us, huh?"

Jake nodded. "We'll do all right here. You just find Shelby and the kid. Oh, and while you're at it, that Murdock fella, too."

Chapter Nineteen

Shelby made to move her arm, felt something block it, and rolled the other way. A bright ray of sunlight fell on her face. Her eyes fluttered open at the sudden warmth; she squinted, moved out of the path of the light, and looked around. Bobby was still snuggled up against her side, asleep.

She lifted her arm and pulled back the cuff of her shirt sleeve to reveal the watch on her wrist. "Eight-thirty?" She shook her head to rid her brain of the last fuzzy fragments of sleep. "Lord, we should have been up and on our way hours ago." She turned to Bobby, grasped his shoulders, and gave him a gentle shake. "Bobby? Bobby, wake up."

The boy shook off her hands and burrowed deeper into the blanket.

Shelby nudged his shoulder again. "Bobby, we have to get up." She slid away from him and scrambled to her feet.

"Ahggg." Bobby rubbed his fists against his eyes.

Shelby stretched her arms wide and took a moment to look around at the surrounding pine forest. Sunlight streamed through the trees, turning the dried needles on the ground to gold and the lush boughs of the trees to emerald. A movement behind a small bush caught her eye and she watched as a jackrabbit bounded from its hiding place and scurried across the ground to dive into another bush.

She looked back at Bobby and felt suddenly wonderful, better than she had in days. Confidence and pride swelled in her breast. She had done what none of the others had been able to do, experienced as they were. She had found Bobby. And to top that off, she'd survived a night out in the wilderness, with no more company than a child. Of course, she had to admit, it had probably been nothing more than a lucky break that had enabled her to find the boy; nevertheless, she'd found him and the others hadn't. She was going to make it at the Double K, and nothing or no one could persuade her differently now.

She quickly rolled the blankets and tied them to the saddles. "Okay, back to camp," Shelby said cheerfully, ignoring a momentary lapse of confidence in her ability to find the way. Cupping her hands, she helped Bobby mount his horse and then swung up on Lady.

She was looking forward to seeing Cody's reaction when she rode into camp. She could imagine his anger at his finding she'd ridden out to join in the search after he'd instructed—no, *ordered*—her not to. He had probably gone into a rage, and when she hadn't returned to camp last night, he'd most likely convinced himself she'd gotten lost. He'd probably determined by now that they'd find her huddled somewhere, out of her mind with fear, having gone over the brink into looney-tune land. She couldn't wait to see his face when she rode back with Bobby Rothman in tow.

Shelby smiled to herself. Cody Farlowe was in for one big surprise.

She looked at the sun, then back at the landscape, and nudged Lady. The horse broke into a smooth walk. "Amazing how much different things look in the daylight," Shelby said, smiling back at Bobby.

"Do you know how to get us back to the camp this morning, Miss Shelby?" he asked.

"I think so, but just to make sure, we're going to go up on that hill over there and get a view of the valley. If we're lucky, we'll see the smoke from the breakfast campfire and ride toward it."

"What if they already ate?"

"Then we'll find our way without it." She wished Bobby wouldn't ask questions that brought back her doubt. She was feeling good. She was confident. She knew she could do it. Couldn't she? She tried to remember her Girl

Scout training, realized how long ago that had been, and suddenly felt older than time.

They crested the top of the hill. The valley spread out below them for miles, a blanket of lush meadows broken by thickets of emerald pines and golden cottonwoods. On the valley's opposite border, a range of snow-tipped mountains created a jagged horizon against a crystalline blue sky.

Shelby felt the breath catch in her throat. It was the most beautiful, most magnificent sight she had ever witnessed.

"I don't see any smoke, Miss Shelby."

Shelby turned her attention back to the valley floor. She let her gaze move slowly, looking for the white wisps of smoke that would tell them exactly where the Double K campsite was. Long seconds later she frowned. Bobby was right, there was no smoke.

"What are we going to do?" he asked, clearly not too sure Shelby could get them back.

"Well, let's see. The sun's over there." She pointed. "And the herd's been moving away from it each morning . . . so that means they are somewhere over there." She pointed in the opposite direction. Shelby smiled. Maybe she remembered more of her Girl Scout training than she'd thought.

"We're going to ride down to the valley. Once we get there, it will be a cinch to find the herd." She turned away and urged Lady down the hill. It would have been nice to have spotted smoke from the Double K's campfire, but she wasn't going to worry about not seeing it. She'd get them back to the camp.

An hour later they still hadn't reached the valley floor. She didn't remember doing this much climbing. She reined in and looked back at Bobby. "You thirsty?" she asked, lifting the canteen toward him.

"No, but I'm hungry."

She sighed. That was the understatement of the year. They'd both missed dinner last night, and breakfast this morning, with only a candy bar apiece to tide them over. If Bobby was as hungry as she was, a roasted elephant wouldn't fill him up.

"We shouldn't have much farther to go," she said, hoping she was telling the truth. "Just a bit farther, Bobby, and we'll be back at the campsite."

Cody lifted the binoculars to his eyes and scanned the horizon. He moved his gaze first over the valley floor, then let it rise to the small hills just below and to his left, but the thick growth of trees prevented his spotting anyone. He couldn't even see the other searchers, let alone Shelby, Bobby, or that fool actor. His jaw clenched. Every time he thought of Lance Murdock, anger and jealousy warmed his blood. The man was not only a fool, he was a conceited, pompous, egotistical fool. Taking off alone on a search in countryside he was totally unfamiliar with had been an utterly stupid move.

Of course, Shelby had done exactly the same thing, but Cody couldn't quite make himself think of her as a fool. Instead he categorized her as a stubborn, unrealistic troublemaker who refused to give up when she was beaten. This was exactly the type of thing he'd been afraid would happen if she stayed around the Double K. City women always found a way to get themselves into trouble. Maybe not on purpose, but they managed to get there all the same.

He shoved the binoculars back into his saddlebag, cursed softly under his breath, and urged Soldier back down the sloping bank of the hill. "Come on, Soldier. She's out here somewhere and we've got to find her."

He turned the horse north, away from the valley, away from the camp and the other searchers. He'd head farther up into the hill country. He looked up at the sky. The sun was directly overhead, its blistering rays beating down on the earth mercilessly. Noon. They'd been searching now for more than five hours, and still nothing. No one had spotted a thing.

A horse whinnied in the distance.

Cody reined in and cocked an ear toward the sound. He waited, nearly holding his breath, for the sound to come again.

Long seconds later, the horse whinnied again. Cody jerked Soldier's reins to his left and urged the big horse down the steep bank of hillside toward where he thought the sound had originated. The trees grew thickly in this area, their branches intertwining and blocking out the sun to leave the thicket in deep shadow.

"Help! Someone help me!"

The voice was weak, faint and pleading.

Cody spurred Soldier to more speed. He raised an arm in front of his face to ward off the pine branches that loomed in his way as the horse hurried through the forest. He missed one protruding limb and it slapped against his rib cage, nearly knocking him from the saddle and the air from his lungs.

Several yards farther into the copse, he saw a horse standing in the shadows, its saddle askew, almost sideways. The animal looked up at Cody as he approached, and whinnied.

Disappointment welled in Cody's chest and left an empty feeling in the pit of his stomach. It wasn't Shelby's mount. He swung from the saddle and slowly approached the horse, which seemed skittish and ready to bolt.

"Hold on there, boy," he said softly, moving steadily but cautiously forward, his arms outstretched on either side of him. "Easy does it, Samson," Cody continued, recognizing the gelding. "Relax, now. Come on, boy."

"Help! Is someone up there?"

Cody spun around, looking for the body that went with the voice and seeing no one. Hollywood! He'd recognize that voice anywhere. He

246

grabbed Samson's reins and wrapped them loosely around a nearby pine limb. "Where the hell are you, Hollywood?" he yelled.

"Down here."

Cody looked around, puzzled. "Where the hell's *down here?*"

"In the ditch . . . ravine . . . gully . . . whatever you call the damn things," Lance answered, his weak tone now also tinged with exasperation.

Cody quickly scanned the nearby surroundings. He didn't see a gully. "It would help if it were lighter in here," he mumbled. He stepped around a tall, sprawling bush. His outstretched foot met nothing but thin air, and his body began to sway forward. He flailed the air with his arms, struggling to maintain his balance and shift his weight backward. He landed on his rear with a thump on top of the bush that had prevented his view of the gully.

"Son of a . . ." He got to his feet, muttering a string of curses that could turn the air blue, and brushed himself off. Broken thorns and twigs flew from his shirt and pants.

"Cody?" Lance called.

"Yeah, I'm here. Keep your pants on."

"I . . . I think my leg's broken."

"Oh, great, that'll help lots trying to get you the hell out of there." Cody walked over to Soldier and took the coiled rope from his saddle horn and a flashlight from his saddlebag. He tucked the flashlight under his arm and, unlooping the rope, tied one end to the horn and ordered Soldier to stay put. He held the other end of the rope in his gloved hand and returned to the edge of the gully, flicking the flashlight on and pointing it down inside the ravine.

Lance lay in a crumpled heap almost directly below him.

"How in the name of blazes did you get down there?"

Lance looked up and scowled. "That damn horse stopped when he was supposed to jump. Unfortunately I didn't."

Cody lowered himself into the ravine and hunkered down beside Lance. His right leg was twisted at an odd angle beneath his left. "I'm going to have to straighten that leg out so we can make a splint for it. Only way to get you out of here."

"So do it," Lance snapped.

"It's going to hurt."

"Can't hurt any worse than it already does."

Within minutes Cody had climbed back up the ledge, retrieved two dried branches to use as splints, and a roll of gauze bandage from his saddlebag. He lay them out beside Lance and then prepared to straighten the man's leg. "You ready?"

"Yes."

Cody gripped Lance's calf with one hand and his ankle with the other. "Sorry I don't have a piece of leather for you to bite down on," Cody said, trying to divert Lance's attention from what was about to happen. "How about a bullet? I can get one out of my rifle."

"Very funny."

Cody straightened Lance's leg in one swift move.

"Aghhh, jeez almighty," Lance screamed, his face contorted in agony. Sweat covered his brow.

"You okay?" Cody asked. He pressed the branches up against either side of Lance's leg and began to wind the gauze around them.

"I've been better," Lance gasped. "Have you found Shelby and the boy yet?"

Cody's face hardened. "No."

"Guess I wasn't much help, huh?"

"You tried."

Lance stared at Cody, surprised. He'd expected the man to break out in a rage, to yell and declare him a fool. He hadn't expected any kind of acknowledgment of his effort to assist in the search.

Cody stood, then bent down, grabbed Lance under the arms, and hoisted him to his feet. "All right, I'm going to tie this rope under your arms. Soldier will back up when I tell him and pull you up. I'll hold your leg from down here as long as I can to keep you from bumping into the side of the gully."

Lance nodded.

"When you get up there, take off the rope and throw it back down so I can get out."

Minutes later, Cody struggled up the side of the ravine, recoiled the rope, and returned it to

249

his saddle. He straightened the saddle on Lance's horse and helped him to mount.

"You going to be okay?"

"I'll make it," Lance said, his face twisted in pain. Getting up onto the saddle and swinging his broken leg over the horse's rump had been sheer torture. He'd thought about riding with both legs on one side, sidesaddle, but figured that would be worse. If he lost his balance and fell, he'd probably end up with two broken legs.

"All right, let's go." Cody swung up onto Soldier's back and grabbed the reins of Lance's horse. The two men started out of the forest and back toward the valley and the Double K camp.

Halfway back, Lance called to Cody. "Listen, I can make it on my own from here. You go on and find Shelby."

"I'll see you back first."

"I can make it," Lance argued.

Cody reined in and turned to look at him. The man had more grit than he'd given him credit for, but that didn't lighten Cody's mood any. He wouldn't feel good again until he'd found Shelby. "You're a guest at the Double K, Hollywood, and it's my responsibility to see that you don't get hurt any more than you already have been." He turned back in his saddle and touched his legs to Soldier's side. "And I'll find Shelby."

Twenty minutes later they rode into camp. Jake was the first to spot them and came running. "What the hell happened?" he called out, noticing Lance's leg.

"Broken," Cody said simply.

"I can see that." The men helped Lance dismount and move to sit at one of the tables. "You want Tom to drive him down to the doc's in town?"

"No," Lance interrupted. "I'm staying until I know Shelby's safe."

Jake looked quickly at Cody, but the younger man refused to meet his gaze. A small muscle in Cody's jaw twitched, the only physical sign that the actor's words had bothered him.

"I'll get you some grub," Jake said, and hurried toward the barbecue pit. He returned minutes later and handed Lance a plate piled high with chili, green salad, and steak. "Where'd Cody get to?"

"Over there, by the horses," Lance said. He plunged into the food like a man on the verge of starvation.

Jake walked up to Cody, who was preparing to mount. "Here, eat something before you go back out," he said, holding out a plate of food.

"I'll eat later." Cody slipped his booted foot into the stirrup and swung himself up from the ground. "Always trying to force food down my throat when I've got better things to do," he mumbled.

Suddenly the entire camp erupted in a cacophony of shouts and screams.

Chapter Twenty

Ruth Rothman ran forward. "Bobby! Bobby! Oh, my baby, you're okay." Hank Rothman was right on his wife's heels.

Cody dropped back to the ground and spun around.

Jake shook his head, and a trace of a smile tugged at his lips. "Well, I'll be damned. She did it."

Shelby's smile was radiant as she and Bobby rode into camp and heard the cheers and shouts of the guests. She felt a wave of relief at having finally found the camp, and an incredible weariness. She was near exhaustion from the intense fear she'd experienced during the night, the lack of sleep and food, and her worry all morning of whether she'd really be able to get them back to the camp.

Jake moved toward her and she waved at him, then her gaze slid past the old wrangler to where Cody stood, staring at her. He looked so good. She wanted to slide off of her horse and run to him, throw herself into his arms and feel the security of his embrace, his warmth, and his strength.

Ruth Rothman pulled her son from the saddle and wrapped him in her arms, tears of joy and relief streaming from her eyes. Hank Rothman moved to stand beside the still-mounted Shelby. He reached up and took her hand in his. "Thank you, Miss Hill. I don't know what else to say. Thank you."

She saw the tears glimmering in his eyes and felt a knot in her throat. "He's a brave little boy, Mr. Rothman. You can be proud of him."

The man nodded and went back to join his wife and son, who were walking toward their tent.

Shelby slid from Lady's back.

"You did good, Shelby," Jake said, smiling. "I'm right proud of you."

"Thanks, Jake, but I—"

"Just what the hell did you think you were doing, riding out after I told you not to?" Cody thundered.

Shelby and Jake both jumped and turned at the angry question, which sounded more like an accusation. Cody stood only two feet away from them, his eyes spitting fire, his jaw clenched in his fury. His stance was one of total rage.

For one brief moment she wanted to find a hole and crawl into it, to hide from his wrath, then her newfound self-confidence resurfaced. She drew herself up, stiffening her spine and throwing back her shoulders, and stared him straight in the eye. "I wanted to help find Bobby."

"It was a fool thing to do, Shelby. A damn fool thing. Do you know all the things that could have happened to you out there?"

"Nothing happened."

"Nothing?" he roared, and his tone made her wince. "Instead of looking for one lost kid, we had to look for two. No, make that three."

Shelby's defiant expression turned to one of confusion.

"Hollywood followed you and got lost," Jake said softly, leaning over her shoulder to speak close to her ear.

"Lance? Is he all right?"

"No, he's not all right," Cody said. "He managed to fall off his horse and break his leg. Lucky it wasn't his fool neck."

"Cody, I . . ."

"Go home, Shelby," he said, his voice a deep, cold growl. "Go home where you belong." He turned abruptly and strode across the camp.

Shelby watched him, dumbstruck, as he mounted Soldier and rode out of the camp without a backward glance, his hat pulled low over his forehead, his back stiff, shoulders taut.

She looked back at Jake. "Well, I certainly feel better knowing how glad he is that I got back."

Jake chuckled and scratched at his whiskery chin. "Missy, don't be too hard on him. That

254

boy's got a war going on inside him, and he ain't figured out which side he's rooting for, that's all."

Shelby frowned, not understanding Jake's words.

"You'd better go on and see that Hollywood fella. He refused to go on into town to let the doc tend to his leg until they found you."

Shelby hurried toward the picnic tables where Jake had pointed. She saw Lance stretched out on a bench, his eyes closed. "Lance?" she whispered, bending down beside him. "Lance, are you okay?"

His eyes fluttered open. "Shelby." He sat up quickly and grimaced.

"Lance, you've got to let Tom or the sheriff take you to town to see the doctor. I don't want your leg to set wrong, and I'm sure you don't, either."

"I just wanted to make sure you were all right."

She smiled. "Thank you, I'm fine, but now we have to see to you."

Just then two shots rang out, echoing loudly within the forested landscape. Shelby turned to stare into the dense forest.

"Damn, my head could have done without that," Lance said, lifting a hand to his temple.

"They're letting the other searchers know we've been found," Shelby said, repeating what Jake had told her earlier about the procedure they'd agreed on at the start of the search.

255

"Your foreman was pretty mad that I went out on my own to look for you."

"He wasn't exactly thrilled that I went out to search for Bobby Rothman, either."

Lance reached out and took Shelby's hand. His thumb gently caressed the ridge of her knuckles. "Ride into town with me, beautiful?"

Touched by his sweetness and show of concern, Shelby placed her other hand on top of his. "I can't, Lance. We've already lost time getting the herd to the ridge, and I've got to get the other guests back to the ranch. I hope they won't ask for their money back, though I wouldn't blame the Rothmans any if they did."

"Are you kidding?" he said, smiling for the first time in hours. "This is the most excitement any of them have probably ever had. They loved it." He paused. "Well, maybe the Rothmans didn't, but it all turned out okay." He lifted her hand to his lips and kissed it. "I was worried about you, beautiful," he said softly, his tone changing to one of tender intimacy.

Shelby felt her cheeks warm, but her heart didn't flutter, her chest didn't get tight, her pulse didn't race, and desire failed to coil hotly within her. She rose to her feet, still holding his hand, and looked down at him for a long moment. She felt a niggling of regret. The man who sent her senses reeling off course appeared to want nothing more than for her to go away, and for the man who seemed anxious to get her into his life, albeit temporarily, she could muster

256

nothing more than compassion and friendship.

Not knowing what to say, she pulled her hands from Lance's grasp and turned toward Tom, who was standing with a few wranglers near the barbecue pit. "Tom, I want you to drive Lance into town and see that the doctor fixes up his leg. Have them send the bill to the Double K."

"Yes, ma'am," Tom answered, hurrying toward the chuck truck.

Lance struggled to his feet. "You sure I can't change your mind?" he asked.

She turned and looked back at him. He was talking about more than riding to town with him in the truck, she knew that, but it didn't matter. She'd given her heart to a man who didn't want it, and now she had to find a way to get it back, but going with Lance Murdock wasn't the answer.

The moment they broke from the pine forest and entered the flat, green meadow, Cody gave Soldier his head and let the horse run flat out. He felt the wind on his face and the sun on his back and exulted in both. His body moved gracefully, fluidly blending with the motion of his mount. Horse and rider were one.

A startled deer, grazing on the tall meadow grasses, sprinted out of their path, and Soldier swerved slightly to avoid the fleeing animal, but didn't slow his pace until they entered a copse of cottonwoods. They wove their way through the golden trees, swerving around the thin trunks, dodging under the spindly limbs, until they once again broke into the sunlight and found themselves in yet another wide meadow.

They traveled for more than an hour without stopping, then Cody tugged gently on the reins and took control of Soldier's pace and direction. They headed upward, toward the mountains, climbing ever higher, leaving the valley floor and the meadows behind.

By the time evening approached, Cody and Soldier had traveled farther and faster than they ever had in one day. But the image of Shelby Hill still would not fade from Cody's mind, nor would the longing for her that lived in his heart and warmed his blood.

Night crept over the land, seeping into the crevices of the forests, engulfing the meadows and rolling hills, devouring the warmth of the afternoon and enveloping the earth in a blanket of cool darkness. With the passing of day many of the land's creatures returned to their burrows, nests, and dens, while still others, the night animals such as the owl, coyote, and wolf, woke from their sleep to venture out to hunt and roam. Their sounds echoed in the canyons and woods, wafted for miles on the soft night air, and clung to the mountainous terrain they called home.

Cody threw a few more dry tree branches onto the fire he'd built earlier, laced his fingers

258

behind his head, and lay back on his saddle. He stared up at the sky, and let his thoughts drift back over the events of the past day and night. He'd been worried sick over Shelby when she had been missing, scared that something terrible had happened to her. For those long hours, nothing else had mattered to him, not the fact that a little boy was also missing, not the fact that another adult guest was missing, only that Shelby was out there alone, on her own, at night, and most likely frightened to death. He'd played that scene over and over in his mind, until he'd become almost crazy with worry, driving himself to search for her long hours after his body ached with exhaustion and pleaded with him to stop.

When she'd ridden into camp unhurt, proud of the way she had found the lost child and survived the night in the wilds, he'd felt such relief, such overwhelming thankfulness, that it had rendered him nearly faint. All night he'd been so afraid for her, so frightened that when they finally found her she would be hurt, or out of her head from fear, or worse. Never once had he considered the possibility that she could handle the situation, and that's what had driven him to anger. All this time he'd been wrong about her. She was more like Katie than he had been willing to see and admit. Maybe Katie Hill-Randall had been a little more country in her heart, growing up adoring cowboy movies and horses, while Shelby hadn't. Maybe Katie had purposely sought out this type of life, while Shelby had had it thrust on her. But now Cody saw that the two sisters had the same kind of grit, the same courage, smarts, and stubbornness it took to operate a place like the Double K.

Still he wasn't convinced that Shelby would stay. That she *could* do it, yes, but willingly stay here and build her life around the ranch, no.

Even if she did stay, what difference did that make to him? There was still no life together for them, no hope of a lasting relationship. And maybe that was the real reason he kept running away from her. She was his employer, the owner of the Double K, one of the most well-known and prosperous dude ranches in the country, and she was financially worlds beyond him. He had experienced what it felt like to live with a woman whose bank balance had almost as many digits as he had fingers. He'd felt like a kept man. Cheap. Bought and paid for. During his time in New York with Lisa he had lost his self-respect, and he had almost lost himself. He wouldn't go through that again. He couldn't go through that again, not for anyone.

He stared up at the black sky, an endless shroud that enveloped the earth each night, wrapping it in slumber. It was a beautiful time, he thought, his favorite time, a time when he could rest and forget the trials of the real world or the trivial problems of his day.

Suddenly a shooting star sped across that ebony sky, a tiny but radiant streak of fire that passed over the earth in an arcing trail. From Cody's prone position on the ground, he watched it flash overhead, admiring the brilliance and simple beauty of the sight. Just before the streaming, fiery star disappeared from sight, he did something he hadn't done in years: he made a wish.

Several miles away, Shelby sat at one of the picnic tables, having a warm glass of milk. She hadn't been able to turn off her churning thoughts, hadn't been able to douse the longing for Cody that ate at her insides. The comfort and dark, warm nothingness of sleep had eluded her, leaving her tossing and turning on her bedroll long after the other guests and wranglers had retreated to their own bedrolls and closed their eyes for the night.

Finally, resigning herself to the fact that sleep was not going to come without a little help, she'd resorted to the one remedy that usually worked when something kept her awake. She'd slipped into her clothes, pulled on her boots, which, after Cody's tale of creepy-crawly things looking for a home, she had started to keep *inside* her bedroll when she slept, and stole from her tent to the chuck truck. After getting the milk, freezing cold from being kept in a cooler filled with ice, she'd poured it into a pan and set it on the still-simmering fire of the barbecue pit.

Minutes later, having started to enjoy the quiet of the slumbering campsite, Shelby sipped the milk slowly, but the comforting, relaxing feeling it normally gave her did not come. Instead she sat staring up at the sky, wide awake, thoughts of Cody filling her mind and her heart. What had gone wrong between them? Why had he changed so abruptly from the warm, caring, sensitive man who had made love to her, to the cold, hard person who acted as though he wanted nothing more than to rid himself of the sight of her? What had she done, or said, in those few hours between night and day that had caused him to change?

Shelby threw that last thought aside with more than a touch of anger. She hadn't done anything—that's what was so confusing. If she'd said something or done something, she could understand his attitude, the change in him, but she hadn't. She was certain of that now. She'd thought over every conversation, every interaction she'd had with him since they'd made love, and each time she came to the same conclusion: she had neither done nor said anything that would have caused such a drastic transformation.

Shelby took a sip of her milk and stared up at the dark, endless sky. It was so beautiful, and seemed near enough to reach out and touch. It was totally different from what she'd always seen while living in the city. Here, in the open countryside, the sky was a deep black, not the sickly grayish black that blanketed the never-sleeping cities she'd lived in. And the stars were brilliant, shimmering sparks of light rather than simply dull little spots of weak illumination.

Suddenly a shooting star streaked across that ebony canopy, tails of radiant yellow-white flame trailing behind it as it shot across the sky in a wide arc, speeding toward its destiny, toward its eventual death.

Shelby watched it pass overhead, mesmerized by the majesty of such a simple sight, by its pure beauty. She watched the trails of fire that the star left behind sputter and dissipate as the flying ball of flame continued on its way through the night, and just before it disappeared into the blackness beyond her vision, she did something she hadn't done in years: she made a wish.

Chapter Twenty-one

"Time to get moving," Jake announced.

Shelby scooped up the last piece of syrup-soaked pancake from her plate and popped it into her mouth, then hurriedly rose. She moved away from the others who'd been crowded around the picnic table and placed her plate and utensils in the plastic bucket Tom had set out for dirty dishes. Approaching Jake, she lowered her voice and asked, "Did Cody ever return?"

The older man looked slightly uncomfortable, and just a bit put out. He shook his head. "No, and don't think he's not going to get a piece of my mind when he does."

"You don't think anything's happened to him?"

"Nothing that a good, old-fashioned kick in the—" Jake looked suddenly sheepish and clamped his jaws shut.

Shelby laughed. "You may be right," she said, though she wasn't so sure that the solution to Cody's problem was quite that easy.

"You ready to head out?"

She nodded and began to walk beside him toward the horses. "I'm almost sorry to see the drive end. I never knew how much I could enjoy the open countryside."

"There'll be other times," Jake said, knowing his words were true. He glanced at Shelby out of the corner of his eye. She would stay, he was certain of it, and if Cody would start using the smarts the Almighty gave him, he'd stop acting like such a damn fool.

"What's our agenda for today?" Shelby asked, forcing herself to sound and act light-hearted.

"We'll stop for lunch at Shadow Landing—that's about a mile past where we'll leave the herd. Tom will be there with the truck and we'll have us a little party to celebrate the end of the drive. Katie always did that. Guests really seem to eat it up, you know?"

"Sounds great. Let's go." She swung up onto Lady's back and looked around at the campsite. Tents and bedrolls had been packed away before breakfast. Now all the guests were attending to any last-minute necessities or mounting their horses, and Tom and his assistant were seeing to the clearing and cleaning of the campsite.

"Okay, folks, let's go," Jake called loudly, waving his arm over his head.

The morning passed quickly, too quickly for Shelby. She had begun to relish the adventure of the drive, the beauty of the countryside, and the uniqueness of her new life. She had only one regret: that she couldn't share her newly discovered feelings with Katie, that she couldn't turn to her sister and say, *You were right, Sis. This is the life. This is where I belong.* She couldn't do that, but she could live her life on the Double K and keep it running. She had hoped, deep down in her heart, that Cody would be there to share that life with her, but it looked as if that had been an inane hope, a foolish wish.

She was on her own, as she'd always been, but that was okay, too. Cody had shown her what real love was, let her feel and experience it, and though her heart cried at its loss, she cherished the memory. Someday, maybe, another man would come into her life and offer her love, but somehow, even as the thought entered her mind, Shelby shrugged it aside, rejecting it. There would never be another Cody Farlowe. He had stolen her heart, her entire heart, as surely as if he'd reached in and taken it physically from her, and she knew she would never get it back. It was his forever, and she'd just have to learn to live with that.

By the time the sun was high in the sky, blazing down relentlessly on the sprawling Montana countryside, they were approaching the last curve in the landscape before reaching their final destination.

Jake rode up beside her. "This is it, Shelby. We're here."

They rounded a small hill and the western ridge came into view. Shelby's breath caught in her throat as she took in the magnificent scene before her. It was a sight right out of a magazine or oil portrait, yet the colors were even more vivid, more alive.

She turned to Jake, puzzled. "I thought we were taking the herd to a ridge. This is another valley."

Jake smiled and shook his head. "Yep. The western ridge, that's what it's called. 'Cause of those mountains over there." He pointed to the opposite end of the valley.

She looked back out at the scene before her. On the far border of the valley a range of mountains rose in the distance, majestic, their ragged peaks covered with streaks of pure white snow. Gray rock gave way to a thick, emerald green quilt of pines growing at the base of the mountains, which in turn gave way to golden cottonwoods, which in turn became acres and acres of lush, green meadow, where rich, succulent-looking grasses grew knee-high in a plush carpet.

"It's beautiful."

"Yeah, well, the cattle don't care none what it looks like, just so's it gets them through the winter. Sometimes if the weather gets too bad we truck bales of hay up here to 'em or bring 'em down closer to the ranch. Especially the young'uns."

"I never knew there was such beauty out here. Katie told me she always wanted me to come up here and stay, but I just couldn't see it." Tears filled her eyes, and her voice broke as she continued. "I wish I could have . . . I wish . . ."

"She knows, missy, she knows," Jake said, reaching over and patting her hand. He leaned back in his saddle. "You know, Katie used to sit and talk to me sometimes out on the porch after the young'uns went to sleep and Ken was doing the books. She always said if she could ever get you up here for a while, that she knew you'd stay." She'd also told Jake that she thought Cody Farlowe was the perfect man for her sister, but Jake wasn't about to tell Shelby that, especially with Cody running around out there, Lord knows where, acting like a young fool.

"Did she really, Jake?" Shelby asked, looking at him hopefully.

The old man nodded. "Yep, she did, and now you're here. Katie knows, missy. Don't you make no mistake about that. She knows you're here, and she knows you done good."

Tears coursed down Shelby's cheeks. She leaned across the space that separated their two

268

horses and pressed her lips to Jake's leathery, line-creased, bewhiskered cheek. "Thank you, Jake," she whispered.

"Ah, hell," the old man said, waving her away. "Go on, now. Ain't nothing to thank me for. You done all this yourself, missy. You coulda just tacked a For Sale sign on the entry gate and toodled back to L.A. or wherever in that flashy little car of yours. But you didn't. You stayed. And what's more, you dug in and started doing for yourself, learning our ways. Maria told me how you helped out in the kitchen the first few days you was here. You didn't have to do that, and lotsa women wouldn't have. And Bonnie told me you two already took an inventory of the general store."

"Well, yes, but—"

"But nothing," Jake interrupted. "Shelby, stop beating up on yourself. You didn't have to come on this drive. It's a hard ride, and most likely more work than fun. But you came, and if it wasn't for you, that little kid might have had to spend the night out in the woods all by his lonesome, 'cause we sure as hell didn't find him. You did."

"Yes, but—"

"No more buts. You made it this far on your own, missy. You don't have to thank me for that. *You* did it, Shelby." He pointed a finger at her. "You."

Shelby felt a sudden surge of self-confidence.

It swept over her like a tidal wave, filling her with energy. Her tears dried and she smiled. "You're right, Jake," she said, laughing. "I did do it, didn't I?"

"Damn right."

"Then what are we waiting for? Let's party!" She nudged Lady's sides and urged the mare toward the two trucks in the distance, their red-painted bodies like beacons on the opposite side of the wide meadow.

When she and Jake rode into camp, Shelby's jaw almost dropped open in delightful surprise. Tom and his assistant had really outdone themselves. Paper streamers of white and red were looped about the trees, trailing from branch to branch, bush to bush. Balloons of every color imaginable hung from the streamers and were tacked in huge bouquets to tree trunks. The hot tub was set up and bubbling, a row of balloons attached to its outside rim. There was even a wading pool for the children. Bottles of champagne, wine, beer, and sparkling waters sat perched in huge buckets of ice, and on the barbecue several huge roasts were rotating slowly over the grill, sending off such inviting aromas that Shelby's mouth immediately began to water, and she wasn't even hungry!

Behind her the guests began to whoop and holler and spur their horses toward the campsite.

"Now, this is what I call a campsite," Eva

Montalvo said, moving her horse up beside Shelby's. She winked at Jamie as he continued on, then turned to Shelby. "Cute, isn't he?"

Shelby smiled.

"Oh, I know what you're thinking. You're afraid I'm going to try to steal one of your wranglers, right?" She went on before Shelby could answer. "Well, relax, honey, he's all yours. Not that I didn't try, mind you, but he's a country boy and I'm a city girl, and that just isn't a good match. This is a great place to visit, but heavens, I could never live here. And Jamie, poor man, could never adjust to the city. It'd eat him up."

Shelby stared at Eva, the woman's words echoing in her mind, pounding at her. Was that what had been eating at Cody? That she was from the city?

Eva urged her horse forward and waved at Shelby. "See you later, sweets," she called, catching up to Jamie.

Why hadn't she realized that was why Cody had backed away from her, why he'd changed so? He believed she couldn't adjust to life on the ranch, that she wouldn't stay. Isn't that what he'd constantly been telling her? Every time something happened, every time he'd had to rescue her, he'd told her to go back to where she belonged, and even though she had no intention of leaving, of returning to the city life, Cody refused to believe that. Country and city don't mix. Isn't that what Eva had said?

Deep in thought, Shelby moved Lady in among the other horses, tethered near the side of the campsite, and slid from the saddle. The other woman in Cody's life, the one Jake had told her about, had been from the city. She'd refused to live in Montana, and Cody had gone to the city, but the relationship hadn't worked. Shelby felt a pull at her heart. Maybe Cody had been terribly hurt, she thought. But what did it matter that she'd figured it out? She could go to Cody, tell him that he could trust her not to leave, that she'd fallen almost as much in love with Montana, with his homeland and the ranch, as she had with him. But it wouldn't do any good; she knew that in the same moment she had the idea. Cody was not a man who could be convinced by mere words. Shelby wondered how long it would take to convince him with actions.

She walked over to a bench that had been set in the shadow of the trees bordering the clearing and sat down. Somehow she had to figure out how she was going to convince Cody Farlowe that she had absolutely no intention of going anywhere and, most important of all, that they belonged together.

On a hill overlooking the campsite, Cody sat on a tree stump and lifted the binoculars to his eyes. He could see everything from this vantage point, the streamers and balloons Tom had draped from the trees, the decorated hot tub and wading pool, the buckets of drinks, and the food cooking on the barbecue. He moved the binoculars over the area, looking for Shelby. He saw Jamie and Eva, and wondered briefly if he was going to lose one of his best wranglers to an infatuation and the big city. Bobby Rothman ran across the camp, streaking through Cody's view, and directly behind him ran the other children, all making a beeline for the wading pool.

A billowing cloud of dust rising from the ground in the distance beyond the campsite, beyond the surrounding trees, drew his attention. He lifted the binoculars slightly to get a better view, and adjusted them to the longer range of sight. A truck was barreling across the landscape, approaching the campsite, but it wasn't a vehicle from the ranch.

Cody lowered the glasses and frowned. Who could be coming out to the campsite now, when in a few hours everyone would be back at the ranch? He raised the glasses to his eyes again and brought the truck into focus. He made out the color—blue. The cab had a white roof, and there was some kind of insignia, painted in white, on the door. Doc's truck!

He felt a moment of panic. His heart beat madly, accelerated by the fear that filled his veins. Something had happened. Someone was hurt, and it must be bad if they'd sent for the doctor rather than going into town. Cody turned back toward the campsite, straining through the glasses to see everything, to identify everyone, to find Shelby.

People were everywhere, laughing, popping bottles of champagne and dousing all within arm's reach with the white, foaming spray. Even the Double K wranglers had joined the festivities. Music was obviously playing because Cody could see several couples dancing, bounding around the center of the campsite in a square dance.

A frown pulled at his brow. No one seemed alarmed, yet something *must* have happened. *Where the hell is she?* he thought, the words echoing endlessly in his mind. *Where is she?*

Then he saw her, sitting alone in the shadow of the trees. She had one foot propped on the bench, her arms wrapped securely around her bent knee and her chin resting on top of her folded arms. Where everyone else was laughing and having a good time, Shelby looked lost. Cody's heart somersaulted within his chest and did a nosedive into the pit of his stomach. Is this what he'd done to her? Taken away the spark that had made her so special, so alive?

His first impulse was to jump on Soldier and race down to the camp, to drag Shelby into his arms and promise to make everything all right again, to protect her from all the hurt and worries of the world. But he didn't move. What he could offer her would never be enough. He knew that, cursed that, but it wouldn't, couldn't change. No matter how much he wanted to make a life with Shelby, to love her, he knew it was impossible.

Chapter Twenty-two

The truck pulled up alongside the campsite and the passenger door swung open. With some degree of difficulty Lance climbed down from the cab. A cast covered his leg from just below the knee to his exposed bare toes.

"Son, at the rate you're going, you're going to fall and break the other leg," Jake said, moving up behind Lance. He looked up at the driver of the truck. "Hey, thanks for bringing him back out, Doc. Wouldn't want one of our guests missing the party." After sharing a few more words with the town's only doctor, Jake helped Lance hobble into the campsite.

"Where's Shelby?" Lance asked.

"Hey, look, everyone. Lance is back," someone shouted.

Suddenly all the guests swarmed around him, steering him toward one of the food-laden tables as he was pummeled with questions about whether he was all right and how long he'd have to be off his television show. The redhead who'd had her eye on Lance since the beginning of the drive seemed only interested in who was going to take care of him once he returned home.

Half an hour later, Lance finally managed to extricate himself from the group, promising to return shortly, and hobbled away in search of Shelby. He found her sitting on the bench, still deep in thought, almost oblivious to her surroundings and the gay festivities.

He sat down next to her and bent to catch her lowered gaze. "Hey, beautiful, where are you?" he asked softly, reaching out and catching her fingers in his.

"Lance! What are you doing here? Your leg?" She looked down.

Lance lifted his leg, showing off the thick, white cast. "All set, see? Want to autograph it? Everyone else has."

"I can see that. And what's this?" she asked, pointing to the bright red imprint of a set of lips.

"Would you believe me if I said a secret admirer?"

"Out here?" She laughed. "Not quite, Romeo."

"Uh-oh, I guess I blew it, huh?" He tried to look crushed, but even with his acting talent, it didn't work.

Shelby suddenly became serious, and her tone softened. "If I'd met you when I lived in California, Lance, things might have been different, but now . . ."

"Yeah, I know. Now there's Cody."

She looked up, surprised that her feelings for Cody were that evident.

Lance chuckled. "Much as we rankle the hell out of each other and I hate to say it, Cody's a good guy, Shelby. Probably better than me."

"Lance . . ."

He caressed the fingers he still held in his. "No, really. Hollywood's no place for a relationship, at least not one that you want to last. And actors are a hell of a gamble." He leaned over and pressed his lips to hers. "Have a good life, Shelby. You deserve it."

"Thank you, Lance."

He smiled widely, his eyes lighting with mischief. "But for now you're still a single babe and there's a party going on. Come have a drink with me. Toast what might have been?"

From his vantage point high above the Double K's campsite, Cody watched Lance exit the truck and, leaning on Jake for support and balance, hobble down into the crowd of guests. He breathed a sigh of relief as he saw everyone swarm around the actor, everyone except Shelby. She didn't move from her position on the bench at the far side of the campsite.

But half an hour later, Cody had to hold

278

himself in check to keep from charging down the hillside. He held his breath as he watched Lance Murdock rise from his seat and walk toward Shelby.

"No," he whispered, unaware he was even doing it. "Don't go near her. Damn it, no. Just turn away, Murdock. Go the other way."

Lance sat down next to Shelby and reached out for her hand.

"Son of a . . ." Cody cursed, but he couldn't stop himself from watching, couldn't force himself to lower the binoculars and look away.

He tortured himself, keeping his eyes riveted on her, his heart dying a little each time she smiled at the actor, laughed with him, or let his hand caress hers. He sensed their moods change, saw their laughter die as Lance's face turned serious, and held his breath as he watched Shelby's mouth move in answer to the actor's comment. But he couldn't read the movement of their lips, and he couldn't hear her words.

Suddenly Lance bent forward and pressed his lips to Shelby's, and Cody's blood pressure skyrocketed. His fingers ached to encircle the man's throat and send him into the next world.

Jumping to his feet, he stalked to where Soldier stood, jammed the binoculars into his saddlebag, and swung up onto the large gelding's back. "All right, boy, take us home," he urged, turning Soldier away from the group below and pointing him toward the ranch. He was consumed with jealousy, and he had no right to be. He'd made his decision earlier that day, and sitting there watching her was only prolonging the inevitable, only torturing himself. The sooner he got on with his plans, the better off they'd be.

The Double K group rode through the gates that led to the main ranch house just a few minutes before dusk settled over the land. They were a weary gathering, guests and wranglers alike, and rode quietly, almost no one talking. The wranglers were tired from the double duty of overseeing the movement of the herd and making sure the guests remained safe and had a good time, while the guests themselves had held up well on the four-day drive. Even the Rothmans had forgotten about the scary episode with their son and enjoyed the day. The entire group had partied hard all afternoon in celebration of their success, and now exhaustion was ready to overtake each and every one of them, including Shelby.

Maria had a huge dinner prepared and waiting on the rough-hewn pine buffet tables in the dining room, and it was almost more than some could do to drag themselves into the room and fill up their plates. Some didn't make it, going straight to their beds, instead.

The wranglers retreated to the brick-and-log

280

kitchen, and Shelby followed the guests into the spacious dining room. It was one of her favorite rooms of the main house. The walls were of rough logs fitted together, the floors were hardwood covered with colorful scatter rugs in Indian prints, and a wide bay window offered a view of the pastures to the rear of the house and the open countryside and mountains beyond.

Eva Montalvo sat down next to her, and the man Shelby had noticed beside her on the day they'd started the drive took the seat next to Eva.

"Shelby, that was the best time I think I've ever had on a vacation. I'll be back, you can count on that." She winked conspiratorially, and Shelby had no doubts about what the gesture meant.

"I hope I can stay home next time," the man said.

Eva chuckled. "Ralph's my accountant and a good friend, but he doesn't appreciate the Old West," she told Shelby. "He only came to keep me company, even though I warned him I didn't need it."

Shelby smiled at the understatement.

"So, where's that handsome foreman of yours?" she asked. "We're leaving in the morning and I wanted to say goodbye to him."

"Oh, uh, he had some ranch business to attend to," Shelby lied. Every time someone brought up Cody's name, she felt a painful ache in her heart, followed by intense emptiness. "He'll probably be around first thing tomorrow. Maybe you'll see him at breakfast."

"Okay, kiddo. Well, thanks for a great time. I'm heading for my bungalow. Soaking in a tubful of hot water and lilac is something my body has been looking forward to now for days." She laughed fully, a loud laugh that filled the room, then she rose and moved toward the door.

A few minutes later, the dining room was nearly empty. Shelby got to her feet and made her way into the kitchen. Maria was busy at the sink. Jake was sitting at the table, staring down into a steaming cup of coffee. Rumor had it that Jake was sweet on Maria. Shelby slipped onto the bench opposite him and folded her arms on top of the table.

"Has Cody returned to the bunkhouse, Jake?"

The older man nodded. "Yeah, he's out there. Won't talk to no one, though. Near bit my head off when I asked him where in tarnation he'd been. Told me to tell you, if you should ask, that he'd talk to you tomorrow sometime."

Shelby started to rise, but Jake's next words stopped her and she settled back down.

"Missy, never thought I'd hear myself say this, but I wouldn't blame you none if you fired that boy. He's been acting like a damn mule ever since you got here and it ain't right. I thought he'd come around, but I guess I was wrong.

282

He's just too dang stubborn."

"Fire him?" She looked at Jake as if he'd just told her to jump off a bridge. "I . . . I can't *fire* him."

"You dang well can. You're the boss around here, Shelby, you can do anything you want."

"But the ranch needs him. He's the foreman."

Jake leaned across the table and looked straight into her eyes. "Missy, ain't no one man invaluable to the running of a ranch. Not a one. Cody's good, and that boy's like a son to me, but that don't make no never mind right now. He'd be a terrible loss, I admit, but he ain't irreplaceable."

"You *want* me to fire him?" she asked, disbelief lacing her words.

"Of course not, but I don't know what else you can do. He ain't showing you no respect, Shelby, and you can't keep this place going without it. The other wranglers will soon take it back, too, if they see you putting up with Cody's fussin'. Then there won't be no ranch to worry about."

Shelby got up from the table. "There has to be another way, Jake. There just has to be."

Chapter Twenty-three

In the small bath that adjoined her bedroom, Shelby turned on the water in the big claw-footed tub, tossed some rose-scented bubble bath into the rising water, and stripped her clothes off, throwing them in the corner. With a long sigh, she stepped into the tub and slipped beneath the mountainous layer of foamy bubbles, letting the hot water engulf her and begin to soothe the aches and pains she'd garnered on the drive. She lay her head back against the rounded edge of the tub, luxuriating in the feel of the heat penetrating her weary limbs, and closed her eyes. An image of Cody instantly appeared in her mind as he had been the night they'd made love, a warm, caring, sensitive man who had held her in her arms, kissed her, and given her a world of ecstasy she would never forget. She saw his laughing blue eyes and the curving smile of his lips, felt the iron-hard strength of his muscles beneath her touch and the silken threads of his hair slipping through her fingers. She could almost smell his scent and taste his lips on hers, sweet and tender.

Tears stung her eyes as the cherished memory let her relive the joy, but also brought with it the pain of loss.

"Shelby, are you in h— Oh, damn."

Shelby shot bolt upright in the tub, her eyes flying open at the sound of Cody's voice, her heart hammering wildly. She blinked away the tears and stared at him, unable to discern if he was really standing there in front of her, framed in the doorway of her bathroom, or if she was still dreaming, still seeing what had been so vivid in her mind.

Filmy white bubbles clung to her shoulders and arms and dripped their way down her breasts, over the taut, golden mounds, falling from her rosy nipples and slipping down into the canyon of her cleavage to rejoin the mountainous foam of bubbles that surrounded her rib cage.

He whirled around, turning his back to her, and lifted a fist to rest on the doorjamb. He held his body rigid, his shoulders stiff. "I shouldn't have just walked in—I'm sorry. But you didn't answer when I knocked, and the door swung open, and . . . and I thought something might be wrong."

Dumbstruck to realize he was actually standing there, Shelby scrambled from the tub, grabbed a huge white towel from a nearby rack, and hurriedly wrapped it around her.

"I'll go. I'm sorry." He started to move away, walking toward the bedroom door that still stood open and led to the hallway. "We'll talk tomorrow. I'm sorry—I shouldn't have come."

"Cody, no, wait," Shelby cried, tucking one top end of the towel under the other and racing after him. "Please, it's all right. Wait. I want to talk to you."

He paused with his hand on the doorknob and looked back at her. His eyes seemed sad, the light she loved so much, gone from them.

Shelby moved up to stand before him, the ends of her hair wet and draping over her shoulders in dark curls, small, dripping clusters of bubbles still clinging to her arms.

Cody trembled as she neared, straining to maintain the control he had over himself, struggling to resist what he wanted so much to do. "Shelby, I can't stay . . ."

She moved closer. "Why?" she asked softly, her voice barely more than a whisper. "Why can't you stay? What's wrong?"

Cody groaned and, unable to stop himself, no longer able to control the passion searing through him, swept her up into his arms, dragging her against him, crushing her to his length and molding her pliant, sweet body to his long form. His mouth covered hers, and his tongue sought entry to her inner softness, to the sweetness he knew lay behind the delicately curved lips.

Her lips parted, inviting his entry, welcoming the caress of his tongue, and Cody instantly accepted the enticement. He kissed her almost savagely, taking everything she offered and demanding more. An exigence of need, an agony of loneliness and longing, a hunger for something he desperately wanted were all evidenced in the urgency of his kiss. And Shelby responded in kind, wrapping her arms around his neck and holding him, pulling him to her, returning his kiss, asking for more.

Every cell in his body was aflame with the want of her, demanding that he take her, that he satisfy the gnawing hunger that was razing his body. But his mind would not allow him the blind satisfaction he sought.

Lost in a world of sensuality, of dreams come true and hopes satisfied, Shelby was unaware of the sudden change in him, the stiffening of his body, until he put his hands on her waist and forced her away from him.

Cody tore himself away from her. "No, this is wrong, Shelby." He shook his head. "I didn't come here for this."

She stared at him in bewilderment as he stepped back from her. She moved toward him, her hand outstretched. "Cody, please, what's wrong?"

He shook his head again. "We need to talk, Shelby, but not like this." He gestured toward her towel. "Tomorrow. Maybe in your office."

She longed to reach out to him again, but something in his tone held her back. She nodded her agreement. Yes, they did need to talk. It was time for both of them to stop running.

Shelby passed a nearly sleepless night, spending half of it in her bed, tossing and turning, the other half standing at the French doors that led onto the terrace from her room. By the time dawn crept in, settling over the landscape in a rosy haze, she gave up the effort. Throwing the sheet back, she slid from her bed and shuffled wearily into the bathroom, turning the tap on and splashing cold water onto her face. She felt better, until she thought of Cody again.

Jake was right about one thing: she had to do something. She slipped into a pair of jeans and a soft silk blouse, ran a brush through her hair, applied a little mascara to her eyelashes and gold-orange color to her lips.

Halfway down the wide staircase she saw Jake walking across the foyer. He caught sight of her out of the corner of his eye, paused, and waited for her to descend. "Up kinda early this morning, ain't you?"

"I couldn't sleep."

They walked toward the dining room.

"Any particular reason?"

Shelby shrugged, and poured herself a cup of coffee. "Where's Cody?" she asked, moving to sit at one of the tables. The spacious room was empty, most of the guests still in their beds asleep.

"Took a couple of the boys and rode out to the south section about an hour ago. He said there was some fences there needed fixing."

"Are there?" Shelby asked, wondering if this was just another way for Cody to avoid her.

Jake nodded. "Yep, though they been down for months and probably coulda stayed down a bit longer."

"Would you tell him I'd like to see him when he gets back?"

Jake nodded again. "What are you gonna do?"

"I don't know, Jake. Talk to him, I guess. See if he'll tell me what's wrong."

Jake stared into his coffee. He knew exactly what was wrong, but it wasn't his place to tell her. He hoped Cody would before it was too late.

For the rest of the day, Shelby busied herself with the business end of running the ranch. For several hours after breakfast with Jake, she closed herself up in the office that had once been shared by Katie and Ken, and pored over the books, learning exactly what the expenses normally were and the type of profits she could expect. She studied the employees' salaries, and though they were already more than fair, decided to give them all a raise. Maybe it was

289

foolish, but it was something she wanted to do, her way of thanking them for helping her get settled.

Maria brought her in a tray at lunchtime and urged her to take a break, but Shelby refused. She had a lot to learn, and the sooner she did it, the better she'd feel.

By suppertime her body felt as if it had taken on the permanent contours of the chair she'd been sitting in all day. She joined the guests in the dining room for dinner, greeting the new arrivals, chatting with those who'd been at the ranch for a while, and saying goodbye to those who were preparing to depart. Her heart wasn't in it; the smile on her face felt forced, frozen in place, and the gay lilt to her voice sounded flat and insincere even to her ears.

Wandering onto the front porch, she stared up at the darkening sky and wondered if Cody had returned yet. She hadn't seen Jake all day, and Cody hadn't come to the office, so she had no way of knowing if he was back or not.

She stepped from the porch and walked to the recreation hall, which was a separate building next door to the ranch house, built to resemble an old Western saloon. She pushed open the swinging doors and stepped inside. Several guests were playing pool and in another corner a young boy was throwing darts at a target hung on the wall, but none of the wranglers were there.

She stepped back out into the night and proceeded to the next building, the general store. In reality, it was a high-class boutique, but from the outside, with its mops, brooms, buckets, and crates lining the front of the walkway, no one would ever guess at the luxuries to be found inside.

She opened the door and stepped in. A bell jingled overhead. "Hi, Bonnie," Shelby called to the clerk who was taking an inventory of shirts behind the counter.

"Hi, Shelby. Come to work or shop?"

"Work, but I'll probably end up shopping, too. There're too many beautiful things in here for a clotheshorse like me to resist." Shelby looked around at the racks of Western clothes, hats, boots, and fully dressed mannequins. "You know, this place could rival any store on Rodeo Drive."

"Yeah. Katie always did want the best of everything in here. Like these." The clerk held up a pair of women's cowboy boots. They were black eelskin with thin caps of polished steel trimming the toes, and high, wedge heels embedded with colored rhinestones in the shape of a flower. "Just sold these an hour ago to that Eva Montalvo woman. She wants them boxed and delivered to her room in the morning before she leaves. Five hundred bucks. Can you imagine?"

Shelby shook her head in disbelief. Five hundred dollars for a pair of boots. She had never spent that much on one outfit, let alone on one item. "What can I do to help?" she asked Bonnie, moving behind the counter to stand beside her.

"Nothing, Shelby, really. I just finished tallying up the sales receipts for the day, and I was going over a few items I think we're going to have to reorder soon. Everything else is done."

A rack of colorful swimsuits caught Shelby's eye and she gravitated toward them, unable to resist. "When did these come in, Bonnie? They're beautiful."

"This afternoon. Why don't you try some on. It's a terrific night for a swim. In fact, I was in the back room a while ago and could hear some of the guests out at the pool. Sounded like they were having a great time. I was thinking of joining them."

Shelby mulled over the idea. It did sound good, and it was high time she stopped brooding over Cody. Though she'd had her nose stuck in the books all day, thoughts of him had never been far from her mind. She grabbed three of the bathing suits and turned toward the dressing room. "Go ahead, Bonnie. I'm going to try these on. I'll lock up and see you at the pool in a little while."

The first bathing suit, nothing more than two pieces of material that circled her neck, draped over her breasts, and came together just below

292

her belly button, proved to be a little too daring for Shelby's tastes. The simple style of the second suit she loved, but the fuchsia print did nothing for her. Starting to feel frustrated, Shelby pulled on the third suit, and forced herself to look in the mirror. The suit was one piece and black, with a vee neck that plunged daringly but tastefully. Classy but sassy. She smiled. It was perfect. She unpinned the price tag that hung from beneath one arm, glanced at it, did a double take, and almost choked. "A hundred and twenty-five dollars?" she gasped. "I can't afford this." Almost at the same time she spoke the words, realization that she didn't *have* to afford it swept over her and she chuckled in relief.

Grabbing a towel from the pile on a nearby table, Shelby left the general store by the back door, making sure to lock it, and walked to the pool, which was behind the ranch house. She could hear the laughter of several guests long before she arrived at the lit patio encircling the pool.

"Hey, beautiful, come join us," Lance called as Shelby stepped through the gate of the picket fence that surrounded the pool area.

She looked toward one of the umbrella-topped tables situated on the opposite side of the pool from where she stood. Lance, his casted leg propped up on a second chair, was holding court with several young women who Shelby

293

knew had arrived only that morning. "Maybe later," she called. "I'm going to do a few laps."

"We've got a full pitcher of strawberry margaritas," Lance offered, trying to tempt her.

She shook her head and lay her towel across the back of a nearby chair. Eva Montalvo sat at another table, firmly snuggled within Jamie's arms. Shelby smiled, remembering Eva's words about her relationship with the wrangler. Eva spotted her, raised a glass, and waved her to join them.

Shelby waved back, but turned away and moved to the edge of the pool. The huge square of water was like a glistening turquoise blanket. The lights at the bottom of the pool shone brightly and illuminated its entire length. Raising her arms over her head, Shelby crouched slightly, pushed away from the ground, and dove in. She swam smoothly, back and forth from one end of the pool to the other without stopping, letting the cool water invigorate her, the exercise ease the stiffness of her muscles, the quiet solitude soothe her frayed nerves.

After five laps, feeling herself begin to tire, Shelby moved to the chrome ladder at one side of the pool and reached up to grasp its handles. No sooner had her fingers curled around the cold bars than strong hands encircled her forearms in an iron grip. She was lifted the rest of the way from the water. Shaking the wet tangle of her hair from her eyes, Shelby found herself face to face with Cody.

His gaze raked over her and an impish smile tugged at the corners of his lips, then disappeared. "We have to talk."

Before Shelby could respond, Cody threw her towel over her shoulders and, maintaining a grip on her right arm, steered her toward a gate identical to the one through which she'd entered, at the opposite end of the pool.

"Where are we going?" Shelby asked, unsure what was happening. She tried to dry herself off one-handed with a corner of the towel, but found it too awkward to do that and skip after Cody at the same time. "Cody?"

He remained silent and urged her past an array of plants growing out of brightly painted Mexican clay pots, down a winding path that led past a grove of cottonwoods and a small pond, and into the dark shadows of several tall pine trees. He released her arm and she looked up at him, barely able to discern his features in the dim moonlight that filtered through the thick branches.

"Now that you've got me out in the wilderness, will you tell me what this is all about?" she asked, not too happy about being dragged away from the pool in full view of the guests like some disobedient or newly conquered cavewoman.

Cody looked down at Shelby and all his good intentions wavered and began to slip away. Suddenly he wanted nothing more than to feel her arms around his neck, her body pressed up against his, her lips welcoming his kiss. Clenching his hands into fists at his sides and taking a deep breath, he steeled himself against her and forced his traitorous desires aside. "I've decided to leave the Double K, Shelby. I'm quitting." His words were hurried and curt.

"What?" Her voice was little more than a gasped croak.

"I said I'm leaving. Quitting. Moving on."

"I . . . I heard what you said." She pushed her hair back away from her face and adjusted the towel around her shoulders, while she searched for something intelligent to say. "Why?" was all she could come up with.

"I just think . . ." Cody looked away and shrugged. "I just think it's best, that's all. No cowhand really stays put for too long, you know, even on the best of ranches. It's time for me to go."

"But why? Why now?" Shelby persisted. She felt the ache in her heart, felt a wave of emptiness wash over her. He was running away. Without any explanation to her, without telling her what was really wrong, he was running away. The mere thought made her blood boil.

"I told you, it's best this way."

"For who, Cody? You? Me? Jake? The Double K?"

A harsh look came over his face and he held

296

himself rigid. "For everyone, Shelby."

"Oh, really?"

He started at the sarcasm and anger evident in her tone.

"Cody Farlowe, you are the orneriest, stubbornnest, most chauvinistic man I've ever met, and to top it all off, you're a coward."

"Coward?" A blaze of anger lit his blue eyes. "Now, listen here, Shelby. You don't know what you're saying." He wagged a finger under her nose. "I've never backed down or run away from a fight in my life, but this is different."

"Why?"

He sighed deeply. "It just is."

" 'It just is,' " she mocked. "Well, that's not good enough, Cody. The Double K can't run without a foreman, and you're it. Katie trusted you, and so do I. You're the best, and I can't run the Double K without you."

"Jake can do it."

"I don't want Jake to do it, I want you. I don't want anything around here to change from the way Katie had it, at least not yet. I want the ranch to stay the same. I want you to run it." *And I want you to love me,* she added silently.

"Things change, Shelby. You should know that better than anyone. Nothing ever stays the same."

She opened her mouth to retort, but he continued before she could utter a word.

297

"I was wrong about you not belonging here. You're more like Katie than you know. She was right all along. You do belong here. And you'll do all right. But I've got to move on."

"You haven't given me a reason, Cody. I want to know why you can't stay. What's wrong? What did I do?"

Moved by her words, by the absurd idea that she thought she'd done something to cause his decision, Cody grasped her shoulders, held her at arm's length, and stared into her eyes. He couldn't keep it in any longer. He had to tell her, just once. "I love you, Shelby. That's what's wrong. I love you and it's not right. It would never work between us."

"Love me? You love me?" she echoed, feeling such a swell of happiness she thought she'd explode.

Cody released her and turned into the shadows. "Yes."

She moved to stand beside him, laying her hand on his arm. "Why wouldn't it work, Cody?"

A long, ragged sigh escaped his lips before he answered. "Shelby, we come from two different worlds, and even though you've proven you can live in mine, I can never hope to fit into yours."

"Mine? I don't understand. You love it here, and I've come to love it, too. This is my home now. I'm not going anywhere. Our worlds are the same."

298

He turned to look at her. "No, they're not. You're the boss. I'm just the foreman. You could pack a bag and jet off to Paris tomorrow if you wanted. I'd have to save up for months, maybe even a year, to afford that. You bought that snazzy little sports car, and I'll bet you paid cash. It would take me more than five years to pay that—"

Standing on the tips of her toes, Shelby threw her arms around Cody's neck and hugged him to her. "I love you, Cody Farlowe. None of that other stuff matters. Not the money, not the car, the ranch, none of it. Only that I love you, and you love me."

Forcing himself to deny her embrace, Cody reached up, gripped her arms, and pulled them from his neck. He held them against his chest and looked down at her. "It does matter, Shelby. It matters to me. I can't be a kept man, living off a woman's money. I'm no Hollywood gigolo, Shelby. I can't live like that. And after a while, you'd soon get tired of being the one with all the money, the one paying for everything." He dropped her arms and turned away.

Staring at his back, Shelby thought feverishly, remembering all the basics of negotiation she'd learned in college while pursuing her business degree. "Cody, it's true. I have the ranch and more than enough money to live comfortably for the rest of my life. But I don't know how to run the ranch. The Double K was Katie's dream,

Cody. She put her life into building it up, and I'm afraid I can't keep it going on my own, no matter how much money I have to put into it. But you can. You know how to keep it operating, you know how to handle the wranglers, you know more than I could ever hope to learn in five years."

She moved to stand before him. "If you leave, I'll have to find a replacement. Jake can't do everything alone. He's too old. In the time it would take to find someone, the Double K could be severely jeopardized. A few dissatisfied customers can tell a lot of people. Anyway—" she moved closer, so near that her breasts were almost touching his chest "—without you here to nag me and rescue me from all my disasters, I just might lose interest in running this place. I'll give the money away if that's what it takes, Cody, but I can't do it without you. I don't want to do it without you."

Cody looked down at her, a slight frown still pulling at his forehead as he took her in his arms. "I don't know, Shelby."

"Cody, I love you."

"You sure you won't get tired of being married to a penniless cowboy?"

Shelby's heart leaped. "Never," she breathed just before his lips covered hers.

In the velvety blackness of night, hidden from view by the ever-deepening shadows of the pines, Cody sunk to the soft grass and pulled

300

Shelby down beside him.

Hours later, after they had made love beneath a golden Montana moon, they talked long into the night of their plans for a future together. And Shelby knew, at long last, that Katie's dream would live on, as would her own.

DISCOVER DEANA JAMES!

CAPTIVE ANGEL (2524, $4.50/$5.50)
Abandoned, penniless, and suddenly responsible for the bigges
tobacco plantation in Colleton County, distraught Caroline Gil
lard had no time to dissolve into tears. By day the willowy red
head labored to exhaustion beside her slaves . . . but each nigh
left her restless with longing for her wayward husband. She'
make the sea captain regret his betrayal until he begged her to
take him back!

MASQUE OF SAPPHIRE (2885, $4.50/$5.50)
Judith Talbot-Harrow left England with a heavy heart. She wa
going to America to join a father she despised and a sister sh
distrusted. She was certainly in no mood to put up with the in
sulting actions of the arrogant Yankee privateer who boarded he
ship, ransacked her things, then "apologized" with an indecen
brazen kiss! She vowed that someday he'd pay dearly for the lib
erties he had taken and the desires he had awakened.

SPEAK ONLY LOVE (3439, $4.95/$5.95)
Long ago, the shock of her mother's death had robbed Vivia
Marleigh of the power of speech. Now she was being forced t
marry a bitter man with brandy on his breath. But she could no
say what was in her heart. It was up to the viscount to spark th
fires that would melt her icy reserve.

WILD TEXAS HEART (3205, $4.95/$5.9
Fan Breckenridge was terrified when the stranger found her nea
naked and shivering beneath the Texas stars. Unable to rememb
who she was or what had happened, all she had in the world wa
the deed to a patch of land that might yield oil . . . and the fierc
loving of this wildcatter who called himself Irons.

*Available wherever paperbacks are sold, or order direct from th
Publisher. Send cover price plus 50¢ per copy for mailing an
handling to Zebra Books, Dept. 3977, 475 Park Avenue Sout*
New York, N.Y. 10016. Residents of New York and Tenness
must include sales tax. DO NOT SEND CASH. For a free Zebr
Pinnacle catalog please write to the above address.

OFFICIAL ENTRY FORM
Please enter me in the

Lucky in Love

SWEEPSTAKES

Grand Prize choice: _____

Name: _____

Address: _____

City: _____ State _____ Zip _____

Store name: _____

Address: _____

City: _____ State _____ Zip _____

MAIL TO: LUCKY IN LOVE
P.O. Box 1022C
Grand Rapids, MN 55730-1022C

Sweepstakes ends: 4/30/93

OFFICIAL RULES
"LUCKY IN LOVE" SWEEPSTAKES

1. To enter complete the official entry form. No purchase necessary. You may enter by hand printing on a 3″ x 5″ piece of paper, your name, address and the words "Lucky In Love." Mail to: "Lucky In Love" Sweepstakes, P.O. Box 1022C, Grand Rapids, MN 55730-1022C.

2. Enter as often as you like, but each entry must be mailed separately. Mechanically reproduced entries not accepted. Entries must be received by April 30, 1993.

3. Winners selected in a random drawing on or about May 14, 1993 from among all eligible entries received by Marden-Kane, Inc. an independent judging organization whose decisions are final and binding. Winner may be required to sign an affidavit of eligibility and release which must be returned within 14 days or alternate winner(s) will be selected. Winners permit the use of their name/photograph for publicity/advertising purposes without further compensation. No transfer of prizes permitted. Taxes are the sole responsibility of the prize winners. Only one prize per family or household.

4. Winners agree that the sponsor, its affiliate and their agencies and employees shall not be liable for injury, loss or damage of any kind resulting from participation in this promotion or from the acceptance or use of the prizes awarded.

5. Sweepstakes open to residents of the U.S. and Canada, except employees of Zebra Books, their affiliates, advertising and promotion agencies and Marden-Kane, Inc. Void the Province of Quebec and wherever else void, taxed, prohibited or restricted by law. All Federal, State and Local laws and regulations apply. Canadian winners will be required to answer an arithmetical skill testing question administered by mail. Odds of winning depend upon the total number of eligible entries received. All prizes will be awarded. Not responsible for lost, misdirected mail or printing errors.

6. For the name of the Grand Prize Winner, send a self-addressed stamped envelope to: "Lucky In Love" Winners, P.O. Box 706-C, Sayreville, NJ 08871.